VENDETTA

Candy Lane had a natural gift for creating sexual fantasies for men and women. Her ability to fulfill that special human need had brought money and fame—but her life was empty, sad, and scary.

Alone now in the empty beach house, she was stricken by a sudden sense of impending doom. She quickly laid out six lines of coke, but as she picked up the gold straw, she heard a strange sound just below the windows, a scraping sound like leather on sandy cement.

She opened the top drawer of her night table and removed a .25 automatic Beretta. The scraping sound continued.

She clutched her teddy bear to her left breast and gripped the gun in her right hand. She rose naked from the bed and doused the lights.

Her heart pounded as she walked slowly toward the open terrace doors. Her long hair blew wildly in the sea breeze as she stepped out onto the wooden decking.

She pointed the small automatic toward the sounds coming from the narrow beachside path. The approaching footfalls were pronounced. She dropped the teddy bear and, clutching the gun with both hands, extended her arms, pointing the automatic toward the dark corner of the house. It seemed an eternity before the familiar figure emerged into a spill of light. She sighed in relief and slowly lowered the automatic. . . .

Forty-eight hours later, Candy Lane's nude body was found facedown on the wooden terrace.

ABOUT THE AUTHOR

STEVE SHAGAN is the author of the novel and award-winning screenplay *Save the Tiger*, which won the Writers Guild Award as best original screen drama of 1973. His second novel, *City of Angels*, was the basis for the Paramount movie *Hustle*. In 1976, he received his second Academy Award nomination for his screenplay of *Voyage of the Damned*. His most recent novels were the smash best sellers *The Formula, The Circle*, and *The Discovery*. He is currently writing the screenplay of *Vendetta* for Edward Feldman Productions.

VENDETTA

Steve Shagan

A PERIGORD PRESS BOOK

BANTAM BOOKS

TORONTO · NEW YORK · LONDON · SYDNEY · AUCKLAND

for Anne Strauss . . .

*This low-priced Bantam Book
has been completely reset in a type face
designed for easy reading, and was printed
from new plates. It contains the complete
text of the original hard-cover edition.*

NOT ONE WORD HAS BEEN OMITTED.

VENDETTA

*A Bantam/Perigord Book / published in association with
William Morrow and Company*

PRINTING HISTORY

*Perigord/Morrow edition published July 1986
Bantam/Perigord edition / June 1987*

ISBN 0-553-26733-7

Published simultaneously in the United States and Canada

PRINTED IN THE UNITED STATES OF AMERICA

O   0 9 8 7 6 5 4 3

I laugh and my laughter is not within me;
I burn and the burning is not seen outside.

—NICCOLÒ MACHIAVELLI

Chapter 1

"Ramon?"

"Yeah."

"Julito."

"How you doin'?"

"*Como siempre.*"

"When did you get in?"

"Last night."

"Where?"

"The kingfish store."

"Funny, you must be a *sombra.*"

The taped voices were suddenly garbled in a storm of static. Lieutenant Jack Raines glanced at his partner, Special Agent Silvio Martinez. The wiry olive-skinned Cuban-American shrugged. "Pepe lost it here, but there's more."

Raines wiped the beads of perspiration from his forehead and slammed his fist against the groaning air-conditioning unit. "You'd think they'd fix this thing."

Ignoring his partner's complaint, Silvio activated the fast forward button on the recorder. "It picks up here," Silvio said as he depressed the stop button.

"What does *sombra* mean?" Jack asked.

" 'Shadow.' "

"Meaning Julito didn't see Ramon at the kingfish store?"

"Who knows? These are two Colombian *coqueros* talking in prearranged code."

Silvio hit the play button; the reels revolved, and the taped voices resumed with clarity.

*　　*　　*

1

"You went fishing, Ramon?"

"I told you."

"Tell me again."

"Ave María."

"With P.C.?"

"Santa Rosa."

"*Qué bueno.*"

"P.C. came up with it."

"At the kingfish store?"

"He used a new hook."

"What kind?"

"*Alfombras.*"

There was a dead pause. No static. No voices.
Jack glanced at Silvio, but the Cuban-born operative
stared transfixed at the revolving disks. The taped voices
suddenly resumed.

"Where did P.C. fish?"

"Manzanillo."

"How much?"

"A quarter—maybe more."

"How?"

"Ave María."

"*Qué bueno.*"

"Adios, Julito."

"*Vaya bien*, Ramon."

There was a click, and Silvio hit the stop button.
"That's all of it."

"How did Pepe get it?"

"That's his business."

"No way I can meet him?" Jack asked.

"I'm sorry. I can't do that."

"This assignment is like patrolling the jungle at night,"
Jack said wearily. "You never see a face."

"You prefer Homicide?"

"I prefer the old days at Tactical. Gather information
from eighteen divisions and pass it along; stay out of

harm's way. Maybe it's middle-age terror, but I've got a daughter to take care of."

"I understand, amigo. I understand about family."

Raines opened a window overlooking the smog-shrouded intersection of Wilshire Boulevard and Berendo. A hot, acrid breeze floated into the glass cubicle.

"The traffic lights have halos around them," Jack remarked.

"It's the smog."

"No, I need glasses."

"So get them. What's the big deal? You worry too much about getting old."

"I'm getting to that place where you don't know what's gonna go first—your pump or your putz."

"You been seeing any women?"

"The stewardess now and then. Last time I was with her I got looped. I mean, pissed. I woke up in her bedroom hung-over, surrounded by bullfight posters. I felt as though I'd been in a three-way with Manolete."

"Where was the stewardess?"

"She took off for Panama, scribbled a note, and left a pot of undrinkable coffee." Jack sighed. "What do you make out of this tape?"

"There's a shipment on the way. 'Ave María' is the key, but who knows what the hell it means?"

"I'd still like to talk to Pepe."

"You got to leave that to me," Silvio insisted. "When you run a *coquero* who's flipped to our side, it's like handling an illicit love affair. Your relationship with the informer is intimate but fragile. An informer walks on his own grave. I speak from bitter experience, amigo. One mistake, and it's over."

Jack did not press the issue. He'd heard bits and pieces, rumors concerning a female informer Silvio had run in Miami. The woman had been brutally murdered by Colombian dealers.

"It's in your hands, pal." Jack smiled. "Let's get this tape transcribed for Nolan."

John Nolan was chief of the Los Angeles Police Tactical Division—a position he had held for fifteen years.

Nolan was a highly skilled political tactician who had brilliantly picked his way through the bureaucratic minefield of the L.A. police infrastructure. He was blessed with an intuitive perception of where the true political muscle resided. And in a profession not famous for luxury Nolan understood the virtue of showmanship. His spacious office would have served the president of General Motors. It was elegant and stark, comfortable but imposing, every piece of decor designed for effect. Nothing wasted. Nothing misstated. The oak-paneled walls were softly illuminated by hidden ceiling spots, and a huge picture window overlooked the city. The only incongruity was a six-foot sailfish attached to a wooden plaque on the wall behind Nolan's polished oak desk. The fish seemed to be alive, poised for a final leap to freedom.

Raines and Martinez sat in deep leather chairs and watched Nolan chew nervously on a dead cigar while he studied the tape transcript. Nolan was fifty-six, but his fallen face and gray bureaucratic pallor added ten years to his age.

Nolan had reluctantly accepted the FBI director's request to utilize the Tactical Division as the fulcrum in a newly formed drug enforcement unit called Narcotics Intelligence Force Tactical. The men and women serving in the unit had abbreviated the pretentious title to NIFTY. The squad consisted of field personnel, researchers, communications experts, and liaison people who coordinated NIFTY's activities with the federal Drug Enforcement Agency. Any crime committed in the greater Los Angeles area involving the presence of cocaine was automatically reported to NIFTY. Nolan had selected his longtime chief of operations, Lieutenant Jack Raines, to head the special unit. Silvio Martinez had been personally chosen to work with NIFTY by the director of the DEA.

Nolan finished reading the tape transcript and closed the manila folder. "Goddamn gibberish," he muttered, and relit the cigar. "You guys call me in on a Saturday night to listen to this shit?"

"This is a rare tape, John," Silvio said.

"It might as well be in hieroglyphics." Nolan struggled to his feet and walked to the picture window and stared at the multicolored lights illuminating the southern sprawl of the city.

"I never wanted this narco work." Nolan spoke to the window. "Two dead agents in the last six months. Five flipped informers cut to pieces, and despite all our efforts, we're still caught in a snowstorm." He turned from the window. "We're fighting a hundred-billion-dollar industry with nickels and dimes."

He crossed back to his desk, sank heavily into his high-backed leather chair, and glanced at Silvio. "Can you make anything out of this tape?"

"*Kingfish* means 'Rafael Ordóñez.' *Fishing for kingfish* means 'organizing a shipment for Ordóñez.' *P.C.* is Pedro Cisneros; he's Ordóñez's right-hand man. My guess is there's a snowstorm forming somewhere off the Pacific coast of Mexico."

Nolan reopened the folder containing the tape transcript and asked Silvio, "What the hell does *alfombras* mean?"

"Means 'rugs' or 'carpets.' "

"I suppose there's no point in my asking what *Ave María* signifies."

"Could be anything." Silvio shrugged.

Nolan got to his feet, circled the desk, and paced the thick beige carpet. "We'll never stop the shipments. The only way to hurt them is to cripple their money-laundering operations."

"That's damn near impossible," Silvio said.

"Why?" Nolan asked.

"Smurfs."

"Smurfs?"

"Thousands of legitimate citizens who earn extra money laundering for street dealers. They deposit just under ten thousand in local banks so it's unreported, then wire it to Panama or the Bahamas or Switzerland."

"But that's peanuts," Nolan replied. "The important money is laundered by the mob and the banking community." He shook his head in dismay. "The mob I understand. But our most prestigious banks are transferring billions in unreported narcodollars, and all they get is a slap on the wrist from the Treasury Department."

"What do you want us to do about this tape?" Jack asked.

"Alert the Mexican coastal patrol; send Commander Álvarez a copy of this tape. Maybe he can make some sense out of it."

As the two detectives rose to leave, Nolan said, "It was right and proper for you to call me. It's Saturday night for all of us." He sighed. "I forget that sometimes. Go home. Get some sleep."

Chapter 2

Standing on the terrace of his high-rise apartment, Jack Raines sipped his scotch and stared at the pinspots of light dotting the Hollywood Hills.

He had placed a call to his daughter at her summer camp but had just missed her and left word. Toward the conclusion of her high school semester Jenny had applied for a summer job as a junior counselor. She was accepted and placed in charge of eight-year-olds.

It seemed to Jack as if she had matured in a rush, as if the "little girl" had been magically replaced by a grown-up teenager. Jenny was blessed with her mother's beauty. She had inherited Laura's tall, curvy figure, pale hair, and luminous gray eyes. His late wife's presence was indelibly stamped on his daughter's appearance and mannerisms.

They had been divorced for five years when Laura died, and overnight Jack had had to assume the dual role of mother and father. Once Jenny had moved in with him, certain problems began to surface—the kinds of emotional problems bachelor fathers seldom encounter. Jenny had displayed considerable courage and understanding over her mother's sudden and violent death, but she deeply resented Jack's occasional relationships with other women. It had never occurred to him that his own daughter would be jealous of his meager social life. Only with the passage of time and numerous frank discussions did she finally accept the fact that her father's infrequent affairs in no way diminished his love for her.

Ironically, it was now his turn to be upset by Jenny's casual dates. The widower's normal anxiety about rearing a teenage daughter was compounded by his profession. He'd seen unspeakable crimes committed upon girls of his daughter's age, but he could not in good conscience hold Jenny hostage to his work. It had required a painful and patient exercise of tolerance and trust for him to loosen the reins of responsibility. And Jenny had not betrayed his trust. They now enjoyed an open, honest, loving relationship.

He drained the scotch, sighed heavily, and walked back inside the living room. The distant sounds of traffic coming through the open terrace doors seemed to accent his solitude. He placed a Sinatra cassette on the stereo, and his thoughts drifted back to the tape transcript. He tossed the names and code words around: *Cisneros, Ordóñez, Ave María, Kingfish*. He thought about coca paste now being refined in local chemical labs and how thousands of middle-class Americans had become active dealers and in so doing stimulated the tidal wave of narcodollars lining the pockets of Mafia laundrymen and their Colombian overlords. The fine white powder was more than just a fashionable drug; it had become a political weapon. The CIA had intercepted a KGB directive detailing the involvement of Castro, Vesco, Qaddafi, and the Bulgarian Secret Service in their alliance with the Colombian drug czar Rafael Ordóñez. The Soviet Embassy in Mexico City had activated a special section of the KGB devoted to aiding and abetting the distribution of cocaine into North America. The coking of America represented a significant Soviet victory in the ongoing East-West geopolitical conflict. The NIFTY task force was hopelessly outmanned, outgunned, and outfinanced; they were like a group of children armed with toy shovels trying to stop a full-blown snowstorm.

The phone rang sharply.

"Hi, Dad!" the slightly throaty voice exclaimed. "I just got back from a trail ride."

"How goes it, beautiful?"

"I'm getting tan, tough, and fat."

"Well, you can use a few pounds after my suppers of frozen chicken."

"I'm stuffing myself; it's all this exercise."

"How are you getting along with the kids?"

"Super. By the way, I met a terrific boy. He's nine-

teen. A full counselor. Goes to Stanford. His name is
Patrick. I like him a lot."

"Well, that's what camp is about—meeting new
friends."

"It's more than friendship."

Jack felt a little heat rise in his throat.

"Don't get carried away by a summer romance."

There was a slight pause before Jenny said, "I'd like
you to meet him."

"I will. I'm planning to come up one of these Sundays."

"Let me know, okay?"

"Sure. You need any money?"

"I could use a little."

"I'll put a check in the mail."

"Thanks, Dad." She paused. "Are you okay?"

"Never better."

"You sound sad, depressed."

"Just Saturday night blues. I'm fine. Be good, and I'll
see you soon. I love you."

"Love you, too."

"Bye, baby."

"Bye, Dad."

He missed her but knew the temporary separation
was healthy for both of them. He picked up his drink and
walked out onto the terrace. He looked off at the scruffy,
formless hills and felt an overwhelming sense of loneliness, the kind of bleak aloneness rooted in scarred memories for which there was neither escape nor antidote. He
raised the glass to his lips and paused, noticing an inordi-
nately bright glow coming from a hillside A-frame across
the canyon.

Chapter 3

Sweating profusely under the hot lights, Sherry Nichols concentrated on the two actresses who lay naked on the black satin sheets. The bedroom's walls and ceiling were mirrored, creating severe lighting problems, but their prisms and reflections presented extraordinary compositional possibilities.

Sherry Nichols was a tall, sandy-haired woman who had achieved a cult celebrity as a director of pornographic films. Her last film, *Lickorice*, had been notable for its neoexpressionistic style and the astonishing debut of Candy Lane, who now squirmed impatiently on the circular bed.

The teenage beauty removed the older woman's arm from around her shoulders, raised herself up and, shielding her eyes from the lights, complained, "It's like we're in a micro oven, Sherry."

"Candy's right. Let's get on with it," the older woman chimed in. "This isn't exactly the ballroom scene in *War and Peace*."

"Please bear with me, Karen," Sherry replied. "These mirrors are tricky."

"I need a line," Candy said. "I absolutely need a line."

"Just hold your position for a minute, baby—okay?"

Sherry then turned to the assistant director. "Where's Lisa Chang?"

"Showering," the tall, skinny youth replied.

Sherry knelt at the foot of the circular water bed and peered through a Bell & Howell viewfinder, focusing on Candy Lane and Karen Dara. She switched lens sizes, taking into consideration the action of the scene, the positioning of all three cameras, and the mirrored reflections.

Beads of perspiration ran down her cheeks as she made her mental calculations. After a long moment she rose and spoke to the director of photography.

"Let's use a thirty-five on the master camera and fifties on the hand-held Arris." She paused. "The Arris will cross-shoot into the mirrors. I want magenta filters on the key lights."

The cameraman nodded and moved off toward a cluster of technicians.

Sherry then smiled at Candy. "Relax, baby, we're getting there."

At age nineteen Candy Lane was already a veteran of fifteen hard-core pictures. Her looks were classic, her beauty was articulated by midnight blue eyes, high cheekbones, a straight patrician nose, and soft, full lips. Her breasts were large and firm. Her stomach was hard and flat, her waist, narrow. Her shapely legs tapered down into delicate racehorse ankles. But her eyes were her fortune. They projected a quality of a helpless carnal sacrifice. A straight film critic had termed her extraordinary sensuality as an "astonishing combination of innocence and perverse calculation."

The success of *Lickorice* had made her a controversial celebrity. She had been voted best actress in the Erotic Film Society's annual awards and had appeared on numerous television talk shows. She would, with childlike innocence, defend pornography as simply another form of cinematic sensuality.

She now received "star" treatment: a limousine on location, a hotel suite, her own makeup man, and a working bonus of high-grade cocaine.

Her career had started with nude poses for pornographic magazines. She then graduated to a fluff—the term used to describe girls who performed off-camera oral sex on the male stars, bringing them up to a preclimax state while the female star waited. As Candy's price and fame rose, so did her use of cocaine. She was an "ice princess"—a three-gram-a-day user.

The older woman lying beside Candy was a major star in her own right. Karen Dara's shapely figure and aristocratic demeanor had served her well. She had once been a

commercial model for a national brand of soap. Her refined all-American good looks had caught the eye of a San
Francisco porn director, who offered her the lead in a
high-budget hard-core film called *Playgirls*. The picture
had been a box-office smash and best-seller in cassette. The
key scene in the film involved Karen and three young girls
in a complex lovemaking sequence that projected a star-
tling documentary reality. Her scenes with men were,
however, notably restrained. Her eyes would glaze over,
and her body, mouth, and hands moved as if robotized.

In one of her early films John Traynor, the reigning
star of male porno performers, had taken personal pleasure
in punishing her during an orgiastic sequence. But once she
had achieved stardom, Karen's contract stipulated that her
scenes with men would be faked with body doubles.

"I'd like another line," Candy whispered.

"Sure, baby." Karen smiled and swung her legs over
the side of the bed and carefully laid out four lines of
cocaine on the glass tabletop. Candy leaned over, snorted
three lines, then dipped her finger into the remaining line
and rubbed the fine white powder over her gums.

"Where's Sherry?" Candy asked.

"Checking on our male stud," Karen replied with sul-
len hostility.

"You really hate him, don't you?"

"You'll never know."

Sherry Nichols entered the living room with its vaulted
ceiling, throw rugs, and Italian furniture.

John Traynor lounged naked on the sofa. His legs
were spread, and two young girls knelt before him, stimu-
lating his enormous organ.

"How you doing?" Sherry asked.

"Getting there." Traynor smiled crookedly.

"You mount Candy at the conclusion of this lez sequence," Sherry explained. "It's three cameras, so don't
worry about angles."

"Gotcha."

"Stella, you come with me," Sherry ordered the red-
haired fluff.

*   *   *

In the kitchen an obese gray-haired man with flattened fighter's features chewed on a huge hero sandwich. He weighed almost 300 pounds and wore a grape-size diamond ring on his pinkie. Leo ("the Whale") Whelan controlled the manufacture and distribution of porno magazines, books, cassettes, and film on the West Coast. He also freely distributed high-grade cocaine to his stars and technicians.

"We're ready, Leo," Sherry said.

The Whale nodded, belched, and grunted at Stella. "You want some snow?"

"Of course, Stella wants some snow," Sherry interjected. "Stella cannot perform without snow." Sherry turned to the naked fluff and derisively said, "Can you, dear?"

"It helps." Stella smiled sheepishly.

The overweight pornbroker took a small cellophane bag out of his jacket and handed it to the redhead. Stella laid out eight lines of the fine white powder and greedily snorted line after line.

"Let's go," Sherry said.

A malevolent, melancholy spirit pervaded the crowded bedroom. The cigarette smoke of the crew drifted up to the mirrored ceiling, flattened out, and hung like a wispy canopy over the naked bodies reclining on the circular bed.

The makeup man applied a final layer of number five pancake to a slender Chinese girl's thighs.

Candy's head rested on the pillow. She stared blankly up at her reflected image in the mirrored ceiling.

Karen Dara was on her feet, stretching and flexing her back muscles.

The fluff, Stella, wired on the eight lines of coke, brushed her long red hair furiously.

Sherry Nichols addressed the Oriental girl: "Get on your mark, Lisa."

Lisa Chang walked dutifully to the bed, knelt between Candy's legs, and glanced up at Sherry. "This okay?"

"Fine." Sherry nodded.

Two sound men were chatting and fiddling with the knobs on the Nagra sound recorder.

"Quiet!" Sherry shouted. "Places!"

The master camera was elevated on a small crane. Two cameramen knelt beside the bed, cross-shooting into the mirrors with hand-held cameras. Leo Whelan stood with his back to the far wall, chewing slowly on the remnants of the sandwich.

Sherry's voice was soft and patronizing as she addressed Candy. "You okay, baby?"

Candy nodded.

"Ready, Karen?"

"Yes."

"Remember," Sherry said, "the kiss makes the scene."

"Let's shoot it," Karen replied impatiently.

"This is only a wild track," Sherry advised the sound man. "We'll fill it with music and ecstasy sound loops when we mix."

Lisa Chang peered up from between Candy's legs and asked, "Will my hair get in the way?"

"No. You're playing into camera two." Sherry wiped some sweat from her forehead. "All right, Fred, give us the filters."

The electricians hit some switches, and a dark red light bounced off the mirrors, bathing the naked women in a luminous magenta glow.

"Positions!" Sherry commanded.

Karen and Stella began to nurse at Candy's nipples.

Lisa Chang buried her head between Candy's thighs.

"Candy?" Sherry asked softly.

"Yes. Go."

"Roll cameras!" Sherry barked.

The cameramen shouted in rapid succession.

"Camera one speed."

"Camera two speed."

"Camera three speed."

The sound man shouted, "Wild track. *Cotton Candy*. Scene twenty-three. Take one. Three cameras. End slate!"

Sherry spoke quietly to Candy. "The action starts very slow and builds. I'll give you one-minute calls. Pick up the pace on each minute count. After three minutes I'll cue the kiss."

The bedroom fell silent.

"Action!" Sherry exclaimed.

Candy stared up at the mirrored ceiling as the three women began to perform their sexual wiles upon her.

Time seemed eternal.

The whirring sounds of cameras underscored the silence.

On the two-minute count Candy began to groan, and her hips undulated, pumping up into the Chinese girl's mouth. Her hands pulled Karen and Stella's mouths against her full breasts.

Another minute passed.

"Karen," Sherry whispered, "Stella."

The former soap model removed her mouth from Candy's nipple, and simultaneously Stella's lips slid slowly down Candy's body. Karen caressed Candy's throat, cheeks, and eyes. She then raised herself up and stared lovingly at the blond child-woman for an instant before kissing her deeply.

The cameras, lights, and crew were forgotten as the sweat-soaked women coalesced into a surreal union of naked flesh. Their breasts, thighs, arms, and mouths were refracted in the mirrored prisms, creating an infinity of dazzling sensual images. Their bodies throbbed with a rising intensity, fueled by the fine white powder that had traveled from the jungles of Colombia to the Hollywood Hills.

Leo Whelan, smelling of garlic, moved alongside Sherry and whispered, "This scene alone is worth ten million theatrically. The fucking cassette is out of sight."

Chapter 4

In her chemically charged brain the moving lights were like the eyes of an endless reptile, lidded and half closed as they first appeared, then widening and bright as they zoomed past her.

The top was down on the 450 SL Mercedes, and her pale hair streamed behind her. The convertible sped along the northbound lane of the Pacific Coast Highway. Candy was still snow-blind, and the tension of the filming had wired her nerves. She had been driving for almost an hour and craved a fresh line of coke. Her lips were bruised from the kissing sequence with Karen, and a dull ache throbbed over her right eye.

Karen Dara had left the Hollywood Hills film site after completing the lesbian sequence, but Candy had remained, working in the final scene with John Traynor, Lisa Chang, Stella, and another fluff. Sherry Nichols had kissed her good night, and Leo Whalen had given her three grams of coke and fifty $100 bills.

Streisand's melancholy rendition of "Memory" filled the car as Candy slowed at the second light north of Malibu and swung into the turn lane. The green arrow finally flashed, and she steered carefully across the highway to the beach side and picked up the dimly lit private road. She drove another half a mile before pulling into an open garage adjoining a two-story New England-style clapboard house. She had leased the beach house from a famous film actress currently starring in a Broadway play.

The living room was spacious and comfortably furnished. Two large sliding doors opened onto a wooden terrace that overlooked the sea. Candy had replaced a few of the owner's prints with framed photographs of herself—straight photos, artfully composed against spectacular desert backgrounds. She had paid the photographer $3,000 for the portfolio, hoping to crack some straight modeling work, but nothing had come of it.

She dropped her handbag on the sofa and stepped onto the terrace. The surging sea foamed and roared as it broke angrily against the surf. She drew in deep drafts of the sea air and licked her swollen lips, thinking of Karen. She loved the older woman, but it was hopeless.

Karen could not commit herself to a relationship. Despite her breezy exterior, there was a demon inside her, an inner rage that triggered her shifting moods. She had been caring, generous, and a sensitive lover, but it was always moment to moment. Last summer Karen had gone off to Spain without so much as a good-bye. But in her own peculiar way Karen had given Candy as much love as she was capable of giving. Karen had introduced her to the Order of Shiva, the metaphysical religion that Lisa Chang belonged to. And Candy had found a certain tranquillity in meditation and communication with the inner spirit.

At the very least Karen was someone she could trust.

Candy took a deep breath of ocean air and walked back inside the living room. She noticed the red light blinking on her answering machine and kicked her shoes off, crossed the room, and pressed the playback button on the recorder. There were two messages from Karen and one long-distance call from Pedro Cisneros. She switched the machine back to record and walked wearily into the bedroom.

The canopied bed was covered by a pink cashmere blanket folded down over pink satin sheets; a teddy bear rested against two pink pillows. The bedroom faced the ocean, and sliding doors opened onto a beachside wooden decking.

She removed a small vial of cocaine from her pocket, snorted two lines, and went into the bathroom. She undressed and opened the shower door and adjusted the water taps until the jet stream was piping hot. She stepped inside and turned her face up to the shower head. She closed her eyes and instantly saw John Traynor's immense organ alternately thrusting itself into Lisa Chang and Stella, moving from one to the other like a frenzied stallion in heat. Candy smiled at the irony of Traynor's celluloid image. The male king of porn could not reach orgasm except by prolonged use of his own hand, and only through tricky cutting techniques did Traynor appear to his fans as a stud who could come on cue.

She turned her face away from the shower head and began to soap herself. The name Pedro Cisneros suddenly whirled and flashed in her wired brain. Six months ago she had spent a long weekend with the Colombian dealer at a rented villa in Key Biscayne. Leo Whelan had asked her to deliver a bank transfer check to Cisneros in the amount of $5 million. The money represented narcodollars that had been laundered through Whelan's Galaxy Films Distribution Company. The pornbroker offered her $5,000 as a fee for "courier" services; she agreed only after Whelan had consented to her request that Karen accompany her.

Candy had heard that Pedro Cisneros not only directed Rafael Ordóñez's smuggling operations but also served the drug czar as an accomplished and ruthless enforcer.

The rumors had frightened her, but during that long weekend she never saw the dark side of the soft-spoken Colombian. Cisneros had been a perfect gentleman, both kind and solicitous. He urged her to quit the porno business and kick her drug habit. He mentioned the possibility by which certain pressures might be exerted on studio chiefs so that a film career for her in straight motion pictures might be attainable. She had listened with rapt attention but in the end shook her head and with resignation said, "No one has ever crossed over from porn to straights."

As the night wore on, she switched from coke to grass and slipped into a deep lethargy. She had a vague recollection of Cisneros's carrying her into the bedroom, undressing her, covering her up, and whispering something to her in Spanish before leaving.

She awoke at noon, and over a cup of coffee Karen informed her that Cisneros had left the bayside villa by seaplane at daybreak.

Upon her return to Los Angeles she received a photograph she had posed for with Cisneros and Karen. The color print was followed by sporadic phone calls from odd places: Panama City, Mexico City, Rio, Lima, and on several occasions Key Biscayne. Taking Karen's advice, she politely rejected Cisneros's numerous invitations to visit him in Colombia.

Candy shut the shower taps, wondering if she had made a mistake; perhaps Cisneros could have helped her career.

Back in the bedroom she placed a vintage Neil Diamond cassette on the stereo. She then removed a cellophane bag from the stereo's undercarriage containing a half kilo of 70 percent cocaine. Karen had warned her that anything over 50 percent was dangerous, but as Candy's habit increased, she required the more potent variety. She laid out six lines on the glass-topped night table and snorted them quickly.

She felt the instant arctic flash as the drug exploded in her brain, and her thoughts raced backward in time like a reel of tape spinning in reverse. She stretched out naked on the silk sheets and clutched the teddy bear to her breasts. She remembered her first soft-core nude poses, followed by raw beaver shots, graphic lez spreads, and on to porno loops, then full-length hard-core films, grinding them out day after day until Sherry Nichols selected her for the starring role in *Lickorice*. The film had brought instant stardom, fame—and paranoia. She woke up frightened every day. Only after ingesting five lines of coke with the first cup of coffee did her terror subside.

She desperately wanted out, but to what? How could she ever equal her present income? She could never go back to school or work at some mundane office job. She was earning almost $200,000 a year.

She rose and, carrying the teddy bear, walked over to a framed review of *Lickorice* written by a straight film critic. She studied the words "Candy Lane is the most beguiling child-woman ever to grace the pornographic screen. Miss Lane projects a tantalizing combination of innocence and acquiescence. Her initial reluctance gives way to sensual surrender performed with incredible calculation."

"See, Teddy," Candy whispered to the stuffed toy.

She suddenly burst into tears and sobbed as she walked back to the bed. "A real—a real film critic said that about me."

She sat down on the bed and stuck her forefinger into the bag of coke and rubbed the white powder across her gums, numbing them.

She hugged the teddy bear and remembered that even as a child she had felt her life was late, as if her dreams had been in a contest with time.

She had always wanted the things she saw in films and on TV: beautiful clothes, wondrous tropical islands, elegant restaurants, discos, and charge cards—just flash them and magical things were yours. But people like her did not acquire material wealth by waiting for it to happen. You had to work and scheme. You had to know what it was you had to sell. By the time she was fourteen Candy had known what that special commodity was. She had a natural gift for creating sexual fantasies for men and women. Her ability to fulfill that special human need had brought money and fame—but her life was empty, sad, and scary.

People stared at her in public not with adulation but rather with the macabre curiosity they displayed when slowing down to see an accident on the freeway.

Alone now in the empty beach house, she was stricken by a sudden sense of impending doom. She quickly laid out six lines of coke, but as she picked up the gold straw, she heard a strange sound just below the windows, a scraping sound like leather on sandy cement.

She opened the top drawer of her night table and removed a .25 automatic Beretta. She slid the cylinder back, charging the weapon, and slipped off the safety.

The scraping sound continued.

She clutched the teddy bear to her left breast and gripped the gun in her right hand.

She rose naked from the bed and doused the lights.

Her heart pounded as she walked slowly toward the open terrace doors.

Her long hair blew wildly in the sea breeze as she stepped out onto the wooden decking.

She pointed the small automatic toward the alien sounds coming from the narrow beachside path. Her palm gripping the gun was sweaty, and she shivered in the cold night air. The approaching footfalls were pronounced. She dropped the teddy bear and, clutching the gun with both hands, extended her arms, pointing the automatic toward the dark corner of the house. It seemed an eternity before the familiar figure emerged into a spill of light. She sighed in relief and slowly lowered the automatic.

Chapter 5

Six hundred miles northeast of Bogotá, the village of Santa Rosa lay hidden in a subtropical valley, sequestered between the remote and inaccessible mountains of La Guajira. The population of Santa Rosa numbered fewer than 10,000 souls, but its cocaine refinery produced $25 billion worth of street "snow."

A minuscule percentage of this incredible revenue had raised the Guajira Indians from grinding, hopeless poverty to an economic level rivaling that of their fellow citizens living in the cities of Bogotá and Calí.

The Indians had for centuries chewed the raw coca leaf to guard against cold, hunger, and illness but regarded the refined cocaine as a white man's devil. The Indians believed the economic rewards derived from the coca leaf were a God-given blessing, and the instrument of that gift was Don Rafael Ordóñez, chosen by their Incan deity, Manco Capac, as his servant on earth.

Rafael Ordóñez was a Colombian aristocrat, whose Indian ancestry was mixed with that of the Spanish conquistadors. He had been educated in England and spoke five languages fluently. He was a brilliant administrator, with a remarkable talent for organization.

At age fifty-seven Ordóñez maintained his movie-star good looks. His thick shock of hair was as white as refined cocaine. His face was tanned from swimming and deep-sea fishing. He was fastidious and dressed impeccably, but his wardrobe almost never varied: Cartier sunglasses, Tanino Crisci shoes, white linen suits hand-tailored in Milan, and English sea cotton polo shirts. He wore the designer clothes even when visiting the refinery, which was situated in the heart of a rain forest.

The jungle complex contained facilities for 500 employees and a contingent of armed guards. There were air-conditioned dormitories, dining rooms, and a warehouse lined with floor-to-ceiling bins that stored stacks of $100 bills. The refinery was bordered by paved runways on which Learjets and sleek twin-engine Cessnas landed with bales of raw coca leaf and from which they took off with capacity loads of refined cocaine.

Ordóñez's partnership with feudal landowners in Bolivia, Peru, Ecuador, and Brazil assured him a year-round coca leaf cultivation of six million acres.

The shipments of refined cocaine were supervised by Ordóñez's cousin, Pedro Cisneros, under whose expert direction the drug was smuggled into the United States through an ingenious maze of couriers, private aircraft, high-speed boats, and mother ships operating throughout the chain of islands and cays stretching across the Caribbean.

Once he had assumed control of the fragmented Colombian drug industry, Ordóñez turned his attention to the American Mafia. In the fall of 1978 a highly trained squad of Colombian assassins invaded the Mafia's Florida domain. A bloody three-year drug war erupted in the city of Miami. In July 1981 an armistice was arranged—on Ordóñez's terms. The Mafia would no longer deal or distribute cocaine. It would hereafter confine its activities solely to money-laundering operations for which it would receive a 10 percent fee.

Ordóñez enjoyed his daily inspection of the refinery. The visits afforded him an opportunity to maintain personal contact with his employees. He felt like a general dispensing largess to his troops in return for their undying loyalty. The Indian laborers waved to Ordóñez and Cisneros as they walked past heaping piles of green coca leaves drying in the early morning sun. In addition to their employment in the transport and refinement of the coca leaf, the Guajira Indians constituted a human radar network: Ordóñez was always informed in advance of occasional Colombian Army patrols.

Ordóñez further ensured his safety by the assiduous use of bribes. He had deposited $10 million in the Bank of

Panama, in numbered accounts belonging to Colombian narcotics agents, military officers, and federal district judges. Ordóñez's credo was simple: "Offer a man a bribe; if he refuses, offer him a bullet."

The cousins entered the huge warehouse and stood in the doorway watching Indian laborers spraying DDT into the bins of $100 bills. Big gray rats feeding on the money scurried from bin to bin, but the chemical poison served only as a temporary deterrent.

"We must reconstruct this warehouse," Ordóñez said. "I want it twice the size with glass-encased bins."

"They say rats will survive the nuclear winter," Cisneros remarked.

"Perhaps, but they cannot eat glass. Let's get some air, Pedro."

They strolled through the streaky sunlight, past chemists wearing protective face masks as they blended the coca paste with sulfuric acid, lime, and potassium permanganate. They stopped for a moment at a tin-roofed shed containing heaping piles of fine white powder: concentrated cocaine, a drug so potent that a single line ingested produced instant heart seizure and death. This pure, lethal quality was cut with dextrose and lactose, before shipment to the United States, where it underwent further cutting, taking the potency down to less than 20 percent.

Ordóñez smiled, thinking of the incredible profit: One dollar's worth of coca leaf transformed itself into $300 worth of cut street snow.

The cousins halted at the edge of the rain forest, watching a four-wheel-drive Bronco jeep bouncing toward them. The Bronco braked, and the Indian driver jumped out and walked quickly to Ordóñez.

"*¿Qué pasa*, Manuel?" Ordóñez asked.

"*El alemán llega.*"

"*Gracias.*"

"*A su servicio, patrón.*"

"That kraut is always on time," Cisneros remarked.

"A national trait, Pedro."

"He's not one of us."

"We can't be all things, Cousin. For the moment we need this German."

They heard the distant scream of jet engines approaching the airstrip.

"Bring him to the villa," Ordóñez said.

Cisneros nodded and climbed into the jeep.

"Pedro!" Ordóñez called.

The driver had already placed the jeep in gear. Cisneros gripped the Indian's hand and turned to Ordóñez.

"Is *Ave María* in place?"

"Yes."

"When do you go?"

"Tomorrow. La Paz to Manzanillo."

"Good. By the way, Cousin, do you still communicate with the American girl?"

"What girl?"

"The blond girl—the courier of Whelan. I believe she makes pornographic films."

"Candy Lane . . . yes, once in a while I phone."

Ordóñez shoved the sunglasses up on his forehead and stared at his cousin with a curious mixture of amusement and menace. "It would be better not to do this," he said softly.

The three men were seated on the veranda of Ordóñez's Moorish estate. A blue striped awning shaded them from the tropical sun, and hidden speakers played lilting Peruvian music. Ordóñez had a passion for the sensual percussion and haunting flutes of native Peruvian music. The vast floral grounds of the estate were enclosed by high walls covered with lush purple bougainvillaea and topped by shards of glass. Wild coconut palms shrouded the grounds, providing shade for the constantly patrolling armed guards.

Kurt Ohlendorf had been speaking for the past five minutes. Cisneros and Ordóñez nodded occasionally but did not interrupt the sixty-eight-year-old financial wizard. The former director of the Reichsbank was tall and gaunt, almost cadaverous. His prominent nose was discolored by thin blue veins, and his watery gray eyes were laced by a network of fine red lines. Tufts of gray hair sprouted from his ears, and his thin lips were dry and cracked.

Ordóñez was anxious to dispense with the meeting. His Spanish wife and eldest daughter were vacationing in Madrid, and his coffee-colored blue-eyed Brazilian mistress waited upstairs in the guest bedroom.

Pedro Cisneros appeared to be concentrating on the German's recitation of current money-laundering operations, but his mind turned over Ordóñez's offhanded admonition regarding his phone calls to Candy Lane. He was well aware that Ordóñez never spoke of personal matters without good cause. The slightest deviation from accepted business procedure meant death. No words, no accusations—you were hit. Even as he puffed calmly on the Cuban cigar, Cisneros knew his cousin's mention of Candy Lane was symptomatic of something else.

"We have in this last quarter washed four billion dollars," Ohlendorf said, "but there are problems. The Bank of Boston has been exposed by the federal banking people for transferring, without record, two billion dollars to Switzerland." Ohlendorf wet his lips and continued. "Our bank accounts in Panama are reaching a dangerous limit. If there is ever a political upheaval, our deposits are vulnerable. Our accounts in Liechtenstein, Switzerland, West Germany, and Italy are fast approaching a point of no return." The gaunt German swallowed some beer and said, "We are drowning in cash."

Ordóñez calmly uncrossed his legs and lit a Bolivian cigarillo. His expressive black eyes were impossible to read behind the designer sunglasses. There was a moment of silence punctuated by staccato screams of jungle birds perched in the tall palms.

Ordóñez then spoke in a warm, fraternal manner. "You have, as always, been very precise, Kurt."

"Thank you, Don Rafael."

Ordóñez rose and stared off at the lush tropical vegetation. "We must find new avenues for laundering," he said quietly.

Ohlendorf nodded. "If not, we will be forced to curtail production."

Ordóñez watched a foot-long green lizard dart across

the Italian marble floor. "You both know my feelings. The answer to our problem resides with our Mafia partners."

"That's dangerous," Cisneros cautioned. "We have a historic arrangement."

"Arrangements are subject to revision," Ordóñez countered, and turned to the sweat stained German. "How much did they launder for us last year?"

"A little over one billion."

"I want to double that figure. Go to Los Angeles. Speak with Davis. Tell him to present my demands to Angelo Maffatore."

"All right, but—"

"There are no 'buts,'" Ordóñez interrupted. "The Mafia is a decrepit organization. The eagles are gone: Luciano, Costello, Gambino, and, most of all, their Jewish godfather, Lansky—a great man, Lansky. This young generation is infiltrated by FBI informers. They're careless. They lack the cunning and courage of their fathers."

"We don't want a war," Ohlendorf said.

"There will be no war," Ordóñez replied firmly. "Tell me, Kurt, what are the Mafia's annual receipts from pornography?"

"If one takes into account cassettes, books, films, and magazines, I would say in excess of six billion."

"And how is this revenue deposited?"

"Through a network of legitimate corporations in the U.S. and Canada. Perhaps as many as two hundred separate bank accounts."

"We'll pass the additional billion through those accounts and offer to raise their fee to twelve percent."

"And if they refuse?"

"I have no expertise in matters of cinema"—Ordóñez smiled—"but it would seem to me you cannot make films without actors."

Chapter 6

Candy Lane's nude body lay facedown on the wooden terrace. Clouds of green bottle flies swarmed over her legs, buttocks, and back. Her skin was blistered and scarlet from exposure to relentless rays of summer sun. A black line of ants had risen up through the wooden slats and feasted on dried blood and brain fluid that had leaked out of the gaping hole in her left temple. The Beretta automatic glinted in the sunlight inches from the dead girl's stiff fingers. A piece of her right thigh had been torn and mangled. The sickening sweet stench of decaying flesh rose from her body and seeped through the open terrace doors, fouling the close air in the bedroom.

Wearing surgical gloves and mask, the chief coroner for the city of Los Angeles, Gabriel Torres, knelt over the bloated corpse.

Jack Raines stood on the terrace, watching Torres conducting his forensic ritual. Raines was no stranger to violent death. His tour of duty in Vietnam and his years spent on the homicide detail had steeled him to the sight of violated human beings, but the malodorous stench of putrefied flesh transcended the visual horror; its rank cloying odor clung to the brain and penetrated the soul.

His eyes narrowed against the sun as he studied the scene on the beach. Halfway between the terrace and the surf a square section of beach had been roped off. Four Malibu police officers wearing sunglasses and sweating in the July sun restrained a curious crowd of surfers, joggers, bikini-clad sunbathers, and neighbors. A local newscaster was questioning an elderly white-haired woman. The woman had been taking her usual sunrise stroll along the beach when she heard the snarling sound of a dog coming from

Candy's terrace. The woman had moved tentatively toward the wooden decking before freezing in horror. A large mongrel dog seemed to be gnawing on the thigh of a nude girl lying motionless on the terrace. It took the woman a long time to realize that the nude figure was not sunbathing—and that the dog was not being playful.

The woman ran back to her house and phoned the Malibu sheriff's office. The squad of detectives and uniformed police arrived at the scene at 7:15 A.M. Once the bag of cocaine had been discovered in Candy's bedroom, the chief of Malibu detectives, Paul Lescano, phoned Tactical and alerted the NIFTY division.

Jack and Silvio had arrived at 8:30 A.M. along with a small army comprised of fingerprint men, lab technicians, coroner, chemists, and police photographers. The sounds of organized chaos endemic to police investigatory procedure filled the house.

Jack felt the rising rays of sun on his cheeks, and beads of sweat oozed out of his forehead and streaked down his face.

He lit a cigarillo and stared out to sea. A colorful fleet of sailboats wheeled and tacked in the Pacific breeze, darting gracefully back and forth as if performing a nautical ballet.

Torres belched loudly through the gauze mask and clutched his stomach. "Bag her hands," he ordered his attendants.

The coroner rose wearily, slid the surgical mask from his mouth, and smiled wanly at Jack. "I'll be a while, amigo."

The white-clad morgue attendants gently turned the dead girl over. The swarming flies buzzed angrily, rising like a black cloud. Candy's face was blue. Her open eyes were covered by a white film. Her long pale hair was stiff and darkened by dried blood.

Jack tossed his cigarillo over the terrace and went back inside. The crowd of print men, uniformed police, and plainclothesmen moved up and down the stairs and in and out of rooms with a careless nonchalance, as if they had lived in the place all their lives.

Silvio stood beside a police photographer who changed

lenses and snapped a few more shots of a valentine drawn in cocaine atop the bedside table. The valentine was bisected by an arrow, and the initials P. C. appeared in the heartshaped sections.

"That should do it," the photographer said.

"When you get them developed," Jack said, "have them sent to my attention at Tactical."

"Right, Lieutenant." The man wiped some sweat from his forehead. "Christ, the stink of that cunt is enough to put you on a permanent diet."

A sudden flash of heat rose in Jack's throat. His right hand shot out reflexively. He grabbed the photographer, spun him around, and slammed him against the wall.

"The name of the victim is Candy Lane," Jack rasped.

"Sure, sure. Sorry, Lieutenant."

The portly photographer hurried off. Jack opened his shirt at the neck, slipped off his tie, and removed his jacket.

"Take it easy, Jack," Silvio said quietly.

"What about that coke?" Jack asked.

"Chemist is breaking it down now."

The Malibu chief of detectives, Paul Lescano, tapped Jack on the shoulder. "We've got the prints, photos of the victim, and that valentine. They're getting ready to take her out to the meat wagon. Since this case has been turned over to NIFTY, I think you ought to talk to the press. I don't envy you, Raines. Celebrity porno star. Cocaine. This is a prime-time case."

"Can you assign a man front and back for the next couple of days?"

"Sure."

Lescano waved to his men. The plainclothesmen, uniformed troopers, and print men left the bedroom.

Two morgue attendants came into the bedroom, wheeling a gurney cart upon which rested the remains of Candy Lane, the outline of her shapely figure barely discernible encased in the black body bag.

"We're going out, Lieutenant," the attendant said.

"Just put her in the wagon," Jack replied. "Don't say a goddamned word to anyone."

Silvio noticed the small crescent scar on Jack's right

cheek had turned scarlet and his soft brown eyes were
cold and menacing.

"Be careful with the press," Silvio cautioned.

Jack nodded, turned, started out, and stopped abruptly
as something on the bed caught his eye. A smiling teddy
bear was propped against the pink silk pillows. The eyes of
the inanimate toy seemed to project a childlike innocence.

A convoy of disparate vehicles was parked in random
positions at the front entrance: an ambulance, a morgue
van, a coroner's van, three Malibu police cars, Jack's '71
GTO Pontiac convertible, a black Toyota belonging to
Gabriel Torres, and a TV mobile unit. A cluster of press
cars was parked on the edge of the single-lane road leading up to the Coast Highway.

The TV crews rolled their tape and the photographers' motorized Nikons clicked and buzzed as the attendants wheeled Candy Lane's body to the rear of the morgue
van.

Ignoring the press, the coroner's men opened the
van's rear door, slid the body inside, folded the gurney,
closed the door, and walked quickly to the front seat of the
van. The driver gunned the engine; the van wheeled
around and took off.

Jack came out of the front door and was immediately
surrounded by a crush of reporters hurling a noisy barrage
of disjointed questions.

"How long was she layin' out there, Lieutenant?"

"Was she working on a porno?"

"Was it a coke hit?"

"What'd they kill her with?"

A television anchorwoman with crooked teeth, platinum hair, and a fixed nose wormed her way through the
crowd. A cameraman hefting a miniature TV camera followed the woman. Jack knew her. Everyone knew her.
Gloria Hunnicutt was the reigning queen of network television show biz gossip.

She spoke with a slight lisp, constantly wetting her
lips. Ms. Hunnicutt was reputed to be an extraordinarily
gifted practitioner of fellatio who employed her devastat-
ing talent with unerring professional precision.

She smiled at Jack. "When you're through with these

'locals,' let's you and I have a private interview. You won't
be sorry. I'll say something very complimentary about
NIFTY."

"Forget it, Gloria."

"I can't do that, Lieutenant. I have thirty-five million
Americans just panting for your comments. After all, Candy
Lane was a big star."

He watched her lizardlike tongue flick across her lips.
The legendary TV gossip woman smiled seductively. "When
you're through with these clowns, I'll be waiting."

She sauntered off toward the house. The barrage of
questions from the press assaulted Jack.

"Hold it! Just hold it!" he shouted.

The gaggle of press people fell silent.

"I'll say this once."

The newsmen held small Sony recorders close to his
face.

"You people ready?"

"Go ahead, Lieutenant," a man from the Associated
Press replied.

"The nude body of Candy Lane was discovered by a
neighbor at six-ten A.M. this morning. She was killed by a
single twenty-five caliber bullet fired at close range into
her right temple. A Beretta automatic has been identified
as the gun from which the shot was fired."

"You mean murder weapon, don't you, Lieutenant?"
a journalist shouted.

"There is at the moment no indication of homicide. It
appears that Miss Lane took her own life." Jack wiped
some sweat from his forehead and took a deep drag of the
cigarillo. "A half kilo of cocaine was found in the victim's
bedroom." He did not mention the valentine with its
initials P. C., nor did he mention the dog bites. "The
coroner, Gabriel Torres, will perform an autopsy. The
results will be made public in the next seventy-two hours.
The investigation into Miss Lane's death is continuing."
He turned abruptly and started back toward the house. As
he reached the front door, a smiling Gloria Hunnicutt
blocked his path.

"Out of the way, Gloria."

"I insist on talking to you, Lieutenant."

"I've just given you an official statement."

"You gave *them* a statement. They haven't got thirty-five million Americans by the balls. I do."

Jack began to hyperventilate. The sun, the heat, the smell of death, the violated teenage girl, the teddy bear—all of it began to rush into his throat. "Drop it, Gloria."

"Oh, I can drop it, sweetheart; it's my viewers who demand answers."

"Just tell your viewers that Lieutenant Jack Raines said they can all go fuck themselves."

He brushed her aside and reentered the house.

A profound silence pervaded the living room. Jack studied the beautifully composed straight photographs of Candy. She had truly been a breathtaking beauty. Her looks, her figure, even her slender, delicate fingers were perfectly formed. He wondered what the impact of that beauty had been like in person.

Silvio Martinez came down the steps and walked up to him. "That was some girl."

Jack nodded. "After Torres finishes, let's go through her things. I want to notify her parents before the goddamn six o'clock news."

"Okay. By the way, that coke was seventy percent pure."

"Christ . . ."

"Damn near lethal."

"How the hell would she get that quality?"

"It's rare, but not impossible to come by. It takes a very connected dealer."

"Cisneros?"

"I doubt it. He's a smuggler, not a dealer."

"What about Whelan?"

"He may be a laundryman for Cisneros. If he is, he can get any quality he wants."

They crossed the living room to the answering machine with its blinking red light. The phone messages covered a three-day span. Karen Dara had phoned twice on Saturday night followed by one message Sunday afternoon. There was a week-old message from Pedro Cisneros. Leo Whelan had phoned at 2:00 P.M. the previous day.

There were additional calls from Lisa Chang, Sherry Nichols, and one touching message from Candy's father asking how she was and would she please phone him.

"That's it," Silvio said.

"Okay. Take the tape."

Jack walked over to a VCR unit connected to a large TV screen. Beside the unit a layered cabinet held a small library of cassettes. The straight film cassettes were separated from the hard-core. Jack perused the titles of the porno tapes: *Flesh and Fur, Apple Turnovers, High Society, Playgirls, Sugar Drops*, and *Lickorice*.

The bedroom was strangely peaceful; a palpable tranquillity had replaced the morning's chaos. The stench of decayed flesh had been dissipated by the fresh sea breeze blowing in from the open terrace, and for the first time Jack was aware of the rhythmic sound of waves breaking against the beach.

Gabriel Torres sat on a huge hassock, studying his notes attached to a clipboard. The Italian automatic resting on his lap was tagged and carried the code number assigned to the case. A spent cartridge was enclosed in a glassine bag. The Mexican-born coroner chewed on a cigar as he made a final notation. He picked up the gun, got to his feet, belched loudly, grimaced, and clutched his prominent belly. He glanced sheepishly at the two detectives.

"Forgive me, compadres, but I am a very sick man."

Raines had worked with Torres on numerous cases over the years and was familiar with the coroner's idiosyncrasies. You never rushed him. Torres was a man who collected his thoughts before he spoke.

"I've been suffering from gas. Belching and farting. I don't know what the hell is wrong with my stomach."

"Stop eating those goddamned frijoles," Silvio said.

"It's not my diet; it's my work."

"You look beat, Gabby," Jack said.

"I did not sleep last night. I spent the night dissecting what was left of a torso belonging to a young man found alongside the San Diego Freeway." Torres spoke English with a Mexican cadence and accent. "From what I could tell the victim was no more than seventeen. He had recently been sodomized. But whoever did this, whoever killed him is himself dead."

"How so?" Jack inquired.

"The blood samples of the victim were infected by a virulent AIDS virus." Torres smiled. "Sometimes justice is rendered by natural forces; not often, but sometimes."

"What about our dead little girl?" Silvio asked.

"Yes. Well, this is, of course, preliminary. There are many questions that will be answered only when I get her on the table." Torres displayed the blue steel automatic. "It's a twenty-five caliber Beretta. The clip accommodates nine slugs. One was fired. Eight remain. Here's the shell casing." He handed Jack the small glassine bag and said, "Ballistics will test-fire the gun to be certain this casing was ejected from this particular automatic. The victim died no less than forty-eight hours ago."

"Could she have been dead longer than that?"

"It's possible. There is advanced rigor mortis, and the sunburn and windburn make it difficult; but I'm certain she's been dead for at least forty-eight hours." Torres glanced at his clipboard. "There are powder burns on her right temple. The slug's trajectory appears to be lateral. The exit wound is two and a half inches in diameter. The bullet passed through the brain and shattered some skull bones as it exited. Her teeth are undamaged. Her jaw-bone's intact. Death was instantaneous. Her brain was destroyed on impact.

"The bite marks and torn flesh on the right thigh are unmistakably canine. Probably some rabid stray mongrel. People dump their unwanted dogs up in the hills. The animals are driven mad by hunger."

"You'd better alert the county animal control."

"I've taken care of it, amigo."

"What about the coke?" Silvio asked.

"The quantity of ingested cocaine, alcohol, or alien drugs will be determined by lab tests. The victim shows no traces of semen in any orifice, but there are indications of recent intercourse, both anal and vaginal. There is a slight swelling on her lower lip." He dropped some cigar ash into a ceramic ashtray. "That's it, compadres. I will by tomorrow afternoon have a complete report."

"What's your best guess, Gabby?" Jack asked.

"Suicide." He shrugged his broad shoulders. "But then again she could have been forced to lie down. The killer could have executed her, wiped his prints, wrapped the victim's hand around the gun butt, then placed it a few inches from her fingertips. But that's conjecture. I leave those mysteries to you." Torres started for the staircase, stopped, and turned. "She was a very beautiful girl. I wonder how she came to this." He paused, removed the cigar from between his teeth, and shrugged. "Maybe it's just America."

Jack walked over to the night table and studied the cocaine valentine with its bisecting arrow and initials P. C.

"Pedro Cisneros," Silvio suggested.

"You think Candy might have been a courier?"

"She may have made an occasional drop."

"Look at this," Jack said, indicating a leather-bound book on the bureau. "*Remembrance of Things Past*—Marcel Proust. What would Candy be doing with Proust?"

"Improving her mind," Silvio said.

"Probably a gift from some Hollywood swifty looking to fuck her through intellectual panache."

"Open it. Maybe there's an inscription."

Jack thumbed the first few pages, stopped, and read aloud, "To Candy with love, dreams, and eternal desire— Jeff Kellerman."

"You weren't wrong," Silvio said.

Jack snapped the book shut. "That pompous cocksucker probably promised her a straight role in his next picture."

Jack circled the bed, crossed to the far wall, and examined the framed review of *Lickorice*.

"She was obviously proud of this," he said.

"But why frame the goddamn thing?" Silvio asked.

"She was just a kid, not much older than my daughter. She had to be thrilled by kind words from a respected critic." Jack glanced at the smiling teddy bear and sighed. "Let's go to work."

Time passed unnoticed as they moved from room to room, sifting bureau drawers, closets, handbags, jewelry, cosmetics, medicine chest, record albums, refrigerator and freezer, the backs of framed photographs, under beds, under sofa pillows, potted plants. They shook out books that lined the living-room wall. They combed the grounds and searched through Candy's 450 SL Mercedes before returning to the bedroom.

They dropped all pertinent material on the bed: canceled checks, checkbook, diary, personal phone book, several letters, and a photograph of Candy and Karen Dara, seated on either side of Pedro Cisneros at the edge of a kidney-shaped pool. The photograph had been printed in a fast photo lab in Key Biscayne and was dated January 15.

Silvio thumbed through Candy's phone book, jotting down certain numbers. Jack read the letters. One was to her younger sister, Joyce; the other, to her father. The content of both letters was remarkably similar and almost exclusively dealt with her plans to cross over from X-rated films to straight movies.

There was a birthday card from her father still in its envelope. The return address read: "William Langley, 10567 Edna Way, Studio City, California."

"Her father's name is William Langley," Jack said. "Check her phone book."

Silvio turned the pages to the L's. "Got it. A Valley number for home and an Orange County number for office."

"It's two forty-five. Try the office number."

"You want me to tell him over the phone?"

"Better than the six o'clock news."

"I'm no good at this kind of thing," Silvio said.

Jack picked up the small directory and punched the buttons on the pink phone and waited. A female voice answered, "Avionics Industries."

"Mr. William Langley, please."

"One moment . . ."

Jack stared at the teddy bear.

Silvio sat on the edge of the bed, going through canceled checks.

"Mr. Langley's office," another female voice answered.

"This is Lieutenant Jack Raines, Tactical Division, Los Angeles Police. It's urgent that I speak with Mr. Langley."

There was a dead pause, and the voice said, "Can you please repeat your name?"

Jack complied.

The secretary said, "One moment."

"Hello?" The voice was reedy and tentative.

"Is this Mr. William Langley?"

"Yes . . ."

Jack identified himself again before asking, "Are you the father of Candy Lane?"

"Yes—what's happened?" Langley blurted.

There was no "right" way to break tragic news. You had to be fast, official, and precise.

"Mr. Langley, your daughter was found dead early this morning at her Malibu home. It appears she took her own life."

There was a whooshing sound as if a gulp of air had been ingested and exhaled.

"My God . . ." He gasped. "You're certain, Lieutenant?"

"Yes. I'm certain."

There was a long pause, and Jack knew the man was fighting for composure.

"Where is she?" Langley finally asked.

"Her body has been removed to the county morgue, where an autopsy will be performed."

Silvio did not look up, forcing himself to concentrate on Candy's checks.

"County morgue . . ." Langley whispered.

"Mr. Langley, if you will phone 555-6000 tomorrow afternoon, I will arrange for an officer to accompany you to the morgue. You'll be required to identify your daughter's remains, sign some forms, and claim her body."

"But—how did this happen?"

"Do you have that number?"

"Yes, 555-6000."

"You can phone me Wednesday morning. We'll arrange to meet at your convenience; by then I should have all the pertinent facts concerning your daughter's death."

"Will," he stammered, "will this be in the papers?"

"I'm afraid so. But I'll do what I can to minimize the publicity."

"Thank—thank you, Lieutenant. I must go home now. I have a younger daughter. She's in school. I must pick her up."

Jack hung up and walked slowly out onto the wooden terrace. The odor of death was gone, but dark blood smears stained the wooden decking.

On the beach a single patrolman stood a few yards from the house, which was encircled with official yellow tape. The morning crowd of curious onlookers was gone. Surfers rode the breakers. A few people sat in high-backed chairs, sunning and reading. A pair of joggers loped along the shoreline. Sea gulls cried and circled, seeking sand crabs. The afternoon sun painted flashing white sparks into the vast expanse of blue sea.

Jack tried to shut off the echoes of William Langley's stricken voice. He thought about Jenny. Same generation as Candy, facing the same temptations, the same pressures. How do you protect children against what's out there? The question was unanswerable.

Silvio came out on the terrace. "She was paid by five different companies. The principal one seems to be Galaxy Films Distribution Company. In any case, Leo Whalen signed all the checks."

"We'll pay the Whale a visit."

"There are addresses and phone numbers in her book belonging to her fellow actors."

"How do you know that?"

"It's in her diary. They worked in her last porno. I guess they shot all day Saturday and on into the night."

"Where?"

"Up at John Traynor's house on Sunset Plaza Drive."

"What else?"

"Some interesting names in her diary."

"Like who?"

"Sid Davis, Maffatore, and Jeff Kellerman."

"Any comments?"

"She goes on about Kellerman. It looks like they were pretty thick."

"Marcel Proust." Jack sighed disdainfully.

Silvio glanced at the dark stains on the decking, then stared off at the surging sea. "I don't know what it was that pushed her this far, but the goddamned coke didn't help her any. Sometimes," Silvio said haltingly, "sometimes I feel like walking down dealer's row with an Uzi and just blowing those cocksuckers away. Sometimes—" His voice broke.

Jack had heard similar comments from almost every frontline narco cop he had ever worked with. They were a breed apart, afflicted by a consuming, hopeless rage.

Silvio handed Jack a sheet of pink stationery. "I found this pressed between the covers of her diary."

The words were written in block letters:

SHE SMILED ON CUE — A CELLULOID
FANTASY, LOST IN THE LIGHTS,
SEEKING A DREAM THAT
WOULD NEVER COME TRUE.

C.L. 7/8/86

Chapter 7

A handsome woman wearing a black evening gown stood atop the Arc de Triomphe. The amber lights of the Champs-Élysées glowed in the background. The woman held a fluted rose-colored bottle of perfume and smiled seductively as the camera moved into a close-up. She spoke in a husky voice, extolling the virtues of the perfume.

The TV commercial played to a handful of late-afternoon customers in a dimly lit Mexican restaurant on Figueroa Street. Seated on high stools at the Formica-topped bar were two Japanese youths, a Cuban numbers runner, a tired-looking black transvestite, and a bearded Caucasian with long, flowing hair, wearing khakis and a field jacket bearing the insignia of the 101st Airborne Division.

The perfume commercial had nothing to do with their lives, but the people at the bar stared at the TV screen with hypnotic attention.

Jack and Silvio were seated in a booth toward the rear. Silvio had suggested the place for several reasons. It was close to Leo Whelan's office in Chinatown, the food was passable, and the restaurant was a hangout for contact people who worked with Silvio's principal informer, Pepe Montoya.

"What do you make of the names in Candy's directory?" Silvio asked.

"You mean the straight film people?"

"Yeah."

"We should talk to Jeff Kellerman, but we've got a hell of a lot of doors to knock on before we see him."

Jack lit a cigarillo and glanced up at the TV screen. The perfume commercial had been replaced by a daytime soap featuring a scene in a hospital room of a grimacing teenage girl caught in the agonizing throes of childbirth.

"You think someone hit Candy?" Silvio asked.

Jack shrugged. "No signs of a struggle or forced entry, nothing disturbed. Her poem indicates despondency, and she was probably wired on that seventy percent snow. My guess is she was depressed, went out onto the terrace, and blew her brains out."

"That cocaine valentine to P.C. might have been her suicide note," Silvio suggested. "She could have been tight with Cisneros."

"Doesn't add up," Jack said. "How could she have a case on a man who has to slip in and out of the country like a shadow? Pedro Cisneros is on the watch list of every immigration officer at every airport and border crossing in the country. It's like trying to maintain a relationship with a ghost." He paused, inhaling deeply on the cigarillo. "There's one other thing: We're assuming that Candy drew the valentine."

"I didn't think of that," Silvio replied. "Christ, I hope we don't have a homicide on our hands; it clouds what we're really after—tracking that high-grade coke."

Silvio poured the last of his beer and asked, "Did you get hold of Commander Álvarez?"

Jack nodded. "I wired the transcript of Pepe's tape to Mexican naval headquarters in Manzanillo."

"Álvarez runs a hell of a good department," Silvio said. "Maybe his intelligence unit can make sense out of it."

Jack swallowed some beer and sighed. "I can't get that teddy bear out of my head. Years ago I bought one just like it for Jenny."

"Don't equate this case with your daughter. Candy made her choice."

"What choice? Listen, you throw enough money at some teenage kid, give her some celebrity, hook her on drugs, and there are no more choices."

"No one forced her into porn and drugs."

"That's bullshit. She had no one to lean on. She was a beauty loose in a jungle full of predators—mind fuckers. Hell, the last line of her poem says it all: 'lost in the lights,/seeking a dream that/would never come true.' My own daughter could have written that line."

"I tell you again, don't personalize this thing." Silvio stared into his glass. "I made that mistake once." He raised the glass and sipped some beer. "In Miami, in '78, I was second man in the South Florida Drug Enforcement Division. We had a fine Cuban community, all of us refugees. We respected this country. The Americans took us in when Castro came to power. There are no more patriotic Americans than the Cuban community in Miami. When the Colombians started the snowstorm, our kids began to get hooked. I worked eighteen hours a day, seven days a week. But it was pissing against the tide. We could never crack the top echelon. One day a woman, an attractive woman, Maria Vasconsuelos, from a fine Cuban family, came into my office and volunteered to work undercover. She was twenty-eight. Bright. Educated. Determined. That girl did more for the United States than the entire South Florida antidrug unit. She infiltrated the top-level Colombian *coqueros*. She was incredibly brave. I loved her but never made love to her. You understand what I mean?"

Jack nodded but remained silent.

"I ran her too long," Silvio continued. "I got greedy. Her information was like gold. I knew she was taking high risks. I was married. I had two kids. I had personal problems. I had the weight of the department on me. I knew Maria was going too far, but I let her run. Her intelligence was making us all look good. We scored some fantastic coke busts. We damn near nailed Cisneros. Maria put us close to the top, all the way to Ordóñez. I don't know who she slept with, who she conned, or how she got her wires, but I finally decided to take her out of action." Silvio drained his beer. "It was the night of July Fourth. I went out to her house on Calle Ocho, in Little Havana. It was a hot, muggy night, firecrackers and Roman candles. The door was open. I walked into the living room. She was all over the place. It was like someone had smeared the walls with strawberry jam. I fell apart. Booze. Uppers. Downers. Blew my life. My family. The director of the DEA sent me to a rehabilitation center in Virginia. It took two years for me to straighten out. I blamed myself for Maria. I personalized her death."

"I understand," Jack said. "When my wife was killed, I felt the same way. We'd been divorced for five years. But still, I blamed myself. You have to try to forget and go on."

"And never personalize any case," Silvio pointedly added.

The men rose and started out. As they passed the bar, the bearded man wearing the army jacket slid off the stool and grabbed Silvio's arm.

"*¿Qué tal, amigo?*" the veteran asked.

"*Como siempre.*" Silvio smiled.

"*¿Tiene poco?*"

Silvio reached into his pocket and handed the man a twenty-dollar bill.

"*Muchísimas gracias.*"

"*De nada.*"

"*El dragón de purpúreo—a las once.*"

"*Muy bien.*"

Chapter 8

The late-afternoon sun was a yellow smear discolored by the exhaust of 200,000 vehicles converging on the downtown freeway exchange.

The chilled air inside the Pontiac smelled like mustard gas, causing their eyes to smart.

Jack drove the GTO convertible east on North Broadway, through the heart of Chinatown. They passed ancient two-story redbrick buildings bearing signs in Chinese characters that advertised laundries, restaurants, import-export companies, check cashing, and travel agencies.

Jack slid a cassette into the stereo, and the Goodman quartet swung into the original recording of "Here's That Rainy Day."

"You like that old stuff, huh?" Silvio asked.

"Now and then. I guess I was never hip enough to understand rock and roll."

He braked sharply as a mangy dog trotted across the intersection. "It's probably none of my business, but what did that bearded character tell you?"

"Pepe wants to see me tonight."

"Where?"

"A Chinese hash house on Sunset and Descanso called the Purple Dragon."

"You want company?"

"Can't do that."

"Watch yourself," Jack said. "If the Colombians ever find out Pepe's flipped, you'll get hit with him."

He turned left onto Spring Street and cruised slowly for three blocks, checking the numbers.

"There it is," Silvio said, pointing to a two-story redbrick building. A faded sign attached to the roof read "Galaxy Films Distribution Company."

They parked in a dirt lot adjacent to the building. There were five other vehicles in the lot, including a large Volvo station wagon and a 1986 Jaguar with Nevada plates. A pile of flattened cardboard cartons was stacked flush to the building, obscuring the first-floor windows.

A big Oriental man sporting a Fu Manchu mustache came out the rear door, carrying a steel film container in each hand. He wore cotton pants and a T-shirt cut off at the sleeves. The muscles in his arms were the size of grapefruits. He crossed the lot toward the station wagon and grinned at the two detectives.

Jack returned the smile and asked for directions to Leo Whelan's office.

"Go to front door. Press button."

"What about the door you just came out of?" Silvio asked.

"No good. Locked now."

Jack took out his leather holder and displayed his gold badge. "We're police. Can you open that rear door for us?"

"You go front. Press button."

The man brushed Jack aside and walked deliberately to the station wagon. He tossed the film cans onto the rear seat, got behind the wheel, gunned the motor, and grinned at them derisively before stirring up a cloud of dust as he sped out of the lot.

They walked through a narrow alley to the building's front entrance. Jack pressed a button on the door's serrated speaker.

"Can I help you?" A muffled female's voice came through the speaker.

"Lieutenant Raines and Agent Martinez to see Mr. Whelan."

"One moment," the voice replied.

A filthy derelict shuffled toward them. His front teeth were missing, and his eyes were red and watery. His breath smelled as if he'd been drinking formaldehyde. "Got a quarter?" he rasped.

The door lock release buzzed, and they went inside. The wino cursed the two detectives and their ancestors until he had exhausted his rich vocabulary of expletives.

The ground floor was alive with activity. A cacophony of typewriters and ringing phones issued from a warren of open cubicles where men and women pored over ledgers and invoices.

People crisscrossed the central corridor, carrying bits of paper, still shots, posters, and reels of film.

They walked the length of the corridor to a large L-shaped desk where a pleasant-looking black woman operated an old-fashioned plug switchboard. She disconnected several lines, then turned to the two detectives. "Up those stairs; first office on the right."

Leo Whelan's office appeared to have been furnished from the Hill Street depot of the Salvation Army: Nothing matched in color, style, or fabric. A heavy iron safe and three steel cabinets were set against the far wall. A grimy large window overlooked the parking lot, and a variety of porno posters decorated the wall behind Whelan's desk.

The pornbroker's immense belly heaved as he reached for a cigar. "Sit down, fellas." He smiled. "Take a load off."

Whelan raised a match to the cigar, and the diamond ring on his pinkie sparkled brilliantly. Silvio sat on the arm of a worn chintz sofa. Jack remained standing. "How's business, Leo?" he asked.

"Not bad. I'm busting my ass to edit Candy's last picture. Got to ship in two weeks." He blew some smoke. "The wire services broke the news of her death. My phones have been going crazy. I'm gettin' bookings from straight theaters." He paused and shook his head. "Damn shame. The kid was surefire box office. She was on her way."

"To what?" Silvio asked sarcastically.

"Big bucks, that's what. Listen, pornography is just another form of cinema art."

"You call fucking and sucking art?" Jack asked.

Whelan's voice took on a gruff tone. "Let's not get sanctimonious. Erotica is what *you* like; pornography is what the other guy likes. I was crazy about Candy. I paid her more money than any star since Marilyn Chambers. I didn't put a gun in her back. These people come to us. We don't kidnap them. Now, I'll cooperate with you fellas, but spare me the morality."

"You're absolutely right, Leo," Jack said calmly. "Business has nothing to do with morality."

"Damn right. Look at these defense contractors charging the government ten grand for a fucking toilet seat. You fellas wanna little scotch?"

"No," Jack replied. "I'd rather have some of that seventy percent coke you dish out to your stars."

Whelan's puffy red cheeks lost some of their color. "I never in my life touched cocaine."

"We found a half kilo of seventy percent snow in Candy's bedroom," Silvio said. "Any idea how she got it?"

Whelan sighed. "Let me give you some history. These kids start with straight nude photos. They go from soft-core shots to beavers, to lez spreads, to hard-core loops, coking up all the way. By the time I get them, they're snow-blind. Candy Lane was an ice princess—a three-gram-a-day user long before Sherry Nichols discovered her."

Silvio moved toward the desk. "So they get hooked in the farm system, right?"

"It's not just porn. They get hit on by degenerates in the straight film business. Listen, there's maybe ten reliable broads in this whole racket. The men are even scarcer. They burn out faster. It's not easy to assemble a cast of star performers. The last thing I'd do is to give them coke. I run a legitimate business, and I pay my people top dollar. I don't ask them what they do off-camera."

Jack sat on the corner of Whelan's desk. "When was the last time you saw Candy?"

"Close to midnight this past Saturday. She finished her last scene and left."

"Where were you shooting?"

"John Traynor's house."

"The manufacture of pornography is illegal in Los Angeles."

"No shit?" Leo smiled. "That law is on appeal. You want to book me, book me."

"Did you pay Candy that night?" Silvio asked.

"I gave her fifty one-hundred-dollar bills."

"That's funny," Silvio said. "We only found two crumpled twenties in her purse."

"I can't help what you found. I paid her five grand."

"You pay your stars in cash?" Jack asked.

"Whatever they want. If they don't declare it, that's their problem. I don't separate the angels for Uncle Sam."

"You phoned Candy Sunday afternoon," Silvio said.

"That's right. We had printed all the film. I wanted to tell her how terrific it turned out."

Silvio edged closer to Whelan. "You wired Candy. You hooked her. You were her dealer. You and your Colombian friend Pedro Cisneros. You're a fucking laundryman. You and Sid Davis and Angelo Maffatore."

The Whale's great belly heaved as he rose out of his high-backed chair. His tree-trunk arms dangled apelike from his massive shoulders. He placed the cigar in a blue ceramic ashtray and looked straight at Jack. "I know you for a long time, Raines, from the days you worked vice out of Tactical. You were a glory boy but straight. Now you're running this NIFTY squad and you picked up this spic." His right thumb indicated Silvio. "You want my help, tell your spic partner to behave himself."

Silvio moved with swift, deadly grace. His left hand was a blur as it sank into the Whale's belly up to Silvio's elbow. The pornbroker grunted, grabbed his stomach, and fell back, flopping into his chair. Silvio's open right hand played a loud tattoo across Whelan's cheeks. The force of the blows snapped Whelan's head back and forth.

Jack grabbed Silvio and pinned his partner's arms. "Enough!"

Silvio gasped for air, still feeling the rush of adrenaline. "That's for nothing," Silvio rasped at Whelan. "I'll nail you for dealing, you fat prick. One way or the other. But you'd better be civil with me. I got a hundred ways to make rat shit out of you."

Whelan's eyes teared, and purple splotches appeared on his cheeks. "Nolan's gonna hear about this, Raines."

"I apologize, Leo," Jack said soothingly. "But my partner tends to get emotional when he sees dead kids wired out on coke. Now, just answer a few questions, and we'll get out of here."

"I'm listening," Whelan said, glancing warily at Silvio, who had crossed to the grimy window.

"How many different companies do you operate?"

"No comment."

"You ever do business with Sid Davis or Angelo Maffatore?"

"No comment."

"How much you gross in a year?"

"Ask the IRS."

Silvio turned from the window and spoke to Whelan in a calm voice. "You'd better answer him."

Whelan glared at Silvio and rubbed his left cheek. "I personally do maybe four hundred million a year."

"In films?" Jack answered.

"Films, cassettes, books, magazines, and I got a direct mail-order business in the basement. I get hard-core stills by the bulk for a buck apiece. I mount them and send them out for fifteen bucks apiece."

"Is that what comes out of those cartons outside?"

"Yeah."

"Keeping the cartons piled up like that is a fire hazard."

"Well, let them give me a citation."

"So you gross four hundred million?" Jack pressed.

"Give or take a nickel. If I get a hot picture like *Lickorice*, the gross increases. The big thing now is cassettes. No telling where the top is. We got a tiger by the tail. Look, this whole business started as an accident. Lovelace swallowed a giant cock in a seven-minute loop. That wop director spotted her and came up with the gimmick for *Deep Throat*. Picture broke out big; that cunt's tonsils became part of our culture and created a whole industry."

"What does the industry gross?"

"A little better than six billion."

Silvio moved a few feet toward Whelan. "You ever use Candy to carry money?"

"No."

"You know Pedro Cisneros?"

"I heard the name. Never met him."

"What about Rafael Ordóñez?"

Whelan chewed his underlip and shook his head no.

"Did anyone have it in for Candy?"

"Beats me. She was a nice kid. Everyone liked her. I thought she committed suicide. At least that's what's on the radio."

Jack took the photograph of Candy, Karen Dara, and Cisneros out of his pocket and dropped it on the Whale's desk.

"Recognize them?"

"Sure. This is Candy, and the other quiff is Karen Dara. I don't know the guy."

"The guy is Pedro Cisneros. The picture was taken in Key Biscayne."

"So what?" Whelan shrugged.

"This Karen Dara work for you?"

"Yeah, but not exclusively. She's a star. She worked Saturday night with Candy."

"What would two of your stars be doing with Ordóñez's right-hand man?"

"Ask Karen Dara." Whelan sighed. "Is there anything else?"

"I want all the film you shot Saturday night," Jack replied. "Outtakes. Everything. And a list of names and addresses of everyone, cast and crew."

"I could ask you to get a court order," Whelan replied.

"You're right, Leo," Jack said. "We can come back with a court order. It's up to you."

Whelan hesitated, eyeing both men. "What the fuck, I got nothing to hide." He spun around and pressed a button on the intercom.

"Betty?"

"Yes?"

"Is the chink back?"

"Just came in."

"Have him meet Officers Raines and Martinez at their car. I want him to give them all the positive film on *Candy Cotton*. Outtakes, too. And a call sheet with cast and crew."

"Right."

Whelan released the button and relit his cigar.

"Did Candy ever mention the director Jeff Kellerman?" Jack asked.

"No, but he's a well-known DG."

"What's a DG?"

"Degenerate," Whelan replied, then paused, before he asked, "You think someone hit Candy?"

"What do *you* think, Leo?"

"I think you guys were out of line. I cooperated, and you leaned on me. That wasn't right."

"I apologize," Silvio said. "It wasn't personal. I have an aversion to being called a spic."

"Just an expression."

"Well, then, there's no hard feelings." Silvio smiled. "You know, Leo, you really ought to lose some weight. Maybe you ought to start snorting some of that high-grade snow you gave Candy. Coke is one hell of a diet depressant."

Leo waited until he heard the rear door close before rising and walking to the window. He watched the big Chinaman place a dozen film cans in Raines's Pontiac. He wondered if he had made a mistake surrendering the film. But there hadn't been much choice; besides, all they would see was a few hours of unedited fucking and sucking. His cheeks still smarted from Silvio's open palm blows, and his stomach ached from the left hook. He turned from the window and glanced up at the *Lickorice* poster of Candy Lane smiling mischievously. He wished now that he hadn't sent her to Florida with the check for Cisneros. The connection was dangerous. The fucking Colombians were crazy. Candy might have offended Cisneros. The spics might have hit her. Candy's eyes seemed to follow him as he paced the threadbare rug, trying to decide whether or not to phone Sidney Davis.

Chapter 9

In his glass-encased office, eighteen stories above Sunset Boulevard, Sidney Davis reread the text of the front-page story for the third time.

The dapper attorney was a slightly built, soft-spoken man whose nondescript features masked a ruthless intelligence. Despite his bland appearance, he was capable of flashing a dazzling smile which he used with calculated effectiveness.

Davis had graduated from Stanford Law School cum laude and in less than a decade had become a leading attorney specializing in theatrical law. His list of clients comprised a who's who of movie stars, directors, producers, and in one case a major motion-picture company.

His reputation as a brilliant negotiator was without parallel. He possessed a computerlike, instantaneous grasp of complex legal details. Before he entered a negotiation, Davis's private investigators would collect personal data on his adversaries, seeking a skeleton that might be rattled at the appropriate moment. He was a student and admirer of Niccolò Machiavelli's philosophy and subscribed to the Florentine's theory of negotiation: "There is nothing more difficult to take in hand, more perilous to conduct, or more uncertain in its success, than to take the lead in the introduction of a new order of things." Sidney was a listener, a counterpuncher.

His tax-sheltered income was in excess of $1 million a year, and he had invested the proceeds exclusively in real estate. He owned property in Century City, Brentwood, and Beverly Hills and a private villa in the Mexican resort of Manzanillo.

In the fall of 1982 Davis was appointed special counsel to a major Hollywood trade union. The union controlled all the "rolling stock" used in the manufacture of motion pictures. The appointment inevitably led Davis to Angelo Maffatore. The aging mafioso presided over the national council and supervised all Cosa Nostra activities in the Far West. After numerous meetings Maffatore retained Davis as his personal attorney.

It was not the money alone that induced Sidney to accept Maffatore as a client. He had become progressively bored with the practice of theatrical law. A pervasive irrelevance had crept into his psyche. He had begun to feel that life was predictable, that every deal was a replay of the previous negotiation. He was tired of acting as a father figure to insecure actors and actresses.

Angelo Maffatore represented a dangerous but fascinating client. Sidney had always been impressed with power and found a certain exhilaration in being chief counsel to a man who wielded life-and-death authority over a vast illicit empire.

Sidney had taken pains to shield his wife and two sons from his association with the West Coast Godfather. His penchant for secrecy was based not on fear for the physical safety of his family but rather out of consideration for his wife's lofty social standing in Los Angeles's moneyed society.

His own public image was above reproach. There were, after all, nationally renowned attorneys who made no excuses for their representations of infamous clients. As long as an attorney did not cross that fragile line into prior knowledge of criminal intent, he remained legally protected by the law of "privileged" client-attorney information. Sidney had so far managed to stay on the right side of that line.

Having finished the article, he turned back to the front page and glanced once again at the headline: PORNO QUEEN DIES IN MALIBU. A full-length photo of Candy Lane wearing a skimpy bikini appeared alongside the text, which quoted a brief statement issued by Lieutenant Jack Raines.

The girl's sudden and violent death troubled Sidney. Candy was money-in-the-bank, a star performer in Maffatore's burgeoning porno industry operated by Leo Whelan. Sidney had visited the set of *Lickorice* in San Francisco and remembered the child-woman's electrifying sensuality. The loss of Candy Lane's services would be measured in millions. According to the newspaper story, her death was attributed to suicide. Sidney hoped the report was accurate. The police usually closed suicide cases with dispatch. But the discovery of cocaine at the murder site had brought the NIFTY squad into the case.

The buzzer on his phone console sounded.

"Yes?"

"Kurt Ohlendorf is here."

"Send him in."

The German's very presence in his office was a severe test of the fragile legal line binding Sidney. The former Nazi banker represented Rafael Ordóñez, and the purpose of this meeting concerned money laundering. Was he violating his position as an officer of the court by agreeing to meet with Ohlendorf? Probably not. He was not legally responsible for the source of Ordóñez's money, nor was he personally engaged in the process of money laundering. He was merely representing his client's interests in a business matter. The impending meeting with Ohlendorf was simply a logical flow of converging interests centered on his client, Angelo Maffatore. The meeting was not illegal but rather a syllogistic inevitability. The ethics of his position were irrelevant. Lawyers represented clients, not morality.

The office door opened, and Sidney flashed his brilliant smile at Ohlendorf. "Good to see you, Kurt," he said, shaking the gaunt German's hand. "Sit down, please."

"I have only minutes. I must take a flight within the hour for San Francisco. I return to Los Angeles tonight."

"Can I get you a drink?"

"No. Nothing."

Sidney was intrigued by Ohlendorf's history. The Nazi banker had fled Berlin in March 1945 to Switzerland, carrying with him $8 million worth of "Pay the bearer" certificates. He had spent the last months of the war in Lausanne, actively aiding Nazi war criminals escape to the safety of South America.

Ohlendorf cleared his throat and took out a gold cigarette case, extracted a cigarette, and struck the lighter. The smoke rushed out of his nostrils in two thick gray lines. "As you know," the German said, "we are presently laundering one billion dollars through your client's various pornographic accounts for which the Mafia receives a ten percent fee. Now we—"

"I'm sorry," Sidney interrupted, "but I know nothing about my client's business arrangements with Rafael Ordóñez."

"Yes, yes," Ohlendorf said impatiently. "For us, you and I, here in this office, you know nothing." He sucked on the cigarette and spoke through the smoke. "Rafael Ordóñez wishes to revise his agreement with your client. It is his intention to increase the amount laundered by the Mafia from one billion to two billion. This additional money can easily be washed through your client's pornographic cassette companies. Ordóñez wants you to convey his request at once to Don Angelo and that you personally come to Santa Rosa with Maffatore's response."

"I can't promise you an immediate answer," Sidney calmly replied. "Don Angelo is at the moment in New York."

"You can phone him."

"Don Angelo will be back on Tuesday." Sidney smiled. "It's only a matter of forty-eight hours."

Ohlendorf stared icily at Davis and nodded imperceptibly. "I will be staying at the Bel-Air Hotel, and I await your call."

"Have a good trip to San Francisco," Sidney said. "A pity you have to rush back. San Francisco is the jewel of American cities."

"I find Lausanne to be the only civilized city in the world. Thank you for your time, Mr. Davis." Ohlendorf cracked the door open and as an afterthought said, "By the way, Rafael Ordóñez made an interesting observation. It is his belief that films cannot be produced without the services of actors." He paused and pointedly added, "Or actresses. *Auf Wiedersehen, Herr Davis.*"

Sidney walked slowly back to his desk wondering if Candy Lane might have been the first victim of Ordóñez's "observation." He was also intrigued by Ordóñez's request for him personally to deliver Maffatore's response in Santa

Rosa. The Colombian drug overlord was almost a mythological figure in Sidney's mind, and the prospect of meeting him was both frightening and exciting. The loud buzz on Sidney's private line interrupted his thoughts. He leaned forward and lifted the receiver. "Yes?"

"Leo."

"You on a clean line?" Sidney inquired of Whelan.

"Absolutely."

"Go ahead."

"You heard about Candy?"

"Only what I read."

"Those bastards from NIFTY took all the footage of *Cotton Candy*."

"So what?"

"This NIFTY unit isn't vice. They drew the case because the Malibu cops found seventy percent snow in that cunt's bedroom."

"What else?"

"That spic partner of Raines's leaned on me."

"I'll phone John Nolan. Is that it?"

"Not quite. Candy carried a check to Cisneros back in January. Raines has a photograph of Candy and Karen Dara with Cisneros at Key Biscayne."

Sidney turned over the Cisneros-Candy Lane connection. It was a direct link between the teenage porn star and Ordóñez's right-hand man.

"You still there?" Whelan asked.

"Yes, I'm here."

"Are we okay with the Colombians?"

"Why do you ask?"

"I think the fucking Colombians hit Candy."

"What makes you think so?"

"I hear things on the street."

"Good-bye, Leo."

Chapter 10

Jack and Silvio were seated in the small screening room at Tactical. They had viewed ninety minutes of Candy Lane's last film; reel after reel depicted almost every conceivable human sexual attitude and combination. The footage had featured John Traynor alternately mounting Candy, Lisa Chang, and a young girl with long red hair who was obviously wired. In the scenes with Traynor, Candy seemed passive and emotionless, but the Oriental girl and the redhead appeared to be enthralled by Traynor's giant organ.

The screen went dark, and the lights came up as the projectionist changed reels.

"Guy like Traynor can give you a complex," Silvio said.

"You could hang wash on that goddamn thing," Jack agreed.

"I wonder who the redhead is?"

"Probably a fluff they're bringing along," Jack replied. "She's not even listed on the call sheet."

The lights were doused, and the screen lit up.

The huge circular bed was bathed in a magenta glow. Lisa Chang's head was buried between Candy's legs. The redhead's mouth covered Candy's right nipple, and Karen Dara performed the same action on Candy's left breast. A tall, homely woman moved into the scene and redirected Candy's hands so they appeared to be caressing the necks of the two girls.

"That must be the director, Sherry Nichols," Jack said.

The woman moved out of the frame, and the scene continued.

Jack thought Karen Dara was strangely attractive. She did not have Candy's classic beauty, but there was something compelling about her aristocratic demeanor.

The action played for a minute or so; then the redhead pulled her mouth from Candy's nipple and slid down Candy's body. Karen Dara raised herself and kissed Candy lightly and repeatedly before their mouths joined in one long sensual caress.

"That kiss looks pretty real to me," Jack observed.

"If it isn't, someone should give them Oscars."

They ran another forty minutes of film before the lights came up and the projectionist's voice came over the control console: "That's all of it, Lieutenant."

"Thanks, Pete."

"Do we hold this stuff or what?"

"Just store it for now."

Jack rose. "You notice in all the footage Karen Dara never once worked with Traynor."

"I guess some of these women just do lez scenes," Silvio replied.

The intercom buzzed. "Lieutenant?"

"Yeah?"

"Nolan wants to see both of you."

John Nolan was on his feet, his usual gray pallor was slightly flushed, and his voice was thick with anger. He pointed a long cigar at Silvio.

"You may be DEA, Martinez, but as long as you're attached to NIFTY, you're working for me, and my people don't rough up citizens. I don't give a shit if Whelan is pimp, pornographer, or dealer. I won't permit Gestapo tactics." Nolan paused, catching his breath. "This isn't Miami. This isn't Havana or La Paz, and I don't appreciate irate phone calls from important attorneys like Sidney Davis."

Silvio glared at Nolan but did not respond.

Jack intervened. "Listen, John, we started the day looking at Candy Lane's body. It wasn't pretty, and we were not in the best of humor. The truth is Whelan insulted Silvio."

"So he called him a spic—so what?" Nolan asked, the

tone of his voice moderating. "The local press have labeled me a pigheaded mick. You don't use that badge to muscle citizens or suspects—or anyone else." Nolan sunk into his chair. "Christ almighty, we're all over the goddamn six o'clock news. Front page in the *Examiner* and *Times*. The last thing we need is Sid Davis filing a battery complaint against one of my men with the city attorney's office."

"I apologized to Whelan." Silvio sighed. "I apologize to you."

"All right," Nolan grumbled. "Let's put it behind us. I'm not asking you fellows to walk on water, but we're dealing with connected people and a celebrity suicide."

"We could be dealing with a celebrity homicide," Jack added.

"I don't even want to think that." Nolan paused. "Have you notified next of kin?"

Jack nodded. "Candy's father. His name is William Langley."

"Is he anybody?"

"Probably not. He's employed at a place called Avionics Industries, one of those defense plants out near Disneyland."

"We found seventy percent cocaine in Candy's bedroom," Silvio said, "and a valentine drawn in coke with the initials P. C., and a photograph of Candy and Karen Dara with Pedro Cisneros in Key Biscayne."

Nolan scratched a pimple on his jaw and leaned back. "You think Candy may have been a courier?"

Silvio shrugged. "She might have carried a check from Whelan to Cisneros."

"You're the expert. How rare is seventy percent coke?"

"Very rare. It would have to be supplied by an extraordinary source. In this case it might have gone from Cisneros to Whelan to Candy."

"If we could prove that, it would give us the Colombia-Mafia connection we've been looking for. We'll never get Ordóñez, but we might nail Davis and Maffatore."

"There's something else," Jack said. "We found two twenties in Candy's purse, but Whelan claims he paid her five thousand in cash Saturday night."

"Christ . . ." Nolan moaned. "You think some street guys might have hit her and grabbed the cash?"

"It's possible. Might even be a goddamn vigilante. Some nut who wants to cleanse America of pornography. But outside of the missing money, all the evidence points to suicide."

Nolan drummed his fingertips on the desk. "Did that film tell you anything?"

"Pretty raw," Jack said. "But well composed, well shot, well lit."

"Candy in everything?"

Jack nodded. "But the only time I believed she was into it was a kissing scene with Karen Dara."

"You think Candy was gay?"

"I think she was lost and desperate. We found a poem she wrote about chasing dreams that never come true."

"How does a nineteen-year-old white kid from an apparently middle-class family get into this toilet?"

"Who knows?" Jack said. "A distorted view of the contemporary American dream—fame, glamour, money."

"And coke," Silvio added. "She also had some contacts with people in straight films."

Nolan's gray pallor turned a shade lighter, and his troubled eyes narrowed. "No stars, I hope."

"The only prominent name was Jeff Kellerman," Jack replied. "If you believe the gossip, that little prick has fucked everything from mud wrestlers to midgets."

"What did Whelan give you?" Nolan asked.

"Nothing.

"Well, I suppose you've got to run down everyone who appeared in Candy's last picture. I'd like to put some heat on Sid Davis. He's the catalyst. Represents Maffatore, meaning he's wired to the Colombians."

"Let Davis sweat the headlines for a while," Jack said. "Candy's death will generate some heat. Let's hold off on Davis. We've got a hell of a lot of people to talk to."

Nolan stared up at the ceiling pinspots and rubbed his hand wearily over his eyes. "There's no foundation to things anymore. No form. Middle Americans dealing coke. Kids fucking and sucking on film. Pentagon sending money and munitions to banana republics that ship us back drugs.

Corporations selling the government faulty parts. The president honoring the SS. TV making celebrities out of rapists and their victims. The sporting world riddled with coke. Terrorists running wild. It's out of control. No form. No foundation."

"Father Casey has a theory." Jack smiled. "Man is an imperfect creature who inherited a perfect world and proceeded to fuck it up."

"Well, if you listened to the confessions of cops for thirty years, you'd arrive at the same conclusion." Nolan paused. "You hear anything from Álvarez on that Ave María tape?"

"Nothing yet."

"If you need any help, I can give you Phil Brody."

"Leave Phil alone," Jack said. "He's had enough of the street for ten lifetimes."

"Well," Silvio said, "Brody might run down the people on the film crew."

"Yeah," Jack agreed. "That would be helpful."

"Okay," Nolan said, "give Brody their names and addresses. I'll get him on it. Now, keep me informed. I don't want any surprises. And watch yourselves. It looks like a suicide, but we might be chasing a psycho."

Chapter II

The westbound traffic on the Santa Monica Freeway had thinned out and accelerated to a speed that exceeded the legal limit of fifty-five miles per hour.

Jack Raines checked the dashboard clock; the luminous green hands read "9:47 P.M." The car radio was tuned to the all news station. Candy Lane's death had been reported on both the local and the national segments. Jack felt a genuine sympathy for Candy's father. The man was probably already besieged by the press at his valley home, and it was only the beginning. The lurid nature of his daughter's profession and the circumstances of her drug-related death made for high Nielsen ratings. There was no way to keep the lid on a story of a beautiful but doomed teenage girl who had X-rated her way into national prominence.

Jack glanced at the rearview mirror, activated the right-turn blinker, and swung the classic Pontiac into the extreme right lane.

Karen Dara had reluctantly agreed to see him. She had given him directions to her Venice home as if she were talking to a child. The tone of her voice had been unmistakably patronizing.

Jack saw the big green sign FREEWAY ENDS 1/4 MILE and carefully merged the Pontiac with exiting traffic.

He took Lincoln Boulevard to Rose Avenue, climbed the steep hill, and caught his first glimpse of the Pacific. The sea shimmered in the moonlight, but its blue-black surface seemed motionless as if its luminous dips and curves had been crafted on canvas with a palette knife. He reached the foot of Rose Avenue and turned left on Pacific and entered Venice.

The old beach town was a dismal slum sandwiched between the middle-class dignity of Santa Monica and the yuppie glitz of Marina del Rey. He drove past stucco buildings with Moorish arcades—melancholy survivors of a grandiose, failed dream.

In 1904 Abbott Kinney, a wealthy entrepreneur, became obsessed with the idea of transforming Venice, California, into a replica of Venice, Italy. Canals were dug; *palazzi*, constructed. Plans to re-create the Piazza San Marco were drawn. For a brief euphoric moment it appeared that Kinney's vision would become a reality, but in the end geography doomed his Venetian dream. The beach town was too far from the central city. The average Angeleno could not afford to commute, and the old California money preferred the seclusion and virginal beauty of Malibu.

The *palazzi* turned into penny arcades. The unfinished canals became murky breeding grounds for mosquitoes. The site of the Piazza San Marco transformed itself into a maze of narrow streets lined by decaying candy-colored bungalows inhabited by drug addicts, winos, prostitutes, and flute-playing hippies. Street gangs surfaced at night, prowling the dark alleys like packs of jackals preying on anything that moved.

South of Washington Boulevard, Jack turned right and traveled a short block that dead-ended at the beach. He parked and slid the official police sign into the loop on the visor. He locked the car and walked ten feet to the paved strip separating the seaside homes from the beach. Several hundred yards to the south the Venice pier was illuminated by amber-colored lamps. Night fishermen cast their lines into the sea from the circular end of the pier. Far off to the north the ghostly silhouette of the Santa Monica Mountains shadowed the Pacific.

He walked south on the paved strip and stared off at the misty lights illuminating the great sweep of beach that hugged the seaside towns of El Segundo and Manhattan Beach. The lights, the sea, and the curving shoreline reminded him of Mediterranean seaside villages south of Barcelona. He and Laura had strolled along those Spanish beaches a lifetime ago.

He reached Karen Dara's Spanish-style house and

looked back at the Venice pier. It seemed as if someone had waved a magic wand at the pier, separating the squalid tenements to the north from the faded elegance of the beachside houses to the south. He walked up the used-brick path to the front door, gripped an iron ring that hung from the jaws of a bronze lion, and banged it against the heavy wooden door. After a moment her voice came through a speaker.

"Yes?"

"It's Lieutenant Jack Raines."

"I'll be right there."

Karen's screen image was still indelible, and as he waited, Jack wondered what she would be like in person.

"Come in, Lieutenant." She smiled.

She was tall, with broad, straight shoulders. Her ash blond hair parted in the center, and its soft fall framed her patrician face. She had an engaging smile that played in curious counterpoint to her imperious lime-colored eyes. She wore beige linen slacks and a red silk blouse; ivory bracelets jangled at her wrists, and a coral necklace circled her throat. He caught the sweet scent of her perfume as he followed her into the high-ceilinged living room.

The room held an eclectic mixture of antique and contemporary pieces. Copies of *Art and Antiques*, *Connoisseur*, and an expensive black-embossed Italian magazine called *FMR* were fanned out on a Lucite coffee table, along with recent issues of *Vanity Fair* and *Vogue*. The floor was covered with a fine antique Persian carpet. Two huge sliding glass doors opened onto a stone terrace that overlooked the beach. A wet bar acted as a partition separating the living room from a dining nook. A bookcase ran the length of one wall; the opposite wall was decorated with Modigliani prints centered on an expensively framed lithograph.

"Care for a drink?" she asked.

"A little vodka over ice."

He crossed to the far wall and glanced at the lithograph. It was a replica of a propaganda poster painted in the bold expressionistic style of the thirties. The poster depicted a handsome young woman standing defiantly atop a wooden barricade. Her long hair blew wildly in the wind. Her shirtsleeves were rolled up. Yellow shell bursts flashed behind her, and fallen soldiers were sprawled at her feet. She held a rifle in her right hand and a banner in her left that read *"Madrid Resiste Bien."*

Karen handed him the drink. "Interesting, isn't it?"

"I would guess it's a collector's item."

"It is. I found it in the Madrid flea market about ten years ago.

"I know something about the Spanish Civil War. My uncle was in the Lincoln Brigade. He was killed at the Ebro River in 1938."

"I wrote a term paper on that war in my senior year at college," she said.

"Really?"

"Yes, really." She smiled. "Are you surprised by the subject or the fact that I attended college?"

There was something intimidating about her self-assurance and those haughty lime eyes.

"Have a seat, Jack." She smiled again. "You don't mind my calling you Jack"—she sipped her drink—"do you?"

Her delivery reminded him of Lauren Bacall's sexy sarcasm in those early films with Bogart.

They sat opposite each other on a pair of white silk-upholstered down sofas. She lit a cigarette and in a throaty voice said, "You wanted to see me."

"I don't enjoy any of this, and I hope you don't—"

"I don't," she interrupted. "Just fire away, Jack."

"Were you and Candy lovers?"

She crossed her long legs. "Let me give you a little preamble before I answer that. Okay?"

"Sure."

"Good." She sipped the iced gin and sucked the cigarette smoke deep into her lungs. "The men and women who perform in erotic films are far from saints, but neither are they degenerates or monsters. We give the public graphic sexual fantasy on film. If the folks out there didn't want X-rated movies, there wouldn't be any."

"I'm not interested in the public morality. I asked if you and Candy were lovers."

She rose and walked to the partitioned glass doors and stared at the distant lights of fishing trawlers.

"Yes . . ." She sighed. "Candy and I were lovers. But we weren't *in* love. Candy was young. Beautiful. Ambitious. And not terribly bright. A dangerous combination. She was doomed by her incredible sexuality. It just lit up the screen. But she couldn't perform without coke. In the end she was destroyed by it." Karen turned to him and sipped some gin. "Personally I prefer an occasional toke of good grass. I tried to help her. I spent hours with her, talking to her. Trying to get her to be realistic."

"About what?"

"About chasing the illusion that one day she would cross over into straight films. Of course, that pompous bastard Jeff Kellerman didn't help her any."

She crossed to the sofa, sat on the arm, and stared into her glass. "Kellerman promised Candy a role in his new film. He promised her a role in his last film. What he wanted, of course, was to fuck her, to have her do scenes with other people. But Kellerman was a symptom, not the disease. Candy was just over her head. A lot of people took advantage of her."

"Was Pedro Cisneros one of those people?"

"No. To the best of my knowledge she met him only once. I accompanied Candy on a long weekend to Biscayne Bay. Cisneros seemed to be a perfect gentleman."

Jack reached for a cigarette but came up empty.

"Over there. Help yourself," she said.

He crossed to the bar and took a cigarette out of a pack of Gauloises and lit it with an old U.S. Army Zippo.

"Can you tell me why Candy met with Cisneros?" he asked.

"That's a dangerous question for me to answer; besides, I'd be guessing."

"Did Leo Whelan send her?"

"Ask him."

"I have."

"Ask him again."

"I intend to."

"Is there anything else?"

"Do you own a gun?"

"As a matter of fact, yes."

"Can I see it?"

"This way, Jack."

He followed her into the cream-colored bedroom. She placed a Gucci shoebox on the bed, removed the lid, and handed him a snub-nosed .38 Smith & Wesson revolver. He flipped the chamber on the gun; all six chambers were loaded.

She opened her night table drawer and handed him the license authorizing her to carry the weapon.

"Why did you apply for this?" he asked.

"We get paid in cash, and with all due respect to your colleagues, this neighborhood isn't exactly Tahiti. Come on, let's freshen these drinks."

They stood on either side of the bar, facing each other.

"I hope you don't mind my calling you Jack."

"Call me anything you like—just be nice."

"How can I be nice? I'm a bad girl. Porno star. I'm part of the evil scourge that's destroying the moral fiber of this great nation."

"You really hate yourself, don't you?"

"Ah, now the lieutenant's playing nickel-and-dime Freud."

He sipped the vodka and asked, "When was the last time you saw Candy?"

For the first time he detected a trace of fear in her eyes. She chewed her lower lip. "I—I guess it was last Saturday night. I was through early. I won't work with Traynor. Candy had some scenes with him and two other girls."

"I know."

"How?" she asked, surprised.

"I've seen the film."

"Oh." She stroked her hair. "Well, I guess it was close to eleven when I left. I phoned Candy several times later that night and again on Sunday."

"Were you worried about her?"

"Yes and no. I thought, or at least hoped, she had gone home with Lisa Chang. She and Lisa were close, not in a sexual sense, but Lisa had introduced us both to the Order of Shiva."

"What's that?"

"An Eastern religious group. They have a temple in the hills above Zuma Beach. We both got a lot out of that. It's an amazing force. Some of its rituals are on the weird side, but if you open your mind to it, you can channel into your past lives, communicate with the dead, and, more profoundly, touch your inner spirit."

"So you left the film location around eleven Saturday night?"

"Right."

"And you came straight home?"

"Yes."

"You were alone all night?"

"Yes."

"Can you prove that?"

"No."

"Did Pedro Cisneros ever try to contact you?"

"No."

"Did you ever see Whelan with Cisneros?"

"No."

"Do you know Sid Davis?"

Karen nodded. "He came up to San Francisco when we were shooting *Lickorice*."

"Who invited him?"

"Whelan. No one visits the set without Leo's approval."

"Was Davis involved with Candy?"

"No. Sidney is not a player. He's more interested in power than sex."

"Does he represent you?"

"One of his partners. Sidney doesn't bother with performers anymore."

"Do you know Angelo Maffatore?"

"I've met him."

"Where?"

"At his Bel-Air mansion. He hosted a small party back in May. I sort of liked the old man. He was kind and respectful."

She placed her glass on the bar and moved very close to him. The scent of her perfume rose from her wrists as she touched the tips of her hair. She stared intently into his eyes. "I loved Candy in a way that you probably can't understand."

"Try me."

"I can have sex with a man, but I can only make love to a woman."

"You're right: I don't get the distinction."

"Then there's still hope for you." She paused. "I want you to know that if someone took Candy's life, there isn't anything I wouldn't do to even the score."

"I understand. But if she was murdered, it was professional. I'd advise you to let me handle that." He handed her a card. "You can reach me at that number, day or night."

They stared at each other for a moment. "I'll show you out," she said huskily.

She opened the front door and smiled. "For whatever it's worth," she said in that hip Bacall style, "I can still separate what I do offstage from what I do onstage. Drive carefully, Jack."

Chapter 12

The Purple Dragon was located at the eastern end of Sunset Boulevard, in the heart of the Silver Lake district. The restaurant's flashing Chinese characters played discordantly against the surrounding Spanish neon. The luminous cultural clash confirmed the district's polyglot ethnicity. Tens of thousands of illegal immigrants from Mexico, El Salvador, Guatemala, South Korea, and Vietnam had settled in Silver Lake.

The adult immigrants were law-abiding, hardworking men and women who commuted daily to the glittering west side of the city, where they performed menial tasks in homes, restaurants, office buildings, and hospitals. But the youth of Silver Lake lacked their parents' historic acceptance of servitude. They neither understood nor respected the impenetrable American system.

The district's isolated and disenchanted youth constituted an ideal pool of manpower for drug dealers. The Colombian *coqueros* offered the young people astonishing economic rewards for distributing cocaine to a white ruling class that had excluded them from its legitimate enterprise. In a single decade the dismal neighborhood had become a violent but thriving hub of cocaine distribution.

The Purple Dragon represented a convenient contact point for dealers and by tacit agreement had become a tranquil watering hole in an otherwise lawless jungle.

The restaurant was an L-shaped room with a series of glass partitions separating the dining area from the cocktail lounge. The bamboo bar was lined with Latinos, Asians, and a few "uptown" Caucasian dealers.

Silvio Martinez was seated in a booth, sharing a plate of ribs with a thin, almost anorexic, dark-skinned Colom-

71

bian. Pepe Montoya's face was badly scarred by an untreated childhood infection of smallpox. His wily black eyes were in constant motion: scanning tables; searching out faces; darting back and forth as if he were watching a tennis match.

The two men chewed on barbecued ribs and drank cold Chinese beer. Neither man was interested in the food, but they had to maintain the appearance of two friends enjoying a late-night snack.

"Who's in the booth behind me?" Pepe asked.

"A couple of Gualtametecas—dishwashers."

"You got two chinks behind you," Pepe observed.

"So what?"

"Chinks are bad luck."

Pepe swallowed some beer and opened another button on his candy-striped shirt. A huge gold cross hung from his neck and dangled against his bony chest. "Fucking hot in here."

"Yeah. The fans aren't worth a shit," Silvio agreed.

Pepe lit an unfiltered Lucky Strike and blew the smoke up toward the papier-mâché lanterns.

"Fucking quiet in here," Pepe said nervously.

Silvio signaled to the Chinese waitress. The woman came over to the table, and he handed her four quarters.

"Play some Cuban music on that juke, okay?"

"Anything special?"

"A salsa by Celia Cruz."

They sat in silence until the percussive Afro-Cuban music blared from overhead speakers.

"I played the tape for my partner," Silvio said.

"That's your business," Pepe replied.

"Can you give me something about the word *alfombra?*"

"I can't tell you nothing about that tape—not *alfombra,* not *Ave María,* not *kingfish,* not *P. C.* Nothing."

Pepe picked up a rib and chewed the meaty flesh, speaking between the bites. "Ordóñez's laundryman is in town."

"Ohlendorf?"

Pepe nodded. "The kraut met with Davis. He delivered a message from Santa Rosa. Ordóñez wants the wops to wash an extra billion through their legit porno corporations."

Silvio felt an undefined rush of exhilaration, but his face betrayed nothing. He swallowed some beer and listened as Pepe continued. "Ordóñez wants Davis to come to Santa Rosa with Maffatore's answer."

"Suppose he doesn't like the answer?"

"Ordóñez thinks you can't make movies without actors." Pepe wiped the grease from his lips. "Could be a war. I gotta split, amigo."

"One question."

"Yeah?"

"You know where someone could get hold of seventy percent snow?"

"Yeah."

"Where?"

"From me."

In that moment Silvio knew the pockmarked Colombian informer was playing both sides of the street.

Chapter 13

The *Ave María* plowed through the heavy seas fifteen nautical miles off the coast of Manzanillo. Its running lights were doused as it headed due north at twelve knots. The thirty-year-old Panamanian freighter was similar in appearance to any other cargo vessel plying the Pacific coast, but in reality the ship was a floating gem of sophisticated marine telemetry.

Its hull was coated with chemically treated nonreflective paint, making it a difficult target for long-range radar detection. Computerized radar dishes capable of detecting a rowboat at ten nautical miles were welded to steel beams alongside the smokestack. Doppler digital continuous wave radar beams sought out and jammed enemy radar signals. The wheelhouse contained loran, sonar, and a Mitrek supersolid-state high-frequency radio console.

The ship's original Scottish fire-tube boilers had been replaced with General Electric two-gear, destroyer types of turbines capable of doubling the freighter's cruising speed from fifteen to thirty nautical knots.

The *Ave María* carried a mixed cargo of Mexican leather goods, Bolivian sugar, Colombian coffee, and handwoven Peruvian rugs.

The high-tech instrumentation in the wheelhouse was illuminated by soft green lights, and Cuban technicians operated the sophisticated electronic gear. The bridge was quiet except for the creaking sound of the vessel as it rolled and pitched with the movement of the sea.

Pedro Cisneros and the Bahamian captain stood silently on either side of the helmsman. Cisneros and the captain had made numerous runs together in the Caribbean, but this trip was new to both men.

Cisneros had grown a beard and dyed it gray to match his dyed gray hair. He wore blue contact lenses over his brown pupils; the disguise conformed to his expertly forged Panamanian passport bearing the name Pablo Escobar.

He scanned the moonlit sea all the way to the horizon line; there were no visible running lights. Barring any trouble, they would be berthed at San Pedro by 11:00 A.M. tomorrow.

Cisneros had an inordinate personal interest in the success of this particular voyage. He had created the innovative idea and sold it to Ordóñez. It was costly and detailed; legitimate cargo consignments had to be purchased and loaded at three different ports. The ship's movements had to be above suspicion; the arrival at its ultimate destination, exact. It was a gutsy method of smuggling that had never before been attempted. There were certain risks, mostly from DEA informants, but if the plan succeeded, they would have finally eliminated that vulnerable dead-in-the-water transfer of cocaine from the mother ship to high-speed small boats. There would be no need for ship-to-shore radio contact. No fear of air-sea U.S. and Mexican surveillance. They would sail straight into San Pedro, unload their cargo, and depart the following day. The customs agents would undoubtedly open and inspect random sacks of sugar and coffee. The agents were trained to seek out refined cocaine but had no history with coca paste.

Once the ship was berthed, Cisneros would present his passport and seaman's ID card to the INS inspector at immigration. He would be granted a temporary maritime pass valid for the length of time the ship was in port. But his plans did not include a tour of Los Angeles. He was booked on a Pan Am flight departing LAX at 6:00 P.M. for Bogotá. He hoped to be back in time for Ordóñez's meeting with Sidney Davis, but he was getting ahead of himself. They still had 430 nautical miles to go. He stroked his beard and addressed the captain.

"What's our present speed, Cappy?"

"Twelve knots—"

The Cuban radar technician suddenly exclaimed, "I've got a sighting!"

Cisneros and the captain stared anxiously at the Cuban, who quickly made some calculations. "A low silhouette," he said. "Patrol boat due south, moving at eighteen knots."

Cisneros crossed the dimly lit bridge and peered into the green radar viewfinder. The Cuban punched a series of buttons on the computer visualizer, and Cisneros clearly discerned the low silhouette of the following craft.

"We can jam their radar signal," the Cuban technician suggested.

"No," Cisneros said, and turned to the radio operator. "You picking up anything?"

The operator shook his head negatively and removed his earphones.

"What frequency you on?"

"Two-six-three-one-five-Manzanillo maritime."

"Switch over to two-seven-one-four-five-Mexico air-sea rescue allocation."

The operator replaced the headset and fine-tuned the dials, seeking the proper frequency.

"What are they doing outside their twelve-mile limit?" the captain asked.

"It may not be a Mexican coastal patrol," Cisneros replied. "Might be a shrimper."

"Not at eighteen knots," the radarman interjected, "and not with that silhouette."

"Should we kick in the turbines?" the captain asked.

"No," Cisneros replied. "I don't want them to think we're running."

"Do we maintain our present course?"

"Let me think, Cappy."

Cisneros turned the problem over; someone might have tipped the Mexican authorities shortly after the *Ave María* had departed Manzanillo with the leather goods. Then again, it could be a naval craft on routine patrol, but Cisneros's long history in drug-running said otherwise. The Mexicans had probably been tipped, and if so, they would undoubtedly attempt to interdict the *Ave María*. He could let the patrol craft come alongside and hit it with Sagger missiles and blow its radio, then systematically wipe out the crew. But that was dangerous; if the Mexican patrol craft disappeared from its base radarscope, the whole coast would be alerted—air and sea, all the way to Alaska. He could still return to Barranquilla, but Ordóñez had an enormous investment in this shipment, and everything was in place.

The captain and the technicians stared at him, waiting for instructions. Cisneros ignored them and continued to sift the options. The Mexicans were unpredictable. Their coastal patrol boats would be berthed for months at a time; then suddenly, for no apparent reason, they'd send a fucking fleet out. He stroked his beard nervously. He needed a piece of inside information that would give him an edge. In the deadly cat-and-mouse game of drug smuggling the edge was critical.

"I've got them!" the radioman suddenly exclaimed.

"*¡Paloma! ¡Paloma!*" The voice came through the radio amplifier loudly and clearly.

Cisneros and the captain crossed quickly to the radio console; their eyes were riveted to the amplifier.

"*¡Paloma en el aire!*"

"Paloma is the code name of the patrol ship. He's calling his base," Cisneros explained to the Bahamian captain, who spoke no Spanish.

There was a momentary pause.

"*En atención,*" the base replied.

"*Estamos a quince millas al oeste de la base en rumbo al norte,*" the Mexican patrol craft reported.

"They're fifteen miles west of Manzanillo on a northerly course," Cisneros translated.

The radio blared again.

"*¿Qué velocidad lleva?*" the base inquired.

"*Máximo de diez y ocho nudos,*" the patrol craft replied.

The captain started to ask Cisneros for the translation, but Pedro put his forefinger to his lips.

The naval base voice came on. "*¿Cuál es su posición con respeto al blanco?*"

"*Falta diez millas al sur en cruce lento.*"

"*Siga conectado volvere.*"

The voices died, and a low hum filled the void. Cisneros turned to the captain. "The patrol craft reported its position to be ten miles south of the target ship. That's us. The base ordered him to maintain radio contact and wait for further instructions."

There was a momentary pause before the amplifier resumed transmission.

"*Tengo el procedimiento,*" the base directed. "*E avise si el blanco al terra el rumbo.*"

"*Entendido, termino la transmisión,*" the ship replied.

"That's it," the Cuban radioman said.

"That's what?" the captain asked.

Cisneros translated. "The base ordered the patrol boat to keep following and advise if we change course."

The bow dipped severely in a deep trough, and the men grabbed handrails.

Cisneros motioned to the captain, and the dark-skinned Bahamian followed him outside.

They stood on the moonlit foredeck of the bridge. The wind and sea spray were a welcome relief from the cloying heat of the wheelhouse. Cisneros took a pair of powerful infrared binoculars out of a cabinet and scanned the southern horizon. "No sign of lights."

"What do you think?"

"If we maintain this due north course, they'll follow for a while, then have Cabo de San Lucas pick us up. Cabo will alert the U.S. Coast Guard."

"Unless we're just a radar track—an accident," the captain said.

"We can't count on that." Cisneros's eyes smarted from the contact lenses. He took a small vial of Hypo-Tears out of his jacket, tilted his head back, and squeezed a few drops into each eye.

"You okay?" the captain asked.

Cisneros nodded, blinking his eyes. "Change course. Set a westerly heading for Hawaii. We've got to throw them off."

"Suppose they stay with us?"

"They can't follow forever."

"We're due to dock at eleven A.M. If we're late, we lose the berth. We'll have to anchor out."

"We'll sail west for maybe four, five hours," Cisneros replied. "They won't stay with us longer than that."

* * *

They took their supper in the bridge. The radar technician supplied periodic fixes on the trailing patrol craft. The radioman held to the Mexican naval communication frequency. The hours slipped by, each passing minute taking them farther off course, making their on-time arrival in San Pedro questionable. The one positive factor was a steadily calming sea.

"We're almost fifty miles off course," the captain cautioned.

"Trust me, Cappy. We'll make it."

The bridge fell silent except for the low hum and sporadic static emanating from the powerful radio console. The tension in the wheelhouse grew with each passing moment.

The silence was suddenly shattered by the Mexican accented Spanish that blared from the amplifier.

"*¡Paloma llamando a Manzanillo!*"

They rushed to the radio console. The operator held the knobs steady on the frequency.

"*¡Estamos litos Paloma—avise Paloma!*" The command base acknowledged.

There was a long and rapid exchange in Spanish between the base and the patrol vessel before the radio voices ceased transmitting.

Cisneros turned to the captain and smiled. "We're okay. The ship asked if they should notify San Pedro. The base command advised them not to. They think we're a decoy. They suspect their information was incorrect."

"Meaning they did get a tip."

Cisneros nodded. His brain whirled like a computer armed with a bank of information, seeking out a false figure. He had a pretty good idea of how the leak occurred. He would pass his hunch along to Ordóñez when he returned to Santa Rosa.

"As soon as we lose their image on our radar," Cisneros said, "kick in those GE turbines to flank speed, and steer due north for San Pedro. We're gonna be okay, Cappy."

"The U.S. Coast Guard could be waiting for us," the captain cautioned.

"Maybe. But if they are, they'll send out air surveillance when we make U.S. territorial waters."

"Then what?"

"Then, my friend, we'll dump those fucking rugs, and the fish will stay stoned for five generations."

Chapter 14

Reluctantly Jack lit the first cigarillo of the day. He had tried all the "cures" but could not kick his lifelong addiction to nicotine.

He settled in the chair facing the TV set. The network had just relinquished five minutes to local stations. A pleasant-looking woman wearing too much eye makeup and a tense smile recited the local news without a trace of emotion.

"An unidentified man was killed on the San Bernardino Freeway at approximately three A.M. Witnesses indicated the man strolled onto the freeway, sat down, and played a flute.

"Eighteen elderly women were arrested at their West Valley homes early this morning. The women have been charged with the laundering of cash derived from the sale of cocaine. The women known as the Granny Gang have allegedly been depositing large sums of narcodollars in banks throughout the Los Angeles area. The police seized more than five hundred thousand dollars in small denominations."

A commercial for a movie interrupted the newscaster. Jack watched in amusement as a muscular actor single-handedly defeated a brigade of Vietnamese soldiers while rescuing five American POWs. The movie commercial was followed by a denture commercial, which in turn was followed by a commercial for a vaginal douche.

Jack walked to the terrace windows. A damaged yellow sunlight lit up the A-frames and stilt-supported Spanish casitas clinging to the Hollywood Hills. He opened the sliding doors and felt the rush of hot desert wind.

He thought of Karen Dara's parting line: *"I can still*

separate what I do offstage from what I do onstage." She
had been testing him, flirting with him—and despite her
profession, he was intrigued with her; and she knew it.

He closed the terrace doors and walked back to the
TV set.

The local news spot had been turned back to the
network, and the attractive blond anchorwoman smiled
and said, "We switch now to Gloria Hunnicutt in our
Hollywood studios for the inside story on the shocking
death of Candy Lane."

The legendary gossip appeared against a black back-
ing featuring a huge blowup of Candy Lane wearing a
skimpy bikini.

Hunnicutt wet her lips and smiled.

"Good morning to all of you from Hollywood. The
film capital is agog over the drug-related death of Candy
Lane. Your correspondent has learned from unimpeach-
able sources that Miss Lane had ingested a large quantity
of potent cocaine shortly after completing her last X-rated
film on Saturday evening. A valentine drawn in cocaine
was found in Miss Lane's bedroom at her Malibu residence along with a secret diary containing names of Hollywood celebrities who shared more than a passing relationship
with the late porno star.

"Despite efforts by Lieutenant Jack Raines of Tactical's NIFTY squad to withhold details surrounding the
porno idol's death, your correspondent has learned that
Miss Lane's body had been savagely bitten in a cannibalis-
tic orgy. There is at this moment an unconfirmed but
authoritative report that Miss Lane's off-screen activities
involved a notorious Colombian drug smuggler. I'll have
more on this fast-breaking story tomorrow morning."

Hunnicutt paused, and the image of Candy Lane
disappeared from the backdrop. "And now the latest in
the continuing conflict of egos on the jinxed and trouble-
plagued production of—"

A loud buzzer sounded at an electronic panel attached to the phone console. Jack snapped off the TV set
and lifted the receiver.

"Yes."

"Silvio Martinez is in the lobby."

"I'll be right down."

He hung up and stared at the framed photograph beside the console. It was a happy family portrait of himself, Laura, and Jenny at age six, tanned and smiling in front of a Spanish *parador* outside Madrid. But Spain was a long time ago. Before their divorce. Before Laura was murdered.

Chapter 15

Dappled sunlight filtered through tall pines bordering the grounds of Angelo Maffatore's Bel-Air estate.

The aged West Coast Godfather was seated at a glass-topped wicker table on the veranda, sipping coffee and reading the *Los Angeles Times*. The ocher-colored wall of his sprawling Mediterranean villa loomed up behind him. The morning stillness was punctuated by chirping blue jays and hissing lawn sprinklers.

Candy Lane smiled seductively from her prominent position on the front page.

The Mafia chieftain removed his reading glasses and shook his head in wonderment, puzzled by the fact that the death of a middle-class porno actress commanded front-page space. In Italy scandals meant nothing unless they involved powerful politicians or titled nobility. Well, perhaps in a curious way the fact that Americans took a proletarian view of their scandals explained the greatness of the country.

He removed a pair of sunglasses from his breast pocket, put them on, and glanced off at the manicured lawn that sloped gracefully down to an Olympic-size swimming pool. Despite his advanced years, he still managed to swim ten laps a day; the water temperature was maintained at eighty-five degrees year-round. Maffatore loved Southern California. It had been twenty-five years since he migrated from the East, but he still shuddered at the thought of those cold, grimy New York streets.

He brushed his thinning gray hair and traced a pale line of scar tissue that ran from his left earlobe to the edge of his mouth. He then rubbed his right wristbone. The dull ache of an ancient bullet wound had started to throb again. *I'm like an old racehorse*, he thought, *battered and bruised but determined to reach the finish line with dignity*. Lately he had begun to think he had lived too long.

Gambino was gone. Lansky was gone. Luciano. Bugsy Siegel. Costello. All gone. It was a curious irony that he, the foot soldier, should have survived the generals.

As a young man he had survived the Castellmare wars and the Prohibition wars and the great national bloodletting when the disparate clans were organized under Luciano and Lansky. He had survived running numbers in Brooklyn during the reign of Lepke and Murder Inc. He had been stabbed, shot, and beaten, but he had lived to attend the funerals of his enemies. A legend had grown up around him. Luciano had said, *"Maffatore non e' umano."* But Angelo *was* human and felt the deep fatigue and tension of his continuing responsibility. By virtue of luck and cunning he had become the elder statesman of the organization. The passing of the old guard had been a painful inevitability, but the real trouble had started ten years ago in the South American jungles.

He shook his head in disbelief. A goddamn plant. A leaf. A fucking coca leaf growing wild in the Andean jungles had become the most profitable drug in the history of mankind. The Mafia's heroin traffic had been severely damaged by the rising popularity of cocaine. Heroin was a nigger drug, a ghetto drug; cocaine was white, like the moneyed Americans who were hooked on it. The snowstorm was worth $100 billion, and the Colombians controlled everything from the jungles to the American nose. During the Miami drug war Colombian killers would burst into public places and hit anyone in the line of fire. They sliced up women and children with chain saws. They had only two rules: Kill and win. In July '81 Maffatore effected a humiliating armistice with Ordóñez's representatives. The Mafia became a laundry service for the Colombians, washing a billion dollars a year in return for a 10 percent fee. The 1981 agreement had been faithfully adhered to until this moment.

Ordóñez was now demanding that an additional billion be washed through the Mafia's pornographic corporate bank accounts. The fucking spics were never satisfied. But Ordóñez had the edge. If a war broke out, it would be fought in the United States, on the Mafia's turf. A lot of federal heat would come down. A war would be disastrous. He would have to negotiate. He would have to buy time.

The sound of approaching footsteps interrupted his thoughts. He turned toward the house as the uniformed butler ushered Sidney Davis to the table. Maffatore smiled weakly. "Good morning, Sidney."

"Sorry I'm late," the attorney replied nervously.

"Care for some juice?"

"No. No, thanks." Sidney was always tense in the company of Maffatore.

"Coffee?"

"No. I've had enough."

Maffatore nodded to the butler, who left abruptly.

"What are we faced with?" Maffatore asked.

"I told you last night."

"I was very tired. I'm just back from New York. I have jet lag. I'm not as young as you. Tell me again."

Sidney repeated Ohlendorf's proposal, including Ordóñez's "observation" about the difficulty of making films without actors.

Maffatore shifted in his chair, and said, "Now, tell me about Whelan's phone call." Davis related the substance of his phone conversation with Whelan.

The old mafioso's scarred, seamed face reminded Sidney of an artifact: a pitted marbled head, thrown up by the Ionian Sea onto a Sicilian beach. "I warned Leo never to use actors as couriers." Maffatore sighed. "The man lacks discipline. But he's made a fortune for us. Between him and his associates in Detroit and New York we've built a six-billion-dollar industry. Still, I must speak with the Whale."

He shoved his sunglasses up on his head, and his eyes were the color of midnight. "So Ordóñez observes that one cannot make films without actors," Maffatore mused. "Maybe they killed Candy as a warning to us."

"I don't think so," Sidney said. "I think her death is a

coincidence. But we have to respond. Ohlendorf is at the Bel-Air Hotel, waiting for an answer."

"Ordóñez wants you to deliver my response personally to Santa Rosa?"

"Yes."

"Well, you're the counselor. What do you suggest?"

"You have no choice, Don Angelo. In my opinion you have to offer them something."

"Offer them what?" Maffatore asked with a trace of anger. "We launder a billion for them now. The checking accounts of our corporations are swollen with our own cash. What is there left to offer?" He tapped the sunglasses, and they fell back over his eyes. "Let's walk."

They strolled across the lawn into the shade of the pines. Maffatore's hands were hidden in the deep pockets of his silk robe. Sidney draped his blue blazer over his arm. The high buzz of cicadas sounded from the trees.

"We must try to avoid a war," Maffatore said quietly, "although this time the Colombians are vulnerable: Their principal dealers are known to us. Their domestic refineries are known to us. We can hurt them."

"True enough," Sidney agreed. "Since we don't deal or distribute, how would they retaliate?"

The old man removed his sunglasses, and his penetrating black eyes stared at Sidney with genuine amazement.

"If a war breaks out, they'll go after everyone. They'll kill me. They'll kill the council of capos. Union people. Vegas. They'll hit every legit front we got. They don't think, and they don't scare. Ordóñez murdered twenty-four district judges in Colombia, men he couldn't buy."

Sidney felt beads of sweat running down his arms.

"But as you said, Don Angelo, we can hurt them where it counts."

"When you're dealing with spics, forget logic. The fucking Colombians are crazy."

"Not Ordóñez. He has, after all, built an empire."

"He's a brilliant organizer, and he's educated," Maffatore conceded. "But underneath, he's got that mestizo blood. Violent blood. And in the end blood determines a man's destiny." He rubbed the throbbing nerve in his

wrist. "Our strongest card is our pornographic corporate
bank accounts. Ordóñez must expand his laundry or cut
production; we have to hope he'll do business."

A big Irish setter came bounding through the pine
trees and made a beeline for Maffatore. The old man
hugged the thoroughbred dog and whispered, "Easy, Red.
Easy, boy."

He picked up a pine cone and tossed it down the hill.
The dog raced off through the trees, chasing after the
cone.

"All right, Sidney. Call Ohlendorf. Go with him to
Santa Rosa. Tell Ordóñez we are willing to revise our
agreement. We will launder an additional four hundred
million and maintain the present fee of ten percent."

"If he refuses?"

"Sing 'Sorrento.' Tap-dance. Maybe use that smile of
yours, heh? Tell him this is a start. We'll try to accommodate more. Buy time. We can hurt him, but he can shut
down our porno business. We need time to prepare in
case of war. I have to consult with the council."

"I'll do my best."

"I know you will." The old man draped his arm
around the lawyer's shoulders. "But take care. You'll be
tired from the trip. Don't be diverted. Don't accept any
women. Don't talk business to Cisneros or the German,
only to Ordóñez. Don't reject his hospitality, but don't
lose your dignity."

Sidney began to hyperventilate. A ball of fear knotted
his stomach. "The trip worries me."

"Legally?"

"No. My position is simply that of an American attorney representing an American client in a business dispute
with a foreign citizen. No. I have no legal problem. I just
wish we were dealing from a stronger position."

"I wish a lot of things, too." Maffatore sighed. "I wish
it was 1937 and the Brooklyn mob was around: Bugsy
Siegel, Abbandando, Marty Goldstein, Pittsburgh Phil,
Happy Maione, Moey Amberg, Three Finger Brown . . ."
The old man's eyes grew misty as he summoned up the
names with great reverence. "No fucking spic would have

lasted for five minutes on the streets of Brooklyn in 1937."
Maffatore turned his hands palm up in a gesture of help-
lessness. "But then was then. Now is now, and we do
what we can. Don't be fearful. Remember, no one kills
the negotiator. Not even Ordóñez."

Chapter 16

Silvio drove the 1971 GTO in low gear, climbing slowly up the corkscrew road. Jack was seated alongside, studying the *Daily Racing Form*. The Pontiac's windows were closed, and the air-conditioning unit was set at maximum.

"Car handles like a dream," Silvio remarked.

"It's supposed to. I've had it restored six times."

They followed the serpentine drive through an architectural nightmare; it was as if a Disneyland scenic designer had been turned loose in the Hollywood Hills.

Silvio braked sharply as a big coyote loped across the road, heading for the dried carcass of a rattlesnake.

"Fucking jungle up here," Silvio muttered.

Jack nodded but did not look up from the racing tabloid.

"You still play the horses?" Silvio asked.

"Now and then. I enjoy handicapping. It's a deductive challenge like crossword puzzles." Jack folded the *Racing Form* and reflectively said, "Laura used to enjoy the races."

"I always preferred jai alai to horses," Silvio replied. "I knew a Basque jai alai champ in Miami. The guy could climb a wall, gave me a few tips now and then."

Silvio cursed softly in Spanish as they just missed hitting a VW convertible that had veered into their lane. The driver, a young girl with a Chiclet smile and spiked purple hair, waved to them as she whizzed by.

"Kids are crazy," Silvio muttered.

"I guess I've been lucky," Jack said softly.

"Yeah, Jenny's a fine young lady. You did something right."

"Not me. Her mother raised her."

There was a moment of silence before Silvio asked, "What actually happened to Laura?"

"After we divorced, she married a wealthy neurosurgeon, Dr. Martin Sorenson. He owned a big medical complex in Westwood. Sorenson was a man of many interests; one of them was archaeology. He took an artifact out of a dig in Syria. The Syrians came looking for it. Laura walked in on them. They shot her four times.

"I ran the case down—halfway around the world to a cave in Jordan. I was one-on-one with the doctor. He was tough, very tough, a former OSS operative. He came at me with a hunting knife. The floor of the cave shifted. He fell thirty feet to the stratum below and got impaled on a bronze spear held by a Canaanite devil-god."

"Jesus . . ." Silvio whispered.

"He had me cold. That shift in the floor saved my life."

They rode in silence for a while, climbing steadily, passing signs that read FIRE AREA—NO SMOKING.

"Bitch," Jack suddenly muttered.

"What?"

"Gloria Hunnicutt. She took a shot at me this morning on the tube."

"What's the difference?"

"She knew about the coke valentine."

"Probably went down on a Malibu cop or one of the print men."

"Maybe so. She did a number on my partner, Phil Brody, a couple years ago, trying to get an inside story on a murder case."

"Sounds like she'd make a bust-out porno star. We should introduce her to the Whale."

"Whelan may not be long for this world. If Pepe's right, if Ordóñez is putting the screws to the mob and doesn't get a deal, the Colombians will take out the whole porno film industry."

"Maybe Candy was the first hit," Silvio suggested.

"Well, there's that missing five thousand, and we know she and Karen Dara met with Cisneros in Florida.

By the way, did you ask Pepe where Candy might have gotten that seventy percent snow?"

"I asked, but he clammed up," Silvio lied. He couldn't risk Jack or anyone else's knowing that Pepe was both dealing and informing.

Silvio steered around a wicked curve and slowed as they entered a cul-de-sac at the summit of Sunset Plaza Drive. They parked and walked toward the soaring triangular entrance of an A-frame. The main section of the house was nestled below on the canyon escarpment, supported by steel struts.

A pretty redhead wearing a zebra-striped string bikini let them in. "Hi." She smiled. "I'm Stella."

They followed her swishing buttocks down a flight of stairs into a vaulted living room that overlooked a patio-pool area. The walls and ceiling were painted black; the sofas, chairs, hassocks, and carpeting were white. Huge canvases thick with vivid slashes of primary colors hung on the walls.

"You fellas want a cold drink?" Stella asked.

"No, thanks," Jack said.

"I wouldn't mind a glass of ice water." Silvio smiled and followed her to the wet bar.

"You performed in Candy's last picture, right?" Silvio asked engagingly.

"How did you know?"

"We saw the film."

"What a shock. I still can't believe Candy's gone," Stella said, and handed Silvio the sweating tall glass of ice water. She glanced at Jack. "You sure you don't want anything? We've got Diet Coke, beer, and—"

"No," he interrupted. "I'm fine."

She popped the cap on a bottle of Heineken and took a long gulp from its mouth. "Christ, it's hotter than a whore's ass in a lumber camp."

"What time did Karen Dara leave Saturday night?" Jack asked.

"Early. Around eleven. Karen won't do any piston shots."

"Piston?" Silvio asked.

"Fucking scenes. Not that Karen's totally gay. I mean, she's had numbers with men. But she won't do it on film—not anymore."

Jack felt a curious anger at Karen Dara's sexual proclivities being tossed around by the red-haired fluff.

"Did you get paid that night?" he asked.

"The Whale paid us all in cash."

"Did you actually see Leo pay Candy?"

"Uh-huh." She leaned over the bar, giving both men a full view of her ample breasts.

Silvio swallowed some water and asked, "How much did Leo pay her?"

"Five thousand in brand-new, crispy hundred-dollar bills," Stella replied, and peered out at the pool. "Leo's talked to me about starring in a new flick. A kind of tribute to Candy. He's got a straight screenwriter working on it." She turned and faced them. "I feel sort of sad about doing it, but it's a chance. One good role can bust you out. A big chance. I'm sorry about Candy, but . . . well, you know what I mean."

"Yeah, we know what you mean," Jack said. "How many films did you make with Candy?"

"Oh, I don't know, maybe eight or nine. I didn't get on-screen all the time. I fluffed a lot."

"But you knew Candy pretty well."

"Sure."

"Would you say she was depressed?"

"The only time Candy seemed happy was when she was wired."

"How about you?" Silvio smiled. "You blow a lot of snow?"

She laughed, sipped her beer, and said, "We all do coke. I mean, it's like asking the Burger King if he uses ketchup. Like they say, 'Coke is it.' Hey, have you guys spoken to Lisa Chang?"

"Not yet," Jack said. "Why do you ask?"

"No reason. Well, it's just that she's weird. Jealous of everyone. Lisa wants to be a star, but Sherry says people don't identify with chinks."

"You think Lisa Chang might have done some damage to Candy?" Jack asked.

"I don't know. It's tough to tell what a chink is thinking." She paused and brightened. "Come on, John's expecting you."

The pool and patio overlooked the smog-shrouded city. Tops of tall office buildings were barely visible in the pus-colored haze, and a hot desert wind stirred the palms clinging to the hillside.

John Traynor reclined on a lounge, reading the daily *Variety*. He wore reflective sunglasses and a brief bikini. The crotch of the bathing suit bulged as if it contained a grapefruit. His soft, hairless body gleamed with the oily residue of Bain de Soleil. He glanced up from the show biz tabloid as Stella led the two detectives onto the patio.

"Cops are here," she said in her childlike voice.

"Why don't we go inside?" Traynor suggested. "It's a lot cooler."

"Good idea," Silvio agreed.

Traynor rose, slipped a terry-cloth robe on, and glanced off at the thick yellow blanket covering the city.

"They say one day of breathing this stuff is like smoking a carton of cigarettes. I'm thinking of selling this place and moving to Frisco. Great town. No hassles." He tied the robe, and they followed him back inside.

"You fellas want something?" Traynor asked from behind the wet bar.

"I already took care of them," Stella said, and stretched out on the white rug, her back propped up against a hassock.

Silvio remained standing at the patio doors.

Jack studied one of the paint-smeared canvases. "What's the red slash and gold dust supposed to mean?" he asked.

"Whatever it conveys to you." Traynor swallowed some beer. "It's a classic example of abstract expressionism."

"I guess bad art isn't what it used to be." Jack smiled. "But then I'm no expert."

There was a beat of silence as Traynor's faded blue eyes flicked from Silvio to Jack. "How can I help you, Lieutenant?"

"Just answer a few questions."

"Fire away."

"What time did you finish shooting Saturday night?"

"Close to one in the morning. Candy, Lisa Chang, Whelan, and Sherry Nichols left together. Stella slept over."

"Was Candy wired?" Jack asked.

"She was always wired."

Silvio sat on a barstool opposite Traynor and politely asked, "You have any idea where she got the coke?"

"Not a clue."

"You see any on the set that night?"

"Yes. I saw some."

"You just admitted to a felony," Jack stated bluntly.

Traynor's milky complexion flushed. "What felony?"

"Being in the presence of illegal drugs is a crime in this state. We could book your ass right now."

"Look, I liked Candy. I'm shocked at her death. But I'm not responsible for what other actors do on a film set. Why get tough with me? What the hell did I do?"

Silvio glanced at Jack and soothingly said, "He's got a point. After all, John's not a dealer. He's an actor, and he's being cooperative." Silvio was playing the old game of good cop, bad cop.

"I'll ask you once more," Jack said quietly but ominously. "Where did the snow come from?"

Traynor put the beer down and looked at Stella.

"Get lost, Stella."

"Shit. I always miss the fun part." She rose and undid the top of her bathing suit and pulled the string on her bikini bottom. "I'm going for a swim."

The glass patio doors closed behind her.

"Who supplied the coke?" Jack repeated the question.

Traynor chewed his lower lip and sighed. "All I can say is there's always a supply of high-grade cocaine on the set of a Leo Whelan production."

"You're telling me the Whale is the connection."

"I didn't say that."

"Don't fuck around with me, John."

"Hey, Jack," Silvio said, "take it easy."

"You ever meet anyone named Pedro Cisneros?" Jack pressed.

"No."

"Sidney Davis?"

"He came up to San Francisco when we shot *Lick-orice.*"

"Alone?"

"As far as I know."

"Did Candy do any dealing?"

Traynor came around the bar and sat on the arm of a sofa. "She might have. We all have—from time to time."

"Before you became a star?"

"Yeah . . . five, six years ago."

"Who supplied you?"

"A real estate agent who lived at the Marina."

"Is he still around?"

"He was killed on the freeway coming back from Vegas."

"People that hang around you don't have much luck, do they?"

Traynor glared at Jack but did not respond.

"My partner's a little edgy," Silvio said soothingly. "Listen, John, off the record, can you positively say whether or not Candy was dealing?"

Traynor rubbed his hands over his eyes. "She was an addict. She was a star. She had money. I don't know whether she dealt or gave it away."

"The name *Kingfish* mean anything to you?"

"No."

"How about *Ave María?*"

"I think it's a religious song."

Jack walked deliberately across the room and with unmistakable menace said, "Let's cut the bullshit. I happen to know you dealt coke to Candy."

"Did Karen tell you that?"

"What makes you think so?"

"She's been on my case ever since we first worked together."

"Why?"

"I guess I hurt her."

"That's easy to understand. You got a hell of a cock, sonny."

"If it makes you feel better, Lieutenant, I'm burned out."

"That's the price of stardom, I guess," Jack replied. "You know Angelo Maffatore?"

"No."

"You ever involved with the Order of Shiva?"

"No."

"Did Lisa Chang get along with Candy?"

"As far as I know, they did."

"What about Chang and Karen Dara?"

"I don't think anyone's crazy about Karen. She's always throwing her education around. The bitch thinks she's better than the rest of us."

"What do you think, John?"

"I think she's a cunt."

"Did Candy think so, too?"

"Candy was in love with her."

Jack glanced at Silvio. "You have anything else?"

"A couple of things." Silvio looked at Traynor. "Is John Traynor your real name?"

"Yes."

"You have any family?"

Traynor shook his head. "They're all dead."

The patio doors slid open, and Stella, wearing a towel around her waist, entered the living room.

"I want a drink."

Her large breasts jiggled as she crossed to the bar.

"Are we through, Lieutenant?" Traynor asked.

"For the moment," Jack replied, and took out a card and dropped it on the sofa. "Don't leave the city without letting me know."

"Am I a suspect?"

"You're a material witness."

"To suicide?" Traynor asked, puzzled.

"Just let me know if you have any travel plans."

"I'm supposed to start a film in Frisco in ten days."

"No problem," Silvio said. "You just let Lieutenant Raines know where you are."

They started for the staircase, and Jack stopped and turned. "By the way, John, you mind if I ask you a

personal question? You don't have to answer. This is unre-
lated to the case."

"What is it?"

"That giant cock of yours—do you strap it to your leg,
or do you stuff it up your ass?"

Behind the bar Stella giggled loudly. "He wears it
around his waist like a belt."

Traynor glared at her and looked at Jack. "Why don't
you ask Karen Dara?"

Jack felt the heat rising. He started to move toward
Traynor, but Silvio grabbed him. "Let's go."

Silvio steered the GTO carefully around the S curves
as they descended the steep drive.

"I don't know why that creep pissed me off," Jack
said.

"Maybe it's seeing Candy up on the screen with
Traynor's cock in her mouth."

Jack stared out the window for a moment before
sighing. "What the hell do I say to her father? Mr. Langley, your daughter's activities were confined to pornography and snorting coke."

"Candy isn't alone," Silvio said. "A whole new generation of preaddicted American children are being bred.
Torres told me that babies are being born with dead brain
cells, fried on hydrochloride cocaine ingested by the
mothers."

"I wonder if we're just pissing against the tide," Jack
said disconsolately.

"If we save one kid, it's worth it."

They came around a wide curve and saw the sun
spots bouncing off the roofs of cars crawling along Sunset
Boulevard.

"Ask yourself," Silvio said. "You spent a year in Vietnam with defense intelligence. Did you do any good?"

Jack was silent for a moment, then reflectively said,
"I saved one old woman. I was attached to the South
Korean Tiger Division. They were gonna kill this old
woman. I convinced them to let her go. That was my
contribution. In return I have a set of busted eardrums."

"What from?"

"I got stuck with an artillery unit for three days in the Highlands. That goddamn sound, the one fifty-five howitzer; it's the end of the world. I'll never forget that sound."

"But you managed to save one old woman."

"Yeah."

"Well, you're in a different war now. But the goal is the same. If we save one life, it's worthwhile."

Chapter 17

The NIFTY squad's operations center was a huge windowless rectangle that had been hastily converted from a file storeroom to its present status without regard for human comfort. The air-conditioning unit pushed the tepid air around, and the harsh overhead fluorescent lighting occasioned frequent employee visits to the police clinic's ophthalmologist.

Jack walked through the warren of small partitioned offices, oblivious of the cacophony of busy typewriters and ringing phones. He stopped at a cubicle where Sergeant Phil Brody was typing a case report on an old Remington.

"Got anything for me, Phil?"

"I been checking on the technical crew of Candy's last picture."

"Any luck?"

"They went to Musso's for a late bite, but I'm still running them down." Brody paused. "Where's Silvio?"

"Questioning Lisa Chang."

"Why don't I draw those assignments?"

"You're too horny. Your overactive libido would get in the way of justice."

"Last time I had an erection the Dodgers were still in Brooklyn."

"You told me it worked with Hunnicutt."

"She's Superwoman—doesn't count. Torres has been waiting for you. He's been in the crapper, got the runs."

"When he regains control of his bowels, send him into my office."

"You mean, *if* he regains control," Brody said, and poured some coffee from a thermos into a paper container. "There's a William Langley on the way up," he added.

"Thanks, Phil."

"I saw Gloria Hunnicutt on TV this morning." Brody smiled. "You must have rubbed her the wrong way. You ought to give her a little news. Take it from me, that dame can—"

"I know," Jack interrupted. "Get milk out of a crowbar."

"You okay?" Brody asked.

"Fine."

"How's Jenny?"

"Great."

"You look lousy."

"It's that time of the month."

Jack snapped his office light on and tossed his jacket onto a cracked Naugahyde sofa. The furniture was worn, stained, and barely adequate; but the air-conditioning unit worked, and a large window afforded a view of Wilshire Boulevard and, on a rare smog-free day, the distant San Bernardino Mountains. A portrait of a thoroughbred hitting the finish line was the sole decoration on the pale green walls. A framed photograph of Jenny rested on his desk alongside a bottle of Bushmills Irish whiskey.

He sat down, picked up the Bushmills, and took a long swig from the mouth of the bottle. He opened a manila case file marked "Candy Lane" and checked off the names: Sidney Davis, Pedro Cisneros, Angelo Maffatore, Leo Whelan, Karen Dara, Stella Pierson, John Traynor, and Lisa Chang.

In the terse typed record of the case history he underlined three questions: "Seventy percent coke?," "Missing five thousand?," and "Order of Shiva?"

He closed the file and dialed Sidney Davis's office. A pleasant female voice answered and informed him that Davis was out of the country. Jack left word, hung up, and crushed his cigarillo out in an ashtray marked "Palace Hotel, Barcelona." The ceramic ashtray was a souvenir of that long-ago holiday in Spain with Jenny and Laura. There was a knock at the door, and Gabriel Torres entered.

The coroner's skin tone was chalky, and deep blue circles rimmed his eyes. He held a manila folder in one hand and an unlit cigar butt in the other.

"I'm a very sick man, amigo."

"Just don't fart in here. I couldn't take it this morning."

"Ay, compadre. When the stomach goes, the good manners go."

"Between you and Nolan I could open a gas station. Have a shot of Bushmills, guaranteed to kill alien bacteria."

"I'll try anything."

Jack poured the coroner a hefty shot.

"*Salud,*" Torres said.

He drained the whiskey, grimaced, and rubbed his belly. "*Madre de Dios,* that's strong stuff."

"It's the best."

Torres placed the envelope on Jack's desk. "Three pages of forensic conclusions on the late Candy Lane. But I can save you the trouble of reading the Latin." Torres lowered himself onto the sofa and winced. "Jesus, these springs are murder. It's like getting a high colonic."

"Nolan promised me new furniture as a reward."

"For what?"

"The next time we intercept what he terms 'a significant shipment.'"

"Then you'd better get a new ass or burn the sofa."

"What have we got, Gabby?"

"We have a female Caucasian decedent approximately nineteen years of age who received a single gunshot wound to the right side of her head, just above the temporal. The area surrounding the wound is caked with powder burns. Bullet fragments are embedded in brain tissues behind the petrous bone and below the tentorium."

"Keep it in English."

"Okay. The slug traveled laterally, causing massive head trauma, resulting in instant brain death. The firearm has been identified as a Beretta auto load twenty-five caliber. The decedent's prints are on the grip and trigger. The spent cartridge matches those that were test-fired. No traces of semen in any orifice. However, there are vaginal emissions of female chemical hormones and libidous sputum female blood cells."

"Meaning what?"

"The decedent had cunnilingus performed upon her the evening of her death."

"That's on the screen," Jack said. "What about prints?"

"No print taken in the Malibu house matches that of any criminal print in the L.A. files, and the Sacramento computer drew a blank."

Torres rose and relit the cigar butt. "The decedent's torn thigh was caused by canine bites. We found blowfly maggot eggs in her eyes. Time of death occurred between two and three Sunday morning."

Torres poured himself another shot of Bushmills. "You mind?"

"Help yourself."

The coroner drained the glass but did not grimace. "That's not too bad."

"Grows on you. Anything else?"

"Toxicological tests indicate the decedent ingested a large quantity of cocaine. The amount and purity of the drug would contribute to abnormal behavior."

"Like killing herself?"

"I can't say it was the coke, but the depression suffered by heavy users can be severe."

"Have you released the body?"

Torres nodded. "To her father this morning."

"So officially we stay with 'suicide'?"

"Forensically speaking, yes. But you've got five thousand dollars unaccounted for, and that valentine worries me."

"Why?"

"If Candy did not draw that valentine, it could be the signature of a serial killer."

"We don't have a series of homicides."

"Not yet, amigo, but those weird signs around violent deaths usually indicate a deranged serial killer."

The door opened, and Sergeant Brody poked his head inside. "I've got William Langley out here."

"Give me a minute, Phil."

"Okay."

"I'll get out of here," Torres said. "I can't face that man again. Spare him the details, Jack. What the hell does it matter now?"

"I will. Thanks, Gabby."

"*Por nada.*"

Jack walked to the window and stared down at the

antlike shapes of pedestrians on Wilshire Boulevard and wondered what he would say to Candy's father: *Mr. Langley, your daughter suffered erotic misery, family tensions, vaginal secretions, bright lights, cocaine, and failed Eastern philosophy. She was a middle-class refugee who fled to the safety of oblivion.*

"Lieutenant Raines?"

Jack turned and saw a slightly built middle-aged man with fine features set off by sad gray eyes.

"I—I know you're busy," Langley stammered. "If this is inconvenient for you, I—"

"Not at all." Jack indicated a straight-backed chair. "Please sit down, Mr. Langley."

"Thank you."

There was an awkward moment of silence before Langley spoke in a halting fashion. "She was—she was a beautiful child, always respectful . . . always considerate. After her mother died, I—I tried to—" He shook his head. "I—" His voice broke.

"Mr. Langley, you don't have to spell it out for me. I'm a widower myself. I have a daughter going on seventeen."

"Yes. I'm sorry. I don't mean to abuse your time." He regained his composure and asked, "What can you tell me about the circumstances of Candy's death?"

"Your daughter died from a self-induced gunshot wound. Just prior to her death she had ingested a large quantity of cocaine which might have contributed to her depressed state of mind." He omitted the vaginal secretions and the canine bites. Jack cleared his throat and continued. "The coroner has fixed the time of death between two and three Sunday morning."

"Had she worked earlier that night?"

Jack felt suddenly trapped. He had an urge to scream, to put his fist through the window, to carry Langley in his arms through the minefield of self-recrimination. Instead, he calmly said, "Yes, she worked Saturday night."

"Candy told me that she had decided never again to perform in an X-rated film." Langley paused and took a deep breath. "I don't suppose you know the content of her last film?"

"No," Jack lied.

Langley stared at him with a curious intensity. "You found no evidence of—of foul play?"

"There's always that possibility, but it's highly improbable. We're still in the process of questioning her acquaintances, but so far no one we've interrogated had any apparent motive to harm your daughter."

"Where did she get the cocaine?"

"A dealer." Jack shrugged. "A friend, a lover. It's not difficult to come by, Mr. Langley." Jack paused. "Do you know whether your daughter owned a gun?"

Langley shook his head. "No. But we—we didn't see each other too often." Tears welled up in his eyes, and he brushed them away with the back of his hand. "Did you find a note, a message—anything at all?"

Jack opened the desk drawer and removed a small cardboard box and handed it to Langley. "This box contains her private phone directory, some letters, checks, and a diary. The closest thing to a note is a poem between the covers of her diary."

Langley opened the box, picked up the diary, and extracted the small slip of paper. Tears coursed down his cheeks as he read the words. "She smiled on cue—a celluloid/fantasy, lost in the lights,/seeking a dream that/would never come true."

He placed the note back in the diary and took a handkerchief out and dabbed at his tears. "I'm sorry, Lieutenant." He rose wearily and said, "You've been most kind."

"Mr. Langley, I say this out of personal experience: If I were you, I would take your surviving daughter and leave the city. Go off somewhere together. Maybe Europe or the Far East. Give yourself a chance to gain some perspective."

"Yes. Yes, I must do that." He shook Jack's hand. "Thank you again." He started for the door, stopped, and turned. "Curious, isn't it?"

"What's that?"

"A man knows what's right. He believes in certain principles. But for one reason or another he lets those principles slip away, and he tries to regain them; but it's too late, and he knows he'll never be the same again." The stricken man turned and left.

Jack sat down at his desk and lit a cigarillo. He felt old, tired, and helpless. The phone rang. He thought it had to be Silvio calling from Lisa Chang's apartment. He let it ring three times before picking it up. "Raines speaking."

The Tactical switchboard operator said, "I have Commander Raúl Álvarez calling from Manzanillo."

"Put him on."

"Lieutenant Raines?"

"Yes. How are you, Raúl?"

"Good. Listen, we acted on that tape transcript you furnished to us. A freighter of Panamanian registry loaded leather goods here at Manzanillo. The name of the ship was *Ave María*."

Jack felt his pulse quicken. He took a deep drag of the cigarillo and picked up a pen.

"You with me, Teniente?"

"Yes, go ahead."

"One of our patrol craft followed the ship for almost six hours. At first it was headed due north, but it then changed course due west toward Hawaii. We were far outside our territorial waters, so we discontinued following, but it may have been decoying. I thought you should know."

"Thanks, Raúl. I'll get on it."

"Good luck, my friend."

Jack hung up and checked the taped transcript, running down "*Ave María*," "kingfish," "Manzanillo," "a quarter," "*alfombras*." He depressed the phone's intercom button.

"Yes, Lieutenant?" the switchboard operator asked.

"I want to speak with the chief customs officer at Terminal Island. Identify NIFTY, and tell him it's an emergency."

He hung up and crushed the cigarillo out. His depression had been ameliorated by a faint glimmer of hope; the call from Álvarez might be a major break—a break the NIFTY squad desperately needed. The frustration caused by the relentless Colombian snowstorm was demoralizing, and both he and Silvio were approaching a dangerous mental edge. They required more than victory; they required vengeance. Vengeance for Silvio's murdered colleague, Maria Vasconsuelos, for Candy, for her father, for the unborn with drug-fried brains. But against whom do you exact vengeance? Rafael Ordóñez safely tucked away in his jungle fortress? Sid Davis? Angelo Maffatore? Pedro Cisneros? Leo Whelan? Or was Candy just the beginning? Was Torres right? Did the valentine indicate a serial killer, a self-anointed avenging angel determined to wipe out the porno players?

The phone buzzed, and he quickly picked up the receiver.

"I have the chief of U.S. Customs, Robert Higbee."

"Put him on."

"Hello?"

"Yes, this is Lieutenant Jack Raines."

"Robert Higbee, U.S. Customs. What can I do for you, Lieutenant?"

"Can you confirm ship arrivals for the last twenty-four hours?"

"Freighters? Tankers? Cruise ships?"

"This would be a cargo vessel of Panamanian registry named *Ave María*."

"I'll check with the Coast Guard and get back to you."

"Hold it, Chief. I need some additional information."

"Yes?"

"If the *Ave María* is berthed at San Pedro, I want its cargo manifest and to whom its cargo is consigned."

"What else, Lieutenant?"

"If the cargo has been unloaded, I'll need the name, address, and phone number of the trucking line that picked it up."

"If the ship's in, we'll have all that on our master computer. I'll get back to you."

Jack hung up, walked out of his office, and entered the NIFTY operations room and threaded his way through the partitioned cubicles to Brody's desk. The swarthy sergeant was eating an egg salad sandwich, sipping coffee, and puffing a cigarette in almost synchronous fashion.

"What's up?" Brody asked through a spray of egg residue.

"I want you to organize a standby detail comprised of our own men: Fitz, Specter, Santoro, Heinz, and Mirell's coke-sniffing dogs."

"What for?"

"I'll know in a couple of minutes."

A young woman in police uniform came around the partition. "Lieutenant?"

"Yes?"

"There's a call for you from U.S. Customs."

"Tell Mary to hold it. I'll be right there."

Jack reentered his office, came around the desk, picked up the receiver, and pushed the blinking button. "This is Raines."

"Chief Higbee here," the customs chief said. "You'd better take this down, Lieutenant."

"Go ahead."

"The *Ave María* arrived ahead of schedule and docked early this morning. Its cargo has been offloaded and consisted of Colombian coffee, Bolivian sugar, Mexican leather goods, and Peruvian rugs."

Jack felt the euphoric jolt that always accompanied a major break in a complex case.

"You said Peruvian rugs?"

"That's right. Eight hundred to be exact."

Jack glanced at the tape transcript and circled the word *alfombras*.

"Something wrong, Lieutenant?"

"No. Go ahead."

"Everything is consigned to Belgravia Imports in South Gate. The cargo was picked up by Harbor Trucking and Transport, 11047 South Broadway, phone number (213) 555-1136." Higbee paused. "Anything else?"

"Yes. I have reason to believe the *Ave María* is involved in a drug-smuggling operation; unrefined cocaine in the form of paste may have been secreted in those rugs. But I can't be certain. I'm dispatching a special unit to board the ship, search it, and question its captain and crew."

"I'll advise the Coast Guard and San Pedro Operations." Higbee paused. "According to our computer's read-out, the *Ave María* is due to sail at four A.M. tomorrow."

"That gives us plenty of time," Jack replied.

"Yes, but some of the crew have undoubtedly gone ashore."

"They have to come back, don't they?"

"That's correct, Lieutenant. I just thought I'd mention it. Your squad will be met at Pier Eighteen by a Coast Guard officer and an armed detail."

"My people will be on the pier within the hour," Jack replied. "Thanks for your help, Mr. Higbee."

"Anytime, Lieutenant."

He hung up and punched the number for Harbor Trucking. A syrupy female voice answered. Jack identified himself and asked for the supervisor.

"This is Charles Kowalski."

"Lieutenant Jack Raines, Tactical Narcotics Division."

"Yes. My secretary informed me."

"This is a police emergency, Mr. Kowalski."

"I'll help in any way I can."

"I appreciate that. Did one of your trucks pick up a cargo of eight hundred Peruvian rugs at Pier Eighteen this morning?"

"Do you have the name of the ship?"

"Sorry. It's the *Ave María*."

"One minute."

The door opened, and Silvio entered. Jack cupped the receiver. "Take a load off. Have a drink. We got a hell of a break."

"In what?"

"*Ave María*."

"Lieutenant Raines?"

Jack uncupped the receiver. "Yes?"

"One of our trucks picked up those rugs at ten-fifteen A.M. and delivered them to Roma Fashions, 1352 Los Angeles Street."

Jack jotted the information down and asked, "That's curious. According to U.S. Customs, those rugs were consigned to Belgravia Imports in South Gate."

"That's correct, but the shipping manifest specifies the rugs be dropped off at Roma Fashions."

"Isn't that unusual?"

"Not with soft goods. The importer often requires additional work be performed before the goods are delivered."

"Thank you, Mr. Kowalski."

"I hope we haven't done anything wrong."

"On the contrary. You've been very helpful."

"My pleasure, Lieutenant."

Jack hung up, pressed the intercom button, and dialed two digits.

"Yeah?" Brody growled.

"Pier Eighteen, San Pedro. The Coast Guard detail will meet you and the boys on the pier. You board a ship called *Ave María*, search it, and question the captain and crew."

"What am I looking for?"

"Coke." Jack paused. "But don't be disappointed if you come up empty. I may have found it."

He hung up and smiled at Silvio. "*Ave María* is a Panamanian ship. The cocksuckers sailed it right up our assholes."

He picked up his jacket. "Let's go."

"Where?"

"*Alfombras*, amigo—fucking *alfombras*."

Chapter 18

They were parked near the corner, diagonally across from the building's Los Angeles Street side entrance. A backup car with two NIFTY detectives was staked out on the Seventh Street side, opposite the building's loading dock.

Roma Fashions occupied the two top floors of the redbrick factory the crumbling façade of which reminded Jack of those ancient relics that lined Canal Street in lower Manhattan.

They had brought Nolan up-to-date on the *Ave María* break, and he promptly canceled his 5:00 P.M. press conference. The canny bureaucrat instantly perceived he would be far better served announcing a major drug bust rather than dealing with the ongoing investigation into the death of Candy Lane.

During the drive from Tactical to Los Angeles Street, Silvio filled Jack in on his interview with Lisa Chang. Her response had followed the party line. "We all loved Candy. She was simply over her head—snow-blind and lost." Lisa Chang had freely admitted to cocaine use, confirming that the drug was always available on Leo Whelan's pictures, but the Oriental porno actress denied that she bore any grievance to Karen Dara; on the contrary, it was she who had introduced Karen to the Order of Shiva.

They had dropped the subject on arrival at the factory and for the past two hours had focused their attention on the building's entrance. The only activity had been the lunchtime departure and return of Mexican workers. The backup car watching the loading dock had not reported any unusual movement. The corrugated steel gate had remained shut, sealing the loading area.

The windows on the GTO were open, and the hot wind parched their throats and irritated their eyes.

"I still think we ought to go up," Jack said.

"There are no rules in this kind of thing," Silvio said, "but whoever runs Roma Fashions supervised the opening and closing of those Peruvian rugs. They'll never buy us as immigration officers looking for wetbacks. All we'll do is alert them. The time to hit them is when they start refining that paste."

"*If* the paste was sewn into the lining of the rugs."

"It's got to be the way they did it," Silvio insisted. "*Alfombras* on the tape tells us that. My guess is the factory workers opened the linings, withdrew the sheets of paste, and restitched the rugs closed. The question is where they took the paste for refinement."

"Has to be somewhere in the building," Jack said. "Probably in the basement or a hidden room behind the loading dock."

"I agree. The sewing machine operators couldn't stand the refining stench of sulfuric acid."

Jack lit a cigarillo and picked up the radio mike. "Easy red one to Easy red two."

"This is Stillwell. Go ahead."

"Anything?"

"Nothing. The loading gate is still shut."

"Who's with you?"

"Reisman."

"Put him on."

There was a slight pause, and a youthful male voice came through the receiver.

"Yes, Lieutenant?"

"You ever done any acting?"

"I've been fooling you for three years."

Jack glanced at Silvio. "Good sign—the kid has a sense of humor."

"What the hell are you doing?" Silvio asked incredulously.

Jack ignored his partner's question and spoke into the radio mike.

"Reisman?"

"Yes."

"We think the lab might be located behind that loading dock. You with me?"

"Yes, sir."

"They probably have window lookouts on your side of the building, so you've got to make this look real. Take off your shirt, get out of the car, rip the shirt, and rub it around in that muck alongside the curb. Put some crap on your face; then cross the street like you're drunk, enter the loading dock area, and piss against the wall. Take your time zipping up; then recross and walk back toward the corner. As you pass Stillwell, let him know if you smelled an odor of rotten eggs coming out of that loading dock."

"Got it, Lieutenant."

"You'll be watched, so don't overact. You're a derelict, a bum, a wino—not Hamlet."

"Yes, sir."

"We'll cruise by at some point. Now put Stillwell on. Frank?"

"Yeah?"

"Stay on the frequency and keep the volume up. Let me know when Reisman is set."

"Ten-four."

Jack placed the mike on top of the radio unit and turned the volume knob up. There was a low hum of steady static.

"Not bad, amigo." Silvio smiled.

"Well, it might tell us a couple of things: the location of the lab and whether they've started the first stage of refinement." Jack paused. "You have any idea of how much snow is involved?"

Silvio wiped the beads of sweat oozing out of his forehead. "Say they had a three-pound sheet of dried paste in each rug; that would be a total of twenty-four hundred pounds of coca paste. They'd have to start cooking fast. It takes three stages to turn that paste into pure cocaine. Once that's done, they've got to cut it and package it. They'll be at it all night."

The radio crackled. "Easy red two to Easy red one."

Jack picked up the mike. "Go ahead."

"Reisman's crossing."

"Okay. Hold your present position. I'll come up Seventh."

"Ten-four."

Jack swung the GTO slowly out into merging traffic, made a left on Seventh, drove past the loading dock, and double-parked up the street. He set the sideview and rearview mirrors so that they reflected the image of a disheveled wino weaving across the street toward the loading dock.

"You can bet they made him from an upper-floor window," Silvio said.

"Let's hope they buy his act," Jack replied.

Reisman entered the loading dock area, leaned against the wall, and unzipped his fly.

"Easy red one."

Silvio picked up the mike. "Go ahead, Frank."

"I've got Reisman in my binoculars. The kid is actually pissing."

"We've got him in our mirrors. If he doesn't get killed, we'll nominate him for an Emmy."

The fluted steel door sealing the loading dock suddenly rattled and rolled up, exposing an open storage area backed by a cinder-block wall.

Reisman did not glance up, nor did he react to the overwhelming stench of rotten eggs.

Two shirtsleeved dark-skinned men stood on the dock, glaring at the wino pissing against the wall. Reisman grinned drunkenly back at them. One of the men nodded, and his heavyset companion came down the ramp as Reisman zipped up his fly.

Reisman smiled and drooled. "You got a buck?"

The man grabbed Reisman, spun him around, and propelled him toward the sidewalk.

"Get the fuck out of here, you wino *cabrón!*"

"You don't have to get rough." Reisman's speech was slurred as he added, "I can take a hint."

The youthful agent recrossed the street, weaving a zigzag pattern, and passed close to Stillwell's stakeout car.

Jack gunned the GTO and sped to the corner, made a left turn, and doubled back to Los Angeles Street, where he parked once again diagonally across from the building's entrance.

The radio crackled. "Easy two for Easy one."

"Easy one. Go ahead."

"Rotten eggs."

"Ten-four." Jack turned to Silvio. "You were right. They're cooking the paste somewhere behind that dock."

"Easy one." Stillwell's voice again came through the speaker.

"Go ahead, Easy two."

"Three more men have come out on the dock, appears to be an unloading crew. The big guy that shoved Reisman is on the street, looking east." Stillwell paused. "Here it comes."

"What is it, Frank?"

"A truck painted like a parcel post vehicle. It's stopping at the dock. The big guy is waving it in, guiding it into the loading dock."

Silvio grabbed Jack's hand. "Ask him to identify any containers they offload."

"Identify the delivery items as best you can," Jack said into the radio mike.

"Okay."

The static hummed and crackled for a few minutes.

"Looks like five-gallon steel containers," Stillwell reported.

"That's ether," Silvio said.

"And jugs of clear fluid," Stillwell added. "One-gallon jugs."

"Acetone and kerosene," Silvio commented. "Tell him to get the hell out of there!"

"Frank?"

"Yeah?"

"Pick up Reisman on Ninth and Hill. Give him my compliments, and return to Tactical."

"Ten-four."

"The last stage is complicated and volatile," Silvio said. "Ether is not to be fucked with. That's why they brought it in. You don't store that shit. Acetone and ether remove impurities; then they dry the slurry over a bank of hot lights and crush it into cakes of one hundred percent pure, lethal coke."

"What do you think?" Jack asked.

"Let's hit them at one, two in the morning. They'll be in the last stage—tired and woozy from all that ether. Surround the building. SWAT team—and the rammer. Crash it. And rush them. Bulletproof vests, automatic weapons. They may have some soldiers up in those windows. Got to be organized. Lights. Tear gas. Stun grenades. Everything. This is a major haul."

"How big would you say?"

"Twenty-four hundred pounds of paste will give you two thousand pounds of pure coke. When that's cut by eighty percent, you're looking at three hundred million dollars' worth of street snow."

"Jesus . . ."

"It's a ballsy move they made, knowing they were tailed and still sailing right into Pedro."

"What about the guy in charge of the sewing plant?"

"Forget it. They've got to have prearranged signals with the lab gang. If we grab the supervisor, we lose the bust. The chemists will blow the lab up. The whole thing will turn into a fireball. The factory supervisor is paid help. We can run him down anytime." Silvio's eyes glittered dangerously as he added, "It's the *coqueros* we want."

Jack picked up the radio mike. "Easy red one to Easy red two."

"Easy red two. Go ahead."

"Scratch the last order. Double back to Los Angeles Street. Keep a watch on the building's entrance. Anyone other than Mexican workers should be tailed."

"Ten-four."

"Not a bad idea," Silvio said.

Jack turned the engine over, slid the windows shut, activated the air conditioner, and pulled away from the curb. They turned left on Seventh and passed under the Harbor Freeway.

"Will this bust nail Pepe?" Jack asked.

"I don't think so. Anyone could have bugged the

conversation of Julito and Ramon. The *Ave María* lead did not necessarily have to come from Pepe."

"I've got to believe an operation like this had to be supervised by Pedro Cisneros. He may have even been on the *Ave María*, which means Cisneros knows the Mexican coastal patrol was tipped."

"It still doesn't track directly to Pepe. Cisneros will figure that someone got careless, but he can't make a solid case that anyone informed."

Jack stopped for the light at Sixth and Wilshire. "Why do you think Pepe gave us the tape?"

"I'm going to trust you, Jack." Silvio sighed. "Pepe's playing both sides. He gets rich dealing, and if he gets nailed by Ordóñez, he'll ask us to place him in the witness protection program. All he's got to do is walk on water for a year or two, and he's got it made."

They turned left into Wilshire and headed west into a dark red sunset. "Suppose you're wrong. Suppose Ordóñez burns Pepe?"

"That's the game." Silvio shrugged.

Chapter 19

A single ruby eye glowed eerily atop the pyramid-shaped temple of Shiva. The moonlit structure was built on a hillcrest above Zuma Beach. Wooden bungalows and canvas tents dotted the area surrounding the temple. The entire compound was enclosed by an electrified barbed-wire fence.

Inside a large tent Karen Dara, Lisa Chang, and the guru, Meli-Ramdas, sat around a small circular table. They wore white cotton cloaks and held hands; an incense candle burned in a red glass lantern, casting sinister shadows on the canvas interior. Behind the worshipers an eight-foot bronze statue of the multiarmed goddess Shiva watched the proceedings through ruby Lucite eyes.

A woman wearing a purple robe entered the tent and placed a lighted pipe with a long stem on the table. The pipe contained a blend of grass and opium. Meli-Ramdas drew deeply on the bitter-tasting smoke and passed the pipe to Karen Dara. She inhaled the heady mixture and in turn passed the pipe to Lisa Chang. They continued the procedure in a silent, studied fashion until a smear of ash remained in the bowl.

Karen felt as though her brain had floated off into the cosmos.

The guru said, "Let us pray that we may contact the spirit of our departed sister."

They clasped hands, bowed their heads, and began to chant in the language of Esperanto. "*Akcepti morto kaj audi.*"

The wind moaned through the tent as they repeated the words in unison. Karen had no conception of time, space, or form. The table seemed to have risen. The wind died suddenly. The candlelight went out. Candy Lane's reverberated voice came out of the night and echoed through the tent.

"KAAARRRENNN . . ."

Karen felt goose bumps run up and down her arms. She stared into the glowing red eyes of Shiva. The guru and Lisa Chang clutched Karen's hands but kept their heads bowed.

"KAAARRRENNN," the voice wailed.

The Shiva's bronze arms seemed to curl and undulate like headless reptiles, but the light in the statue's ruby eyes intensified.

"AVENGE MEEEEEE. The voice echoed. "IF YOU LOVE ME, AVENGE MEEEEEE. . . ." The voice trailed off into infinity.

Karen's palms burned, and her body was sweat-soaked. She could hear her heart pounding; the sound seemed to fill the tent like the muffled thump of a timpany being struck. The ruby eyes of the goddess Shiva lost their glow. The sporadic rocking of the table ceased. "It is time to give our thanks," the guru said.

They knelt at the velvet altar before the multiarmed bronze goddess and began to chant a mantra in Esperanto. "*Hajlo Shiva.*"

They repeated the words at ten-second intervals.

Karen drove her Coup de Ville Cadillac south on the Pacific Coast Highway. She was still heady from the opium and nerved up by the hallucinatory effect of the séance. The traffic moved fast on the dangerous undivided north-south highway. Karen cruised in the lane adjacent to the oncoming northbound traffic. She considered it safer than the inside lane, onto which merging cars swung out of blind intersections, shopping malls, and taco stands.

She had the rearview mirror flipped to its tinted side, but the flashing high beams of a following car flared repeatedly, almost blinding her. She glanced to her right and crossed into the slower roadside lane.

She thought about the channeled voice of Candy, asking for vengeance, and despite her willingness to accept the séance as gospel, Karen knew the combination of drugs used in the ceremony had a mind-bending effect. Candy's voice might have been imagined or even manufactured, but spiritually she *had* felt Candy's presence crying out to her, and somehow she would find a way to bring peace to the dead girl's restless soul.

The lights of oncoming cars whizzed by like surreal flares. She removed her left hand from the wheel and pressed a series of panel control buttons. The windows slid down, and the wind rushed into the car, tossing her ash blond hair. She tuned the radio to KJOI-FM and caught the strains of the hit song from the musical *Evita*. She thought for a moment about the cop with the sad brown eyes. She had toyed with him, flirting and testing him. She may have hooked him a little, but he had been pretty damn perceptive. He knew that she hated herself. Raines . . . Jack Raines . . . Seducible? Probably. But why bother? Perhaps to try to obliterate the images he had seen of her on the screen.

The black Buick that had been in a rush to pass her had slowed and was cruising parallel to her in the fast lane. She tried to discern the driver's features, but his face was a dark silhouette. Her pulse raced as the Buick slowed and swerved sharply into her lane, positioning itself behind her, its front bumper only a few feet off her rear bumper.

She depressed the gas pedal, and the red speedometer needle climbed rapidly.

The Buick stayed on her bumper, its high beams flashing. Her palms sweated as she gripped the wheel and floored the gas pedal. The Buick increased its speed in tandem, tailgating the Cadillac at 85 miles per hour. Her eyes widened in horror as she saw the taillights of a stalled van just ahead. She swung the wheel and veered into the left lane.

The Buick moved with her.

Her mind whirled. The .38 revolver was in the glove compartment, but her only chance was to get off the highway in one piece. She floored the gas pedal, kicked in the turbocharger, and swerved sharply into the right lane; the speedometer hovered at 100 miles per hour.

Surprised by her sudden maneuver, the driver in the

Buick was left at a distance, trapped in the outside lane. Karen saw the four-way Malibu intersection light going from green to amber. She pumped the brake pedal and swung the wheel hard right. The tires squealed and smoked as the Cadillac spun off the highway onto the beachside road. The big car hit a speed bump at the entrance to a shopping mall and whipped around in a wide circle before crashing into a line of shopping carts and coming to a stop. The shoulder and seat belts restrained her body.

She was sweat-soaked and gasping for breath. The market was closed, and there were no signs of life in the shuttered shops of the mall. She undid the seat belt and opened the glove compartment. She gripped the .38 and flipped the safety to off. She got out, glanced around, took deep breaths of the Pacific breeze, then walked slowly to the front of the car. The bumper was severely dented, but the grille and radiator appeared to be undamaged. The crushed shopping carts had acted as a cushion.

She got back inside the car, turned the ignition on, closed the windows, and locked the doors. She opened her purse and placed it beside her. She could see the gleaming barrel of the revolver. Slie shifted into reverse, turned, and headed back toward the highway. She now had a valid reason to call Lieutenant Raines: Someone had tried to kill her.

Chapter 20

They had come in swiftly, silently, rolling up to pre-arranged assault positions. The heavily armed black-clad SWAT team was fanned out on either side of the loading dock. A huge buglike armored vehicle equipped with a galvanized steel protruding ram was stationed at the base of the loading dock ramp. A flatbed searchlight vehicle with six carbon arc lamps was positioned directly behind the rammer. Police vehicles, SWAT personnel vans, and two ambulances were parked at the north corner of Seventh Street.

Jack and Silvio were standing beside a communications command car; both men were smoking and sweating profusely. The acrid medicinal odor of ether seeped into the street from behind the loading dock.

Jack held a radio mike attached to a long cord that connected to the command vehicle's two-way receiving and sending unit.

Silvio glanced at his watch. The radial dials read "1:18 A.M."

The radio receiving unit suddenly crackled into life. "Easy red command. Easy red command." Jack depressed a button on the mike's receiver. "This is Easy red. Come in, central."

"I have Sergeant Brody for you."

"Put him on."

Silvio moved in, positioning himself to hear the two-way conversation.

"Can you talk?" Brody asked.

"Make it fast," Jack replied.

"We went over that tub with a vacuum. No coke. No grass. Nothing. We questioned the captain and crew. Noth-

ing. But Stillwell and Reisman followed a guy who came
out of the factory. A male Caucasian. Tall, gray hair, gray
beard, blue eyes. He took a Yellow Cab to San Pedro and
presented a passport and seaman's papers to the customs
officer."

"You mean he tried to board the *Ave María* as a
returning crew member?"

"Yeah, a crew member who left the ship this morning
with a twenty-four-hour maritime pass. The man's name
was Pablo Escobar."

"Where's the suspect now?"

"We're holding him."

"Thanks, Phil. Anything else?"

"Yeah. Watch your ass. Don't be a fucking hero.
Ten-four."

"Ten-four," Jack replied, and hung the mike over the
vehicle's window.

Silvio said, "A dollar to a dime the Escobar that left
the *Ave María* this morning was Pedro Cisneros."

The SWAT commander trotted over, carrying an M-16,
his face blackened with soot. "We've scanned the windows
with infrared binoculars. No activity. We're set."

Jack nodded and picked up the radio mike and contacted the NIFTY detail stationed at the building's Los
Angeles Street entrance. "We're going in, Larry."

"Right, Lieutenant."

"You guys hold your positions. No matter what goes
down here, don't leave that entrance."

"Got it. Ten-four."

Jack depressed the button on the speaker. "Come in,
rammer."

"Rammer here."

"You all set?"

"Just give us the word."

"You take your start move from SWAT commander."

"Right. Ten-four."

Jack turned to the SWAT commander. "It's all yours."

"Okay. My guys will fan out behind the rammer; once
we bust that steel shutter, we'll toss stun grenades. There
may be return fire, but the lights and grenades should

give us an edge. Now, according to your information, there's a cinder-block wall behind a storage space."

"We determined that this afternoon," Jack replied.

"Okay, we'll knock that down, and—"

"And you'll be up to your ass in coke," Silvio interrupted.

"Let's hope so."

The commander's furtive eyes shone with a trace of madness, the same fearful excitement Jack had seen on the faces of unlucky troopers assigned to patrol the canopy at night when the jungle belonged to the VC.

"Let's go," Jack said.

"Not you," the SWAT commander replied.

"He's right, Jack," Silvio said. "This is strictly SWAT. Nolan ordered us to stay out of harm's way."

"Your boss knows what he's talking about," the commander said. "You guys have no vests, no automatic weapons, no training. You'll just get in the way."

"I've been around a little noise, Captain."

"Maybe so, but I'm responsible, and I don't want one of my men getting hit trying to save your ass."

Silvio put his arm on Jack's shoulder. "Let them bust it open. We'll follow."

Jack chewed his lip, the adrenaline pumping. He took a final drag of his cigarillo and tossed it away.

"Okay," he said.

The SWAT commander took a walkie-talkie out of his belt and spoke briefly to the team on the searchlight vehicle, then moved off like a departing shadow.

The commander positioned himself on the loading dock ramp and activated the beam of a power flashlight. It blinked twice. The searchlight vehicle's six carbon arc lights came on, brilliantly illuminating the loading dock. The bank of arc lights would blind anyone caught in the beams on the other side of the steel gate. The commander's flashlight blinked again, and the rammer's 350-horse-power diesel engine turned over. The bug-shaped vehicle lurched forward, emitting a cloud of blue-black smoke that drifted up into the hot lights. The SWAT team fanned out behind the rammer as it lumbered forward up the ramp and slammed into the steel gate. Plunging on, the rammer tore a huge hole in the gate. The SWAT team rushed into the opening, tossing stun grenades. The yellow explosions were deafening. Jack and Silvio followed the SWAT team into the loading area and saw three armed men standing stock-still. They were backed up flush to the cinder block wall, paralyzed by the concussion grenades and blinded by the arc lights.

The SWAT commander shouted, "Drop your weapons, and don't move a fucking eyelid!" The handguns clattered to the floor. The SWAT team grabbed the men, shoved them facedown, and handcuffed their hands behind their backs. The commander then signaled the rammer. The vehicle roared forward at full thrust and slammed into the cinder block wall, which disintegrated on impact as if it were made of papier-mâché. The searchlight van moved in tandem, its brilliant arcs penetrating into a wide room secreted behind the demolished wall. The SWAT team's grenades went off, flashing and deafening. The assault team rushed into the room. The smell of ether was overwhelming. Five chemists were tending to the refinement of the paste. Three Colombian bodyguards fired wildly at the assault team. The SWAT team returned their fire with bursts of automatic weapons. The gunmen caught in the blinding light and suffering the shock of grenade concussion were cut down in seconds. A choking cordite smoke filled the room. The SWAT commander ordered the chemists to lie facedown on the floor.

Jack and Silvio came into the lab. The entire operation had taken less than three minutes. Two SWAT men were wounded, one superficially, the other seriously. The paramedics had them in tow. The shredded bodies of the Colombian guards pumped rivulets of blood across the stone floor. The handcuffed dazed chemists were hustled out, their eardrums still ringing from the stun grenades.

Jack, Silvio, and the SWAT commander scanned the room. Sheets of cream-colored coca paste were stacked at the far end of a long table. A brown slurry of treated paste passed through translucent tubes into a filtered gauze soaked in ether and kerosene. The residue was heated by a bank of lights, and the dried compound had been pressed into thick chunks of snow-white lethal cocaine. At the far

end of the L-shaped table the pure cocaine had been cut
by lactose and dextrose and packaged into cellophane bags.

Silvio walked over to the heaping pile of cocaine
bricks and dipped his finger into the caked powder and
rubbed it across his gums. "Jesus," he said, and glanced at
Jack. "Try that."

Jack rubbed the powder across his gums. They numbed
instantly as if they had received a massive injection of
novocaine.

"What's this stuff worth?"

"I wasn't far wrong," Silvio replied. "When this pile
is cut by eighty percent, its street value is close to three
hundred million."

Jack glanced at the fallen, blood-soaked bodies of the
coqueros and shook his head. "It was one hell of a plan,
sewing that paste into the rugs and sailing it into San
Pedro. I have to give them that."

"This operation was too clever and too expensive to
be left to hired help." Silvio sighed. "Too bad we didn't
smoke this out sooner. We might have nailed Cisneros.
Pretty cute having someone take his place. I haven't seen
that one since the old days in Miami."

"How did he manage it?"

"He made himself up to look like the guy that left the
factory. His passport was forged in the name of Pablo
Escobar. Once Cisneros left the ship, he went directly to
LAX and home. The factory supervisor then takes Cisneros's
place so that all the crew members are accounted for."

The morgue attendants removed the bodies of the
Colombians.

The smoking demolished refinery grew quiet, and
Jack said, "I hope this bust isn't Pepe's death warrant."

"Pepe will survive. Don't worry about Pepe." Silvio
smiled. "You're gonna get some new furniture. Nolan has
himself the biggest drug bust in L.A. history. We owe
ourselves a little tequila."

"Well, we can thank Commander Álvarez."

"No, my friend." Silvio put his arm around Jack's
shoulder. "We can thank Pepe. That's why I have to keep
that two-timing little bastard alive."

Chapter 21

The lush grounds of Ordóñez's estate were illuminated by spotlights highlighting colorful splashes of mimosa, hibiscus, and purple-flowered jacaranda. Screeching jungle birds punctuated the stillness, and the sweet scent of night-blooming jasmine permeated the veranda.

Sidney Davis, Pedro Cisneros, and Kurt Ohlendorf were seated around a circular glass-topped rattan table, smoking Cuban cigars and sipping aguardiente, a powerful Colombian liquor made from sugarcane. The men were engaged in desultory conversation, marking time, waiting to be summoned by Don Rafael Ordóñez.

Davis had been met on arrival at Bogotá's Eldorado International Airport and whisked to the private section of the airfield, where he boarded Ordóñez's Learjet for the two-hour flight to the clandestine airstrip at Santa Rosa.

Pedro Cisneros had greeted Davis at the villa and explained that the meeting with Ordóñez would be delayed. He suggested that Sidney freshen up and relax.

By the time Sidney showered and dressed, a servant had appeared with a tray of Colombian-style sandwiches, strips of meat wrapped in a thin cornmeal pancake; a silver tureen of Ajiaco chicken soup; bottles of mineral water; and Bavarian beer.

He had eaten hungrily and been about to lie down when Cisneros phoned, summoning him.

A light breeze wafted across the veranda as Kurt Ohlendorf droned on about the perils of paper currency versus the stability of gold. Cisneros said nothing, his mind still focused on the *Ave María* and the tip that had filtered to the Mexicans. Ohlendorf's flat gray eyes assumed a curious energized light as he said, "Gold will skyrocket as worldwide terrorism increases. The Swiss are already moving out of cash into gold. The Hong Kong bankers—"

His words ceased abruptly as a black-suited Indian appeared in the alcove and motioned to Cisneros.

White concave walls soared to an illuminated stained-glass atrium ceiling, and muted recessed lights cast a soft glow over the spacious air-conditioned living room. Modern Italian chairs and sofas were augmented by seventeenth-century French and Spanish antiques. Large primitive Peruvian paintings hung on the walls.

Wearing his customary white linen suit, Rafael Ordóñez studied a vivid, dramatic canvas depicting the slaughter of Indian peasants by Spanish conquistadors.

Davis, Cisneros, and Ohlendorf stood silently in the center of the room, waiting for their presence to be acknowledged. After a long moment Ordóñez turned and smiled.

"Welcome to Santa Rosa, Mr. Davis." He removed his dark glasses and tucked them into his breast pocket. "Sit down, please. Forgive me, but I am a victim of Julia Codesido."

"Who's that?" Davis asked ingenuously.

"A great Peruvian painter. Let the dilettantes collect pre-Colombian artifacts; I've always preferred Peruvian art, music, and culture."

Davis was struck by Ordóñez's amazing likeness to the late actor Tyrone Power.

"I trust your trip was comfortable," Ordóñez said.

"Yes. I was well taken care of."

"Good. Please accept my apologies for the lack of a formal dinner, but my wife and eldest daughter have just returned from Madrid, and I was duty-bound to take dinner with them. Perhaps if you stay through tomorrow evening, we can serve you an authentic Colombian meal."

"I'm afraid that's impossible," Davis cordially replied. "I must return to Los Angeles tomorrow. I'm booked on the afternoon flight."

"Another time." Ordóñez smiled.

"I was amazed at the modern appearance of Santa Rosa," Davis said affably.

"Yes, well, the hospital, the schools, and the appliance stores all are part of the same enterprise. I sent fifteen students to study in Havana last fall. I have four native-born Guajirans attending the University of Mexico. I do what I can for my people. It's my mission, Mr. Davis. That highway through the jungle to my villa will one day lead to the Presidential Palace in Bogotá."

Cisneros shifted nervously in his chair.

Ohlendorf crossed his long legs.

Ordóñez poured some aguardiente over ice and said, "I am not simply a drug dealer, Mr. Davis. This may sound quixotic to you, but I consider myself a man who finds himself standing at the very edge of a twenty-first-century agrarian revolution. The mestizo Indian has been raped by Europeans and North Americans for five centuries. The coca leaf is the key that will finally open the corridors of power to the Indian." Ordóñez paused, but his ice-blue eyes never left Davis. "The days of bananas and coffee are over. I have been chosen by destiny to lead the Indians in this great revolution. I will not rest until they dominate the political and economic life of South America. It is for this noble cause that I require the continued cultivation of the coca leaf."

Davis said nothing. His jet-lag fatigue had slowly evolved into a rising tension. He had not been prepared for a messianic speech.

"We are drowning in cash," Ordóñez continued. "While we speak, rats are eating hundred-dollar bills, and I cannot order my associates in Ecuador, Peru, Bolivia, and Brazil to cut back their cultivation of the leaf. One hundred thousand Indian families would be reduced to starvation. It is for these humanitarian reasons that I ask Don Angelo Maffatore for his help."

Sidney cleared his throat as his mind raced, seeking precisely the right words. "I'm here to help," he said nervously. "After Kurt visited me, I immediately went to Don Angelo. We don't take our partner's problems lightly."

"That's gratifying to hear," Ordóñez replied.

"We discussed your predicament at great length,"

Davis continued. "We suffer similar problems. Our own money-laundering operations are reaching an impasse; nevertheless, Don Angelo felt obliged to help."

Sidney paused and then dramatically said, "I am pleased to advise you that Don Angelo is prepared to accept an additional four hundred million and to pass this money through some of our pornographic corporate bank accounts."

Sidney's heart pounded as he waited for his host to respond. Ordóñez finally shifted his gaze from Davis and glanced at Cisneros.

"What do you think, Cousin?"

"I think it's a modest beginning."

Ordóñez nodded and turned to the gaunt former Nazi. "And you, Kurt, what is your opinion?"

"I regard the offer as a gesture. Nothing more. We require one billion, and in six months, once we commence shipping to Western Europe, we will require an additional billion."

"Let's not project futures," Ordóñez said soothingly. "The problem at the moment is the one billion."

"Don Angelo is sympathetic," Davis said quickly, "but as I said, we have severe problems. The Treasury Department is cracking down. Many prestigious banks have been fined for transferring unreported money: Hanover Trust, Chemical Bank, Chase Manhattan, Crocker Bank, the Bank of Boston. The government may be planning to recall the greenback. There are rumors of a new currency to be tinted red. We have to launder our own capital very quickly. We therefore consider our offer a generous one."

Ordóñez rose and walked to a spectacular primitive painting of Indian peasants harvesting corn. He studied the canvas for a moment, then turned to Sidney. "I realize you are a messenger. But I caution you not to insult my intelligence."

Cisneros coughed.

Ohlendorf picked at a pimple on his chin.

"I repeat. Don't insult me, Mr. Davis," Ordóñez continued. "You have corporations that deal exclusively in the manufacture and distribution of pornographic cassettes. Is this not so?"

Davis steeled himself, fighting for control. He could not afford to betray fear. "Yes, it's accurate," he replied. "But our cassette business is irrelevant."

"It may *become* irrelevant," Ordóñez replied pointedly. "Cassette sales cannot be policed. They are sold by independent shopkeepers throughout North America and Canada. The IRS cannot tell how many have been rented, copied, or sold. You can therefore show any gross income figure you wish. It is through these pornographic cassette corporations that Don Angelo can accommodate my request."

Davis shifted nervously in his chair but did not respond.

"You will tell Don Angelo, with all due courtesy, he is to launder one billion above the existing figure," Ordóñez said. "And in return, I will raise his fee from ten percent to twelve percent. This is my message, Mr. Davis."

Sidney drained the aguardiente, rose, and poured another drink. "We've already received your message," the attorney said caustically. "The killing of one of our major stars, Candy Lane."

"You're mistaken," Ordóñez replied, somewhat surprised by Davis's aggressive tone. "I read about the girl's death in the *International Herald Tribune*. Pedro knew her and admired her. Why do you think we would harm such a child?"

Davis gestured with his drink at Ohlendorf. "When Kurt visited me, he mentioned your observation regarding the difficulty of our making films without actors."

"You make too much of my 'observation,'" Ordóñez replied impatiently. "Now, let's be clear: one billion at twelve percent. You have a week to respond."

Davis's hand trembled reflexively as he lit a cigarette. He exhaled, and his words came through the smoke. "I think it's unwise and counterproductive for me to carry ultimatums to Don Angelo."

"Do you know anything about our history, Mr. Davis?"

Sidney was surprised by the question. "No, I'm afraid not," he said. "Why do you ask?"

"Because history is man's great and only teacher. Ever since Simón Bolívar achieved our independence from Spain in 1819, we Colombians have been engaged in almost continual civil wars. Two million of our people have been murdered. We are a violent, primitive people. If you fail to impress our desperate circumstances on Don Angelo"—he shrugged—"we may have to hold you personally responsible."

Sidney felt a creeping chill enveloping his chest. "Why me? I have no authority to decide anything. I'm here as Don Angelo's attorney—nothing more."

"Don't hide behind protocol, Mr. Davis. You are a key member of the American Mafia. There's a difference between legal representation and being an active partner. In my view you are Don Angelo's adviser. You must therefore try to understand the Colombian mentality. There is an ancient mestizo saying, *'La mortalidad es la única herencia; el engaño es la única garantía.'* " Ordóñez paused and translated. " 'Death is the only legacy; deceit is the only guarantee.' Our children are raised with this saying."

There was a moment of silence, and the dark-suited Indian bodyguard suddenly appeared.

"My man waits for you, Mr. Davis," Ordóñez said. "I don't mean to be abrupt, but I have other business. Family business. I appreciate your time and wish you a safe return."

"Thank you, Don Rafael."

"Por nada." Ordóñez smiled.

Ohlendorf waited for the attorney to clear the room before addressing Ordóñez. "I must be in São Paulo tomorrow night. I have a meeting with the Banco de Brasil."

"Yes, I know." Ordóñez smiled. "Take care with the Brazilian women."

The German's chalky cheeks flushed, and he turned to Cisneros. *"Auf Wiedersehen,* Pedro."

"Vaya bien, Kurt."

The tall, scarecrowlike figure strode from the room, the heels of his boots clicking against the marble.

Ordóñez picked up the bottle of aguardiente and refilled Cisneros's glass. "Let's go out onto the veranda, Cousin."

*   *   *

A refreshing breeze whispered through the palm fronds cooling the sultry tropical night. A night bird screamed angrily and flew off as the men stepped onto the veranda.

Ordóñez studied the illuminated gardens for a moment before asking Cisneros, "Tell me, Pedro, what do you think about this business?"

"The possibility of war worries me," Cisneros replied. "It won't be like Miami. This time *we* are exposed. The Mafia hit men know our dealers. They know the location of our American refineries. This time we are the targets."

Ordóñez sat on the low veranda wall. "What you say is true to a degree." He sipped the strong liquor. "But remember the Mafia is exposed in other ways. If there is a war, it will be fought in America. It is they, not us, who are under federal scrutiny. And we have targets. We can hit their casino management, their heroin dealers, their bookmakers, their service companies. And we can destroy their pornographic enterprises."

"I hope it doesn't come to war," Cisneros said.

"As I do, Cousin. But we may have no choice. I want you to call Aurelio. Prepare our soldiers with passports and weapon pickups in the States, and alert our Cuban allies in Miami and New York."

Cisneros nodded and drained his glass. "Tell me, Rafael, this girl, Candy Lane, did you have her killed?"

Ordóñez removed his sunglasses, and his eyes reflected a calm menace. "Why do you ask?"

"I have my reasons."

"Suppose I did have her killed," Ordóñez said. "What does it matter?"

"I just wanted to know."

"I'm surprised at your sympathy for this girl. These women who perform in pornography are *putos*."

"That girl touched me. I was saddened by her death." Cisneros sighed. "I never made love with her, but she affected me. Perhaps it was her youth. Her death caused me the same pain that I feel when we are forced to kill Colombian soldiers. Perhaps I've become too tired. Perhaps I've seen too much death. I say these things to you because you're the last family I have."

Ordóñez stared at his cousin for a long moment before responding. "While you were away, I went hunting for jaguar. We caught one in the beam of our lights. Its eyes shone like emeralds in my sights. I could not pull the trigger. In that moment, in the eyes of that jaguar, I realized that kind of beauty is only God's to take. Not man. A man must hunt himself. He must seek out his own truth, no matter what the peril. Only then will he be at peace." Ordóñez paused. "Either you are with me or you are not."

"If I were not with you, I would not trust you with my feelings."

"I understand, Cousin, but when a man becomes too tense, his luck runs out."

The phone on the rattan table rang. Ordóñez picked up the receiver. A muffled voice tersely said, *"El pescado ha silo a garrado."*

Ordóñez hung up and turned to Cisneros. "The *Ave María* shipment was intercepted."

Cisneros winced. "Ah, Jesus. I thought we— It was that tip. The Mexicans must have alerted the L.A. narcs." He shook his head sadly. "I'm sorry, Rafael."

"No, no. You were very brave. Even with the patrol craft following. Your decision to sail into San Pedro was valid and does not require second thoughts." He paused. "On the positive side, we now know there is a leak. A leak that sprang from Pepe, Ramon, or Julito. I want them killed."

"But, Rafael, those men are Colombians. They're family. They were probably victimized by a phone tap."

"Perhaps, but the best way to keep a secret between three men is to kill two of them. Have Ramon and Julito taken out. Good night, Cousin." Ordóñez turned abruptly and left.

Cisneros drained his drink and slumped into a chair.

A night bird screamed.

And from far off the roar of a jaguar echoed through the jungle night.

Chapter 22

The view from John Nolan's office was like a picture postcard of Los Angeles in the thirties. A Pacific breeze had cleared the skies of the yellow, eye-searing smog, and neat rows of palm-lined streets sparkled under a bright sun and cobalt sky.

Jack and Silvio watched with amused detachment as Nolan strutted and preened, chewing on an unlit cigar, still gloating over his triumphant press conference. The media had titled the drug bust Operation Alfombra. Nolan had credited the action to months of painstaking investigation requiring perfect coordination among the Mexican authorities, the FBI, the DEA, and his own NIFTY squad, headed by Lieutenant Jack Raines. Nolan had posed in the bullet-splattered laboratory beside a heaping pile of pure cocaine. The bust was the focus of intense local and national press and TV coverage. The NIFTY squad had received congratulations from Paul Anderson, chief of the Drug Enforcement Agency, the local FBI bureau chief, the city commissioners, the mayor, and the governor.

The only discordant note had been raised by Gloria Hunnicutt. At Nolan's press conference she had ignored the drug seizure and pressed him relentlessly for information about the death of Candy Lane and the dead girl's relationships with Colombian drug smugglers and Hollywood celebrities.

"I'm very proud of you fellows," Nolan said warmly. "You deserve a paid holiday."

"Just make good on your promise." Jack smiled. "I expect some new furniture."

"It's in the works. But first things first. I want you to

drop this Candy Lane business. The coroner says suicide. That's good enough for me."

"We can't let it drop," Jack replied.

Nolan's demeanor changed abruptly, and his voice assumed a tough bureaucratic tone. "This is not a homicide unit. I don't give a shit if the girl *was* murdered. Let the Malibu sheriff's office worry about that."

"You're wrong," Jack insisted. "Candy Lane is the link between the Colombians and the mob, Davis and Maffatore, to be specific, and if my memory serves me, you said you'd give anything to nail those bastards."

"Forget what I said. We're riding a crest now, and I don't want NIFTY bogged down investigating the suicide of a teenage porno actress."

"It may not be suicide."

"So what?"

"So she deserves an honest count."

"The coroner says suicide."

"He also indicated she may have been taken out by a serial killer."

Nolan's tired gray eyes blinked. "What?"

"Torres said the cocaine valentine might be the signature of a vigilante, a nut, a crackpot bent on wiping out pornography. Besides, Candy's five-thousand-dollar salary is missing."

"There's something else to consider," Silvio added. "My informant told me that Sid Davis met with Ordóñez in Santa Rosa. The Colombians want the mob to launder an additional billion dollars through their porno checking accounts."

"What's that got to do with Candy Lane?"

"If Ordóñez is pressuring the mob," Jack replied calmly, "Candy may have been the first victim in a war between the Mafia and the Colombians. We can't let this case drift."

"But it's a dead end," Nolan replied. "You've talked to the people on Candy's last picture and come up empty."

"We haven't seen Jeff Kellerman, Sherry Nichols, or the guru."

"What guru?"

"Meli-Ramdas," Silvio replied. "He runs that Order of Shiva."

Nolan slumped into his chair. "You honestly think this case can nail the mob to coke laundering?"

"It's a shot we've never had before," Jack replied.

"Okay . . ." Nolan sighed. "But do me a favor, a personal favor. Give that Hunnicutt dame something. Anything to get her off my back."

"Get Brody on the speaker," Jack said. "He's a longtime fan of Hunnicutt."

Nolan pressed a button on his phone console. "Helen?"

"Yes, sir."

"Put Sergeant Brody on the speaker."

Jack walked around to Nolan's desk. A moment passed before Brody's gruff voice came out of the speaker. "Yeah, Chief."

"I've got Agent Martinez and Lieutenant Raines in my office. Raines has a special assignment for you."

"Phil?"

"Yeah?"

"When's your birthday?"

"What?"

"Your birthday. When is it?"

"November fifteenth."

"We're going to celebrate it early. I got a steamy piece of news for you to feed Hunnicutt."

"My pencil is poised."

"Tell her that Candy Lane, acting as a courier for Leo Whelan, carried a certified check to the infamous Colombian smuggler Pedro Cisneros, and in return she received a kilo of seventy percent pure cocaine—part of which she gave to her occasional lover and benefactor, Jeff Kellerman."

"Terrific," Brody replied.

Nolan leaned into the speaker. "Brody?"

"Yes?"

"I expect a blow-by-blow account."

"You got it, Chief."

"Okay. That's it."

Nolan released the intercom. "Well, that ought to keep the heat off. Listen, where is that one hundred percent coke being stored?"

"The basement storeroom. It's secure," Jack said.

Nolan blew some smoke toward the ceiling and turned to Silvio. "You think a war is possible?"

"If Ordóñez's demands are rejected, you got a war."

Chapter 23

A huge color slide of a smiling Candy Lane played on the TV screen facing the bed. It was as though the dead girl were alive and had watched the two naked, sweating women make love.

Sherry Nichols put her arms around Lisa and kissed her deeply. "Next time I'll chain you," she whispered.

"You'll kill me."

"I'd love to."

Lisa thought about getting to her feet, but her legs still trembled, and she felt heady.

"Want to do a line?" Sherry asked.

"No. I'm fine."

They both stared at Candy's smiling face on the screen.

"God, she was beautiful." Sherry sighed.

"We talked to her."

"What?"

"At a séance. At Shiva. Candy's voice spoke to Karen."

"That bitch."

"Who?"

"Karen. She tormented Candy."

"It might have been the other way around."

"No. Karen dominated her."

Sherry stared at the projection of Candy's face for a long beat before asking, "What did Candy's voice say?"

"Avenge me."

"You really believe in that hocus-pocus?"

"With all my heart. You just have to be open to it."

The phone rang. Sherry answered, and her eyes clouded. "Okay. . . . Yes. . . . I'll be here," she said, and hung up.

"What is it?" Lisa asked.

"A cop. Silvio Martinez. He's on the way over."

"I've met him," Lisa said. "He's working with a Lieutenant Raines. He questioned me."

"About what?"

"Candy. The Whale. Davis. You. Traynor. Stella. Everything." Lisa rose. "I'd better shower and get dressed. I don't think he should see me here."

"What's he like?"

"He's courteous, but there's something . . . I don't know . . ."

Sherry felt tense and distraught. She sat up and reached for a cigarette.

"Goddammit, Lisa, tell me about this cop!"

"It's hard to define. He's pleasant, but he frightened me."

"You're describing every cop who ever gave me a ticket. What did you tell him?"

"We all loved Candy."

"But why are they investigating? The papers said she committed suicide."

"Maybe that's a smoke screen." Lisa shrugged and started toward the bathroom.

"Lisa!" Sherry shouted.

The slim, curvy Oriental girl turned.

"Come back tonight?" Sherry asked plaintively.

"Cross my heart." Lisa smiled and leaned against the alcove. "Stella told me about the picture you're going to make in Frisco—*Memories of Candy*."

"What about it?"

"Am I in it?"

"Of course."

"Starring?"

"You're Asian, darling. I've got to play Stella as Candy, but you'll have a major role."

Lisa nodded and walked into the bathroom.

Sherry rose, picked up her jeans, and slipped them on. She glanced around the bedroom at framed photographs featuring Candy in various erotic poses. She quickly began to remove the photographs from the walls. Her action bordered on paranoia, but she could not afford to have her private shrine exposed to the police. She had some lingering doubts, too, about Lisa's role in Candy's death. She mistrusted the Shiva business and viewed the summoning of Candy's voice with suspicion. Sherry knew that Lisa Chang's pleasant Oriental charm masked a smoldering envy of her more famous colleagues.

Chapter 24

Jack Raines walked down the dusty western street, passing the decayed wooden façades of saloons, hotels, banks, stables, and blacksmith shops. The street had once been the site of feverish film activity featuring immortal stars who had ridden off into countless rear-projected sunsets. But with few exceptions the western had become an anachronism.

He turned the corner and followed a path along the muddy bank of a jungle lagoon to a clearing that housed a neat row of Spanish-style bungalows. The parking stalls were stenciled with the names of the bungalows' occupants. Jack shook his head in wonderment as he passed Ferraris, Lamborghinis, Mercedeses, Jaguars, and Maseratis. He guessed that American cars were not prestigious enough for the insecure artists who passed in and out of the studio gates.

Jeff Kellerman's bungalow was located at the edge of the murky lagoon. A 350 SL convertible was parked in a stall marked "J. Kellerman."

The sound of soft rock played in the wide reception area. The fake oak walls were decorated with framed posters of Kellerman's films. Several minor foreign film festival awards were prominently displayed in an illuminated glass case.

A heavyset black woman was seated at the reception desk, speaking into the phone while simultaneously typing script pages. Two men wearing jeans and leather jackets stood at the far wall, examining a production breakdown board. Two actresses were seated on a sofa, studying script pages. None of the people in the room paid any attention to Jack as he entered the office and walked up to the receptionist.

"They're going over the board now," the receptionist said into the phone. "I'm sorry. Mr. Kellerman is interviewing actors at the moment. I can't disturb him. . . . Yes, of course, Mr. Steinman. I'll have him return your call as soon as he's clear. . . . Thank you." She hung up and smiled politely at Jack.

"Can I help you?"

Jack flashed his leather holder, exposing the gold badge. "Lieutenant Raines to see Mr. Kellerman."

"Oh, yes, Lieutenant. He's expecting you, but he has someone in with him now. We're casting a new film. Would you mind having a seat?"

"Yes. I would mind."

"I have strict orders not to disturb him."

"Tell him I'm here," he replied firmly.

The men at the board turned and stared at Jack, but the actresses' eyes never left their scripts.

"Just a moment," the receptionist said curtly, lifted the phone receiver, and pressed an intercom button. "Lieutenant Raines is here. He can't wait." She paused and nodded. "Yes. . . . Yes, sir." She hung up and said, "Can you give him ten minutes, Lieutenant?"

Jack felt a ball of heat forming in the pit of his stomach as he recalled Karen's words: "Kellerman promised Candy a role in his new film. He promised her a role in his last film. What he wanted, of course, was to fuck her. . . ."

He moved past the desk and walked deliberately to the inner office door.

"You can't go in there!" the receptionist exclaimed.

Jeff Kellerman was short, slim, and neatly attired. He wore tinted glasses that tended to give him a conspiratorial look. His eyes were slightly crossed. His nose was bulbous, and his lips were thick and cracked. He was seated on the edge of a huge desk, smiling benignly at a tall, bony raven-haired girl. His smile switched to a scowl as Jack entered. "What the hell is this, Lieutenant?" he asked indignantly.

The door opened behind Jack, and the receptionist said, "I tried to stop him, but—"

"It's all right, Martha." Kellerman waved her out.

"You agreed to this time," Jack said.

"I'm sorry, but it's difficult to arrange precise times while preparing a movie."

"What do you think, Jeff?" The actress intruded timidly.

"We'll see, dear, we'll see."

"If you want me to come over to the house, it's okay."

"I'll be in touch," Kellerman said as he sat down behind the desk.

The actress picked up her handbag. "This part is perfect for me," she said. "I know my tits are a problem, but I'll be happy to do silicone."

"We'll talk, Loretta," Kellerman snapped impatiently.

Her eyes registered defeat. "Okay." She nodded and left.

"Have a seat, Lieutenant," Kellerman said.

Jack sat in a leather chair, facing the critically acclaimed director.

"Coffee?"

"No."

"Something stronger?"

"Yeah, maybe a strong dose of Proust."

"What?" Kellerman asked, perplexed.

"Let's skip the bullshit, okay?"

"I don't understand your adversarial attitude," Kellerman said righteously. "I agreed to this meeting without having my attorney present. I intend to cooperate. I loved Candy. Truly loved her. It's a terrible tragedy."

"To her father but not to anyone else," Jack shot back. "Don't fuck around with me, Jeff. You and Candy were tight. From what Karen Dara told me, very tight. As a matter of fact, you promised Candy a shot in your next film."

"You've been misinformed."

"When was the last time you saw Candy?"

"I don't know . . . I guess about a month ago."

"Where?"

"At my home up in Bel-Air."

"Were you alone?"

"Not exactly. Candy brought an actress friend with her."

"Remember her name?"

"Stella something." He shrugged. "A redhead."

"And what happened?"

"We watched one of my films and had a bite. A few drinks and . . . well . . . got it on."

"The three of you?"

"What's this got to do with Candy's death?"

"Answer my question," Jack said ominously.

"I never promoted any scenes. It just happened."

"What about Karen Dara?"

"She came over occasionally with Candy." Tears welled up in Kellerman's eyes. "I meant what I said. I loved Candy. Not just sensually but ethereally, intellectually, poetically. I gave her the Proust book because I wanted to enlighten her. I was like a kid with a crush. Candy was a vision. A dream. I always projected her as a lonely figure in a gray dawn wearing a diaphanous gown, what Pauline Kael describes as 'a Bergman dawn.' I had commissioned a script for Candy. I had . . ." He wiped at his tears. "I—I couldn't resist her. I was overwhelmed by her. We used to lie in bed and watch her erotic films. But I didn't see pornography. I saw beauty, yearning, desire, and talent. I never took advantage of her. We loved each other. We were like two children caught in a sensual but innocent relationship."

The phone buzzed, and he pressed a speaker button. "Yes?"

"Steinman is on the line. It's the third time he's called."

Kellerman's face reddened, and he snarled, "Tell that faggot cocksucker to fuck off. I'll speak to him when I'm goddamn good and ready!"

"What about the production people?"

"Move them to seven."

Kellerman released the speaker button, leaned back, and rubbed his hand wearily over his eyes. "Forgive my language, but you make a hit picture, and they smother you. They take the oxygen out of the air." He shook his head sadly. "I've lost every meaningful relationship because of my obsessive dedication to my craft. But"—he sighed—"I've helped some people along the way."

Jack rose and said, "You're a regular Joan of Arc."

"No, Lieutenant. I'm neither saint nor sinner. I'm an artist."

"I'll bet. Did you do coke with Candy?"

"Cocaine?" Kellerman uttered the word as if it were part of an unknown, arcane language. "Me? Do cocaine?" he repeated incredulously. "Never, Lieutenant. I don't believe in drugs. I believe in the human spirit. Pauline Kael has memorialized my philosophy in print: 'Jeff Kellerman's loving vision of life is exquisitely engraved in every frame.'"

Jack felt a sudden urge to flatten Kellerman's bulbous nose, to smash his puppy-dog face. "Listen carefully, you pompous asshole." His voice thickened with rage. "You promised a gullible, lost child legitimacy. You had no intention of fulfilling that promise. You used her. You were her last hope. Your burnt offerings caused her to go that extra yard into suicide. You may as well have pulled the trigger, and if I track your snowprints to Candy, you'll wish to Christ you had been a nun."

"Snowprints?" Kellerman asked timidly.

"Seventy percent coke. That's what Candy snorted before she killed herself."

"I've got nothing to—to do with that."

"You know Sidney Davis?"

"Of course. Sidney's my lawyer."

"What about Leo Whelan?"

"I know Leo," he almost whispered.

"You get pussy from Leo?"

"Mr. Whelan has on occasion introduced me to several girls."

"Was Candy one of them?"

"No. I met her at a party."

"Whose party?"

"John Traynor's."

Jack walked slowly to the wall and studied a photograph of Kellerman and a famous movie actress huddled together on the stage of a nightclub set.

"What does Leo charge for the kids that come off his pussy farm?"

"I never paid any woman for sex."

Jack turned to the pasty-faced director. "You testified for Whelan in a porno trial back in '83."

"So what?"

"You know Angelo Maffatore?"

"I've met him, but I don't know him."

"You're a key player in Whelan's straight film crowd. You give porn the blessing of respectability, and in return you get pussy and coke." Jack's voice broke angrily like a wave smashing into a quiet cove. "Answer me, you son of a bitch!"

Kellerman shifted in his chair, picked up a leather decanter, and poured a glass of water. His hand trembled slightly as he raised it to his lips and swallowed. "I have nothing more to say to you, Lieutenant."

"That's a good idea, Jeff. And I'll give you a couple more good ideas. Keep your nose out of coke and teenage pussy for a while. I hold you morally responsible for Miss Lane's death. And let me tell you, it wasn't a pretty death. She wasn't wearing a diaphanous gown in 'a Bergman dawn.' She was naked in a hot Malibu sun, and the flies and ants were having a good time, and her thigh was chewed to the bone, and the stench of her corpse is still in my lungs—and if she had been my daughter, I'd turn you into a bag of shit! But you're lucky, Jeff, because her father is one of those old-fashioned Americans who still believe in principles. The poor bastard blames himself because he couldn't play mother and father to Candy. But I blame you. And I'm going to nail your fucking ass, baby!"

Kellerman cleared his throat and weakly asked, "Why me? Candy ran around with a lot of people."

"Not quality people like you, Jeff. Not people who get reviewed by Pauline Kael." Jack paused and pointed his finger at Kellerman. "You shouldn't have played 'star' games with that girl. Principles and morality aside, you should have known that one way or another a man always pays for pussy."

Jack turned and left.

Kellerman felt ill. His stomach was queasy, and there was a dull ache throbbing at the base of his skull. He glanced at the phone, sighed heavily, and dialed Sid Davis's private number.

Jack entered the outer office and asked the receptionist if he could phone his office. The woman indicated a phone on a table near the sofa. "Just dial nine and your number."

Brody's familiar growl came on the line. "You got one message. Karen Dara called. She said it was urgent. I gave her the switchboard number at your apartment."

"Okay," Jack said. "Anything from Silvio?"

"As far as I know, he's still over at Sherry Nichols's."

"I'm going home," Jack advised Brody.

"Right. By the way, I have a date with Gloria Hunnicutt. I'm bringing her that scoop you gave me. I've been taking vitamin E all day."

"Happy birthday, Phil."

Chapter 25

John Traynor was seated on the white sofa, a drink in one hand, the phone receiver in the other. Ceiling spots cast a streaky light across the vivid abstract paintings hanging on the black walls. A vintage album of Crosby, Stills, and Nash played on the stereo.

"So we start shooting the nineteenth?" Traynor asked Whelan.

"Right," the Whale replied. "I'll book your suite at the St. Francis."

"Who's starring?"

"Stella Pierson. Sherry decided with blond hair Stella can play Candy."

"Who else?"

"Karen Dara."

"Shit."

"Relax. You got no scenes with her."

"Who else?"

"Chang and that blond kid that fluffed you in Candy's last picture and some local Frisco talent."

"Listen, Leo, I've got to notify this Lieutenant Raines that I'll be leaving town."

"So notify him. If there's a problem, let me know. Davis is back in town."

"Okay."

"You been taking it easy?"

"Just Stella."

"Good. You better be in shape. This is a high-budget flick. We can't stand around waiting for you to get it up."

"I'll be fine."

"The script is on the way over."

"Okay."

"Later, John."

The line clicked off.

Traynor hung up and crossed the big room to a darkly tinted full-length mirror. He admired his reflection. The newly cultivated mustache and short-cropped haircut made him look younger. He had visited a renowned Beverly Hills dentist who after taking numerous impressions assured the porno star that his crooked smile could be fixed. Traynor had undertaken the image improvements at the suggestion of Jeff Kellerman, with whom he enjoyed more than a passing friendship.

Traynor's relationship with the award-winning film director was expensive. He supplied Kellerman with prepaid fluffs and high-grade cocaine, but Traynor considered the expense an investment in his own future. He knew that his days as the male king of porn were limited. His sexual prowess had diminished severely. He required tremendous concentration and constant stimulation to perform. Sherry Nichols's adroit cutting techniques and use of stand-ins managed to fake his orgasms cinematically, but even Sherry's considerable skills could not disguise a limp dick. His future clearly pointed to Kellerman. He would soon have to call in the IOUs.

He turned from his reflected image and walked across the thick carpet, through an alcove, into the master bedroom.

Stella, wearing panties and an open man's shirt, sat up in the huge water bed, eating Fritos and watching a cassette of *Tootsie* on the big TV screen. She waved to Traynor as he entered the room, but her eyes remained glued to the screen. Traynor picked up the remote control and snapped the set off.

"What did you do that for?" she asked petulantly.

"That was Leo. You're starring in *Memories of Candy*."

Her eyes widened. "Oh, wow!" she exclaimed, and got to her feet and did a jig.

"Hey. Hey," Traynor said. "You bust the mattress and we'll be swimming."

She flopped back down and grinned. "Let's celebrate. Order some chinks, and we'll eat, watch a flick, have a blow, and I'll give you the greatest massage you ever had."

The front-door chimes suddenly echoed in the bedroom's remote sound unit. "Who the hell is that?" Stella pouted.

"Probably a messenger with the script."

He flicked the button on the TV remote unit, and the set crackled into life. Stella giggled as Dustin Hoffman adjusted his girdle.

The doorbell chimed again as Traynor reached the top of the spiral staircase. He peered through the one-way peephole, sighed, and opened the door.

"Surprise. Surprise." Traynor smiled weakly.

There was a soft popping sound. A yellow-red baby tomato oozed out of Traynor's forehead. He fell backward, staining the white carpeted staircase with bits of bone and blood as his body slid down the circular steps.

Stella watched with amusement as Dustin Hoffman posing as an actress auditioned for the director. She then noticed a familiar figure enter the bedroom and waved. "Hey"—she smiled—"what's up?" There were two rapid popping sounds, and Stella's face exploded. The white satin sheets were instantly decorated by polka dots of blood.

Chapter 26

Jack sipped the chilled vodka and watched the city lights brighten in the falling dusk. The suffused light reminded him of that special late-afternoon light at Santa Anita. On a winter Sunday, late in the day, the towering mountains on the far side of the stately track would turn purple, a mauve light would envelop the grandstand, and a hush would fall over the crowd as the thoroughbreds in the feature race paraded solemnly in single file toward the starting gate. And in that moment, in that winter light, if you were high up in the stands, looking out, you felt as though Degas had painted you onto a canvas. In the golden age of glitz there was something reassuring about the old racetrack's enduring beauty and dignity.

He turned from the view, walked back inside the living room, and placed a classic Stan Getz cassette on the stereo. The phone rang as Getz's soprano sax got into the first chorus of "Quiet Nights."

Jenny's voice was like a breath of pure oxygen. "Hi, Dad."

"How are you, baby?"

"Great. Thanks for the check."

"How are your kiddies?"

"Fine. We had some excitement last week. Did you see the fire?"

"Which one?"

"The one at Ojai."

"Yes. It was all over the tube."

"We had to evacuate the camp."

Jack felt a twinge of guilt. He knew her camp was not far from Ojai, but it had never occurred to him that Jenny

152

was in any danger. "I didn't realize the fire actually threatened the camp," he said sheepishly.

"The fire fighters stopped it five miles from the campsite."

"I should have called."

"You wouldn't have gotten through. The lines were down. By the way, the camp director saw you on TV."

"He did?"

"She did—the director's a woman. She said it was something about a big drug arrest. You're not taking any crazy risks, I hope."

"You know me. First sign of trouble, and I'm gone."

"When are you coming up?"

"I'm planning to see you Sunday."

"Try to make it. I miss you."

"I'll do my best."

"Love you."

"Love you, too."

"Bye, Dad."

"Bye, baby."

He hung up, crossed into the kitchen, took a frozen chicken TV dinner out of the freezer, and set the oven dial at 350 degrees.

He entered the bedroom, selected a cassette of *Casablanca* from a tray of alphabetized films, and placed it on top of the TV set. He undressed, walked into the bathroom, and turned on the shower taps. He stared for a moment at his reflected image in the mirror above the sink. The crescent-shaped scar over his right cheekbone seemed to be turning progressively scarlet. Old wounds. New colors.

He stepped into the shower and let the hot needles play across his back and neck. He thought about Kellerman and Traynor, and Candy's fly-specked body, and Langley's sad, defeated eyes. He felt a seething anger welling up inside. He would have to get hold of himself; anger was a dangerous cross to carry when you were in the center of a complex case. He turned his face up to the shower head and soaped himself. His thoughts centered on Candy and the people who revolved in the dead girl's orbit. Was she a suicide?

If so, what had happened to the missing $5,000? Was it Candy who had drawn the valentine? And did the initials P. C. actually indicate Pedro Cisneros? Or might it have been someone else with the same initials? And how did Whelan and Davis and Maffatore figure in the case? Was Candy the first victim in a simmering conflict between Ordóñez and the mob? The questions whirled and flashed. But one image remained constant: Candy's bloated, sun-blistered corpse. He shut the taps off and stepped out of the shower. He toweled dry and promised himself Candy's death would not turn into a forgotten yellowed case file. He would go the distance with this one.

He entered the bedroom and slipped on a pair of faded jeans and a white T-shirt imprinted with blue Hebrew letters, a souvenir of his trip to the Holy Land. He walked barefoot into the living room and slid a Sinatra cassette into the stereo. He placed the TV dinner in the oven, setting the timer bell for fifty minutes. He mixed a vodka and tonic and went out onto the terrace.

Sinatra sang "Witchcraft," and Jack felt a profound loneliness. The stewardess he occasionally dated was flying a steady route between Panama and Lima, and Marge Canova, the police lieutenant who worked at Parker Center, had gone on a Mexican holiday. But even so, there was no substance to both relationships. They were devoid of emotion, full of superficial chatter and meaningless sexual aerobics. The only woman with whom he shared a lingering emotional bond was Gabriella Bercovici, the Italian archaeologist who had helped him track down Dr. Sorenson. They had compressed a lifetime of shared experience into two harrowing months. He still corresponded with her, and during Easter week they had had a marvelous reunion in New York. He thought about the possibility of taking Jenny to Rome during the Christmas holiday and introducing her to Gabriella.

The phone buzzed loudly, pulling him out of his reverie. He crossed to the bar and picked up the receiver.

The desk clerk said, "There's a Miss Karen Dara in the lobby."

"Send her up."

"Hold on a second, Lieutenant."

Jack heard the clerk tell Karen, "Apartment fourteen thirty-four."

"Lieutenant?" The clerk came back on the line.

"Yes."

"She's on the way. Silvio Martinez phoned about ten minutes ago. I buzzed, but there was no reply."

"I was in the shower."

"He left a message. 'Sherry Nichols followed the party line.' "

"Thanks, Arthur."

He hung up and thought about Karen Dara. He could see Karen and Candy up there on the screen, locked in that long passionate embrace. He shook his head in wonder. He understood Candy, Traynor, and the others. But Karen was an enigma. She was bright, educated, attractive, witty, and stylish. Why would she choose to swim in the sewer of pornography? Was it money? Exhibitionism? Or a perverted sense of power? The power to turn on millions of people with her body? He sipped the vodka and shrugged. Who was to say? And who was to judge?

The doorbell sounded. He placed his drink on the bar, walked to the door, and opened it.

"Hello, Jack." Karen smiled.

The sweet, heady scent of perfume trailed after her as she entered the living room. She stood there for a moment, with one foot at a right angle to the other like a high-fashion model posing for a photograph. She wore a white suit over a dark blue silk blouse, and a single strand of coral beads circled her throat. She tossed her soft ash blond hair and said, "Is something cooking?"

"Frozen chicken. Specialty of the house." He stared at her for a moment. "A drink?"

"A gin would be nice."

"I haven't got any gin. Scotch. Vodka. Wine or beer."

"Vodka over ice, please."

She sat on a barstool, watching him prepare the drinks.

"Sorry to barge in on you like this," she said.

"It's okay. I was beginning to climb the walls. Sometimes being alone is terrific. Other times . . ." He shrugged.

"I know." She nodded.

He handed her the drink and raised his own glass. "Cheers."

"Cheers." She smiled.

Sinatra sang "I've Got the World on a String."

"Pretty tune," she said. "No one ever phrased a song like Sinatra." She glanced out at the terrace and saw the twinkling lights of the Hollywood Hills.

"Nice place."

"Works for me—and my daughter."

"I didn't realize you were married."

"I'm a widower."

"Oh . . . how old is your daughter?"

"She'll be seventeen this fall."

"Difficult age."

"So far no problems. I guess I'm lucky."

"The time to be concerned is when she starts college, and the danger isn't always from her peers," Karen said, rising from the barstool and walking slowly toward the terrace. "It's the faculty you have to watch. I had the bad luck to fall in love with a philosophy professor. I was very young, of course, still a virgin as a matter of fact. He destroyed me. I didn't know until later that he had balled the entire female freshman class. His name was Dr. Sanford Mengers. The seniors appropriately nicknamed him Dr. Mengele. He did everything but medical experiments."

"I got a message that you called and it was urgent," Jack said bluntly.

"So, you're not interested in my stunted growth." She smiled.

"It isn't that; I don't want to think of my daughter walking through that academic minefield."

She stared at him, her lime eyes picking up the terrace lights. "Someone tried to kill me," she calmly stated. "It was late. Around one A.M. I had just left the Order of Shiva. I was driving south on the Pacific Coast Highway." She sipped the vodka, and a light wind caught the tips of her hair. "A black Buick tried to run me off the road. He tailgated me at a hundred miles an hour. I took a hell of a chance, but I managed to lose him."

"Did you see the driver's face?"

"No. It was dark, and I was terrified."

"When did this happen?"

"A week ago Tuesday."

"Why didn't you phone me?"

"I don't know . . ." She shrugged her broad shoulders. "I suppose I didn't want to believe it was anything more than some highway freak. But it's been worrying me," She paused. "I mean, after Candy . . ."

"I could be wrong," he said, "but I don't think it's related. From what you tell me, it sounds like one of those lunatics who prowl the highways at night. Professionals don't kill by tailgating."

"Maybe not. But a highway accident would be a clever mask for murder."

"Why would anyone want to kill you?"

She stared at him over the rim of her glass and said, "I have no idea."

"What were you doing up at the Order of Shiva?"

"We conducted a séance."

"Who's 'we'?"

"Me, Lisa Chang, and the guru, Meli-Ramdas."

"Why the séance?"

"I wanted to communicate with Candy's spirit."

"What kind of drugs does the guru provide for his disciples?"

She seemed surprised. "How do you know about that?"

"I worked on the con game squad years ago. Exotic religions are endemic to L.A.—like smog and dead palms. What did Candy have to say?"

"Forget it," she replied curtly.

He followed her back inside the living room. She reached into her bag and took out a blue pack of Gauloise cigarettes. She rummaged through the bag and said, "Shit."

"What is it?"

"Match."

He took out the U.S. Army Zippo, flipped the flywheel, and held the flame to the cigarette.

"Thanks," she said, and indicated the Zippo. "Where'd you get that relic?"

"From an old mamasan in Saigon."

The smoke rushed out of her thin nostrils, and she crossed to the bar. "You really shouldn't make fun of my religion."

"You're right. If you buy it, fine. But I promise you, if I went up there with a few seasoned cops, we'd find a professional sound mixing unit that can trick voices so they reverb and echo—make them thin or thick, change timbre or tonality. We'd also find trick tables and chairs with hidden springs. It's all bullshit, Karen. The game is usually played on wealthy widows anxious to speak to their departed husbands."

"You're really suffering from terminal cynicism," she said caustically.

"We all have our hang-ups." He shrugged. "Can I freshen your drink?"

"No, but I'd like a little grass."

"Can't help you there."

"I didn't think so," she said, tossing her hair and letting him have the full force of her glittering eyes. She removed a small cellophane-wrapped joint from her jacket pocket. "You won't mind, I trust."

"Not at all. Smoking a joint is no longer a felony in this state. In fact, it's probably less harmful than those French nails you smoke."

She lit the joint and smiled. "My, my, a cogent social comment." She inhaled deeply and held the smoke in her lungs for a long time before exhaling. A small cloud of pungent-smelling smoke drifted over the bar. She felt the heady rush of grass and said, "I'll have that freshener now."

He poured some vodka over fresh ice and slid it across the bartop.

"Want a hit?" she asked.

"No, thanks."

"It's Hawaiian. I have a cousin in Maui who mails it to me."

"That's dangerous."

"Isn't everything?" She smiled. "I mean relatively speaking."

"I suppose so."

She leaned across the bar, and the perfume came with her. "You have nice eyes, Jack."

"Thanks."

Sinatra sang "Fly Me to the Moon."

"Who sent you here, Karen? Was it Leo? Sid Davis or Don Angelo?"

"It's not very complicated. I came up here because you're a cop and I'm a citizen. And someone tried to do me in. And now that I'm here and somewhat stoned, it suddenly occurred to me that it might not be too terrible if we got it on. There is definitely something to be said for meaningless affairs."

"I'm flattered. But why me?"

"Because you had an uncle who fought in Spain. Christ, does there always have to be a reason? You're alone. I'm alone. Why not?"

"I'll take a rain check."

"What are you afraid of?"

"You want a list?"

"Are you nervous about performing with a performer? Are you intimidated by my screen image? Or do you think I'd contaminate you?"

"I don't trade on emotional cripples."

Her open hand was a blur as it slapped loudly against his cheek. She started to throw the other hand, but he caught her wrists.

"I'm sorry," he said quietly. "I shouldn't have said that. But it's very late, and I'm very tired."

He released her. She rubbed her wrists and dropped the joint into her bag.

He walked her to the door and held it open. "I'm sorry about that remark."

"It's all right. People have said a lot worse to me."

"It's not all right. I was out of line."

She moved very close to him. "What do those Hebrew letters on your T-shirt stand for?"

"They mean 'smile.' "

"Where'd you get it?"

"Israel."

"From what I read, they don't smile much, do they?"

"Between wars."

She circled his neck with her arm and pulled him close. She kissed him lightly on the mouth, stepped into the hallway, and turned.

"Don't worry about the kiss. My doctor tells me I'm not transmitting anything that a little Lavoris won't cure."

Chapter 27

Four bodyguards were stationed at the huge wrought-iron gates leading up to the main house, and additional patrols protected the private road running below Maffatore's hilltop villa. In contrast with the heavy security surrounding the estate, the rear terrace was a study in tranquillity.

Clouds of steam billowed up from the heated water of the swimming pool. Blue jays chirped in their nests high in the tall pines. Boxes of crimson geraniums decorated the windows of the villa's ocher-colored walls. A gentle breeze rustled the purple bougainvillaea that clung to a high wall on the far side of the terrace.

The men were seated at a large glass-topped table adjacent to the pool, shielded from the sun by a striped umbrella. A sweating Sidney Davis sat at one end of the table, facing Angelo Maffatore. Between them sat Vince Mangano, a wizened, thin-faced man who represented the national council. Mangano had flown out from New York for the meeting. He sipped his coffee and chain-smoked dark brown Sherman cigarettes.

"We been sittin' here for twenty minutes talkin' in circles," Mangano rasped. "Now what is this fuckin' spic all about? Does he wanna do bizness—or what?"

Maffatore's eyes were masked by black-lensed sunglasses. He poured some fresh orange juice into his glass. "I never met Ordóñez," he said.

"You arranged the Miami truce in '81."

"I met with Ordóñez's cousin Cisneros in Cancún, Mexico." Maffatore sipped the sweet juice. "Sidney's just come back from Santa Rosa. Ask him about Ordóñez."

Mangano scowled at the tense attorney. "Well, speak up, for chrissake!"

Sidney wiped the beads of perspiration from his forehead. "I presented our offer to launder an additional four hundred million. Ordóñez insists on one billion, and he'll raise our laundry fee from ten to twelve percent."

"I know all that!" Mangano snarled. "I want your impression of this spic."

Sidney squirmed and reached for a cigarette. He had never before been put on the spot by a member of the national council. He had crossed the line. He was consorting with nonclients who were known criminals. He could no longer hide behind the legal shield of client-attorney "privileged information." His incipient boredom with theatrical law might prove to be fatal, and he recalled Ordóñez's threat: "If you fail to impress our desperate circumstances on Don Angelo, we may have to hold you personally responsible."

Sidney moved his chair closer to the table to avoid a hot slice of sunlight. "Ordóñez is a man who perceives himself as a hero, a contemporary Simón Bolívar. He believes that destiny has chosen him to lead the mestizo Indian in a great agrarian revolution, a revolution based on a single crop: the coca leaf. He's convinced that its cultivation and processing will eventually destroy the ruling white society of North America and Europe. The revenue from the leaf will elevate the Indian to power, and he, Ordóñez, will become the Jesus Christ of this hemisphere."

Mangano rubbed his hand across his leathery face. "You mean to tell me he actually believes this shit?"

"Yes, I do."

Mangano lit a fresh cigarette, inhaled deeply, and said, "I thought Ordóñez was a businessman."

"He's a very astute businessman," Sidney replied, "but he's also a visionary."

"He sounds nuts to me."

"Not so crazy," Sidney cautioned. "After all, cocaine is a mind-altering drug, and if you control the mind, you control everything."

"Spare me the philosophy, okay?" Mangano growled.

Sidney did not respond. He felt like a defenseless animal who had strayed into a dangerous part of the jun-

gle. Maffatore remained silent, his eyes hidden behind
the dark sunglasses.

Mangano suddenly slammed his fist angrily against
the tabletop. "All that fuckin' revolution shit is a smoke
screen. There's no mystery here. Ordóñez thinks we're a
bunch of stronzos. He insults us. If we wash a billion
more, he gives us an extra two percent, and we lock
ourselves out of washing a billion of our own hot money."
He glared at Maffatore. "You understand what's happenin'
to us here, Angelo?"

"Be careful how you speak to me, Vincenzo," Maffatore
replied calmly.

Mangano's thin lips slackened, and his eyes betrayed
a trace of fear. "I didn't mean nothing, Don Angelo, but I
gotta deliver a message to the council. We had a week to
get back to the spic. And I gotta know what we're doin'."

"You tell me." Maffatore sighed. "I'm all out of ideas.
Either we wash the billion or we go to war. Anything you
decide is fine with me."

Mangano's arrogant tone instantly changed to one of
humility. He turned his palms up in a gesture of helpless-
ness and spoke softly in Italian. *"Tu sei il capo dei capi. Tu
controlli tutta l'urganizazione. Nessuno actro po desidere."*
Mangano paused and switched to English. "The council is
in your hands, Don Angelo. We live or die with your
decision."

Sidney sensed the intrinsic fear in Mangano's sudden
acquiescence. The distinguished attorney again wondered
how he had come to this place. What was he seeking
among these predators?

Maffatore removed his sunglasses, and his black eyes
played with Mangano. After a moment he sighed heavily
and shrugged. "Maybe I've lived too long. I buried two
sons—killed in forgotten territorial wars. I buried my sainted
Philomena in her Sicilian village, Lercara Friddi. I couldn't
put her to rest in Brooklyn with her sons. She wanted to
return to the earth of Sicily. Even in death my family was
apart. I'd like to retire to spend my days in peace and
enjoy this"—he gestured with his hands—"this paradise.
I'm old enough to know that success means only one
thing: to be able to walk away from problems."

"Ah, Don Angelo, you'd go crazy with nothing to do," Mangano said soothingly. "You'd die with the cancer. Your heart would go. Your mind would go. A man must have problems to stay alive."

Maffatore glanced at Sidney. "How do we stand with Ordóñez?"

"I'm not sure. We had one week to respond. That week ran out twenty-four hours ago. But I assume Ohlendorf is still waiting for my call."

"Where is he?"

"Lausanne."

"Well"—Mangano turned to Sidney—"you're the *consigliere*. What do you suggest?"

"I'm not a *consigliere*. I'm a lawyer. Don Angelo is my client. Nothing more."

Mangano's small hand shot out and clutched the chalky attorney by the throat. "You speak to me like a stronzo, and you'll be eating your asshole!"

"*Basta*, Vincenzo!" Maffatore commanded. "Enough!"

Mangano released Sidney.

Maffatore rose and walked slowly to the sweat-soaked attorney and squeezed his shoulder. "Vincenzo is right. It's too late to play the lawyer. Not here. Not now. At this moment our problem is also your problem."

"I understand," Sidney said. "I meant to convey that I work for you."

"Well, then you must deal with my problem."

"You know my feeling," Sidney said with resignation. "I'm concerned with the political and economic damage of a war with Ordóñez."

"What happens to us in a war, Vincenzo?" Maffatore asked the council capo.

"We'll get hurt. But so will the spics. We know their dealers, and we know their refineries. And we can throw some of their shipments to the feds. We could hurt Ordóñez pretty good."

"True. But you heard Mr. Davis." Maffatore used Sidney's family name purposefully. "He describes Ordóñez as a self-proclaimed saint, and saints enjoy pain. Ordóñez doesn't care about dealers, shipments, and labs. So we hurt them. The price of snow rises. Meantime, they hit

us. Vegas. Unions. Hotels. Nightclubs. Heroin dealers.
And, more profoundly, our porno business. And the war
will be fought in Miami. New York. Chicago. L.A.—*here*.
Here in America! The feds will be laughing at us. They'll
open champagne. It's a bad thing, Vince." Maffatore stared
off at the skyline of the city. "It's a bad thing," he murmured.

Mangano spoke to Sidney in a warm, confidential
manner. "You were there in Santa Rosa. Is there any way
we could clip Ordóñez?"

"I have no expertise in the fine art of assassination,
but in my view you don't have a chance. The villa is
isolated in the rain forest. One road in and out, policed by
Ordóñez's private army. The grounds are patrolled around
the clock by Cuban guards armed with AK forty-sevens.
The Colombian Army can't get at Ordóñez."

There was a moment of silence, and Maffatore sighed.
"Call Ohlendorf, Sidney. Tell him we'll take the billion at
twelve percent."

The green phone on the table buzzed loudly. Maffatore
picked it up. "Yes?" He paused. "Bring him out."

"Who is it?" Mangano asked, puzzled.

"Leo Whelan."

"What the fuck does he want?"

"We'll see."

Whelan lumbered down the grassy slope, carrying his
jacket over his arm. His shirt was dark with perspiration.
His distended belly heaved as he gasped for breath. He
wiped the sweat from his forehead, and his pinkie diamond flashed in the sunlight. "Excuse my intrusion, Don
Angelo, but—"

"This is Vincent Mangano," Maffatore interrupted.

The Whale nodded.

"What is it, Leo?" Maffatore asked.

"John Traynor and the girl Stella Pierson were shot to
death. It just came over the radio."

Maffatore slumped into his chair. The creases in the
old man's tanned face whitened. "Those cocksuckers." He
swore. "Those fucking spics. They probably killed Candy,
too. They couldn't wait one more day." He glanced at
Sidney. "I told you, blood is everything. Blood is destiny.
Ordóñez has that fucking mestizo blood."

"I can't start production," Leo complained. "There isn't an actor or an actress with any star value that'll go to work. We're out of business. I was gonna start shooting *Memories of Candy* in Frisco. Now I—"

"Shut up, Leo!" Maffatore thundered. "Sit down!"

The Whale sank into a chair and stared at the diamond on his pinkie.

Maffatore leaned across the table to Mangano. "Vince, call New York. Tell the council we're at war."

Chapter 28

The fleet of official vehicles were parked in a cul-de-sac at the entrance to Traynor's A-frame. Press cars and TV mobile units lined both sides of the hilltop street.

Jack walked toward the house, wondering how the press always knew. The media's instant awareness of death reminded him of the almost immediate appearance of circling vultures descending over the jungle canopy after a firefight.

He spotted Silvio standing behind the yellow taped line erected by the uniformed Hollywood Division cops.

Jack flashed his badge, crossed the taped line, and walked up to Silvio.

"It's a bitch," Silvio said.

"Who's been running this?" Jack asked.

"That big guy, chief of detectives, Hollywood Division." They walked to a nearby tan Chevrolet, where a mountain of a man lounged against the car's fender.

"This is my partner, Lieutenant Raines," Silvio said.

The man extended the largest hand Jack had ever seen. "Steve Riddle."

Jack gripped the man's hand and winced against the pressure.

"My orders are to turn this mess over to you," Riddle said.

"Your people touch anything?" Jack asked.

"Not my guys. We got the call a little before eight A.M. and arrived about eight-twenty. The coroner, photographers, lab people, and print men came in about nine-thirty."

"So nothing's been moved?"

"Like I said, we touched nothing." He paused. "Fucking sun is murder."

"Let's go inside," Jack suggested.

"I been in there," Riddle replied.

"Who found the bodies?"

"A Mexican maid."

"Where is she?"

"Sitting by the pool."

"You question her?"

"No. She was in shock. She kept crossing herself and mumbling in Spanish."

"Okay . . . I want to clear everyone out," Jack said. "I'd like you to leave a twenty-four-hour detail—one man in back, one in front—until the property is sealed."

"No problem."

Traynor's body lay head down at the foot of the spiral staircase. A blood smear traced his descent down the white-carpeted stairs. His features were distorted into a claylike protruding mass. A coroner's assistant knelt over the body, placing cellophane bags over Traynor's stiff fingers.

Jack and Silvio sidestepped the corpse as they came cautiously down the stairs. The coroner's man rose and glanced at Jack. "Explosive slug. Pushed his face out. Looks like the fucking Elephant Man."

"Where's Torres?"

"Bedroom."

Silvio followed Jack to the glass doors overlooking the pool. A Mexican woman was seated at a table, staring blankly at two uniformed cops, who were chatting and smoking.

"Silvio . . ."

"Yeah?"

"Go out there. Speak to the woman in Spanish. Calm her down. She's still in a daze. Try to bring her around."

"Okay."

"And get rid of those assholes. What the hell are they doing smoking in uniform?"

"The Hollywood Division," Silvio said derisively.

Jack sighed. "Did Brody manage to contact Karen Dara?"

"Not yet."

"Call him and tell him the guru's number is in my case file. She may be up there."

Stella Pierson sat up in bed. The force of the bullets had slammed her against the headboard. Her face looked like melted clay that had hardened and transformed itself into a protruding multicolored snout. Her open eyes were the last recognizable features of what was once a human face. The white satin bed sheets were splattered with blood spots.

Gabriel Torres handed a specimen slide to an assistant and said, "That's it. You can take her."

The stocky coroner glanced at Jack. "*Buenos dias,* compadre." His eyes were rimmed by circles of fatigue. "I warned you," he said indicating the heart-shaped cocaine valentine on the night table. "Same valentine. Same initials P. C. We got ourselves a serial killer."

"Maybe," Jack replied. "Chemist break that snow down?"

"Yes. It's seventy percent pure."

Two men came in, carrying a stretcher and a black body bag.

"Come on." Torres took Jack's arm. "Let's go outside."

The activity in the living room had perceptibly diminished. The photographers had departed, and the print men were packing their instrument cases. Jack glanced out at the pool area and saw Silvio commiserating with the Mexican maid.

"Let's go in the kitchen," Torres said.

They crossed the living room and walked through an alcove into a sparkling ceramic-tiled kitchen.

Torres removed a silver flask from his jacket and poured two hefty shots of tequila. "Knock that down," the coroner said. They swallowed and grimaced at the bite of the cactus-based whiskey.

"Jesus, what a morning." Torres sighed.

"What have you got?" Jack asked.

"We found a single twenty-two-caliber shell casing on the top step. Traynor must have opened the door and gotten hit six inches from the muzzle. The slug exploded inside his head, forcing his face out. That's why it's a lump. You see that Elephant Man look only from explosive slugs. We found two more similar shell casings in the bedroom."

"Any mutilation of the bodies?"

"Not that I could detect."

"Any idea when they were hit? The time is critical."

"I'd rather run the toxicology before I say anything."

"Just give me an idea."

"They were shot less than twenty-four hours ago. Probably between two and six yesterday afternoon."

"Would you connect this MO with Candy Lane?"

"Well, a twenty-five Beretta automatic killed Candy, and in this instance, the murder weapon was a twenty-two automatic. We don't know the make, but explosive slugs are special. The coke valentine is the same, and all three victims were shot at extremely close range."

"Meaning?"

"They knew the killer."

"That might rule out a vigilante."

"No. Someone close to them may have gotten religion. That's your problem, amigo."

They entered the living room as the morgue attendants carried Stella's black-bagged body up the staircase. Torres squeezed Jack's arm and said, "I'll have something for you in the morning."

"Thanks, Gabby."

The coroner crossed the room to the spiral staircase and trudged wearily up the bloodstained steps.

Jack walked out onto the terrace, his eyes narrowing against the bright sun. Silvio patted the maid's hand, got to his feet, and took Jack aside.

"She's okay. I told her we need her help and not to be frightened. Her English is so-so, but if you speak slowly, she'll understand."

Silvio introduced Jack to the middle-aged woman. Her features were severe, and her black eyes were immobile. Her stoic face reminded him of a carved Aztec head.

"We need your help, Mrs. Lopez," he said softly, and sat down.

Silvio remained standing.

"What time did you get here?" Jack asked.

"Before eight, I think. . . ."

"Try to remember what you saw and what you did."

"I—I ring bell like always. But this is to tell the señor that I was here. Sometimes he stays in bed. I use my key. I open the door and . . . *Madre de Dios*." She crossed herself. "I see Señor Traynor. I see the face. I see the blood. I scream—"

Jack patted her hand. "Go on, please, Mrs. Lopez."

"I cover my eyes. I walk down the stairs. I think to call for police. I try to remember the number. I try to think. I walk into the bedroom."

"Why?"

She seemed perplexed by the question and glanced at Silvio.

"*¿Por qué entra la cámara?*" Silvio asked.

"*No se.*"

"She doesn't know why she went in there," Silvio explained.

"Okay. What happened next?"

"*¿Qué?*" she asked.

"*¿Qué pasa en la cámara?*" Silvio translated.

"I see the girl. I scream. I fall to my knees. I crawl from the room. I go to the phone. I dial, you know, *nueve-uno-uno*."

"Nine-one-one," Silvio translated.

"I remember to call that number."

"That was the right thing to do," Jack said soothingly.

"I talk to the emergency woman. She tells me to stay, to wait for police. I come out here. That's all I saw. That's all I know."

"Thanks for your help, Mrs. Lopez," Jack said, and rose. "I'm sorry you had to see this. I'm sorry you had to be the one to find them. I'll have someone take you home."

Jack and Silvio vacuumed the house: closets, drawers, bookcases, suit pockets, cosmetics, file cabinets, and desks.

They found $12,000 in crisp $100 bills, a valid passport, a phone directory listing names and numbers that closely paralleled those in Candy Lane's personal directory. There was a note in Traynor's memo pad to phone Sidney Davis.

"Looks like they were hit by professionals," Silvio commented. "But if Ordóñez wanted to damage the mob's porno business, why not hit Whelan? Why hit the players?"

"Whelan doesn't have a foot-long cock," Jack replied. "He isn't a star, and he can't direct. The Whale is a businessman. He's replaceable."

They came out of the A-frame into the bright sunlight. The horde of journalists and TV camera crews ignored Silvio as he walked to his car, but the shouting, shoving herd converged on Jack. He faced them and held up his hands. "Hold it! Hold it! Chief of Tactical John Nolan will issue an official statement sometime this evening."

"What time was the killing?"

"Were they making a porn?"

"You find any snow?"

"Who was the dame with Traynor?"

Jack ignored their questions and walked past the gaggle of angry press toward his GTO. He reached the convertible, opened the door, and tossed his jacket onto the passenger seat. His shirt was beginning to show perspiration stains. He took a few rapid breaths of air and got into the car. He turned the engine over and activated the air-conditioning.

"I want to thank you, Lieutenant." The smiling face of Gloria Hunnicutt leaned into the open window. "I ran that item Sergeant Brody gave me."

"What item?"

"The one about Candy Lane and the Colombian Cisneros and how Jeff Kellerman obtained certain favors from Candy. I couldn't say he got snow from Candy, but the phrase 'certain favors' keeps the lawyers at my network happy and does the same job—don't you think?"

"I'm happy for you, Gloria."

"Tell me, did you find another one of those valentines?"

"Ask Brody," Jack said, and put the car in gear. "He's a believer, Gloria. He says you're a very great artist."

"I'm just a good journalist, Lieutenant."

The tires squealed as Jack gunned the engine and roared away from the curb. He checked his sideview mirror and saw a black cloud of exhaust settle over the platinum queen of gossip. He shifted to low gear as he descended the steep drive that snaked its way down the hill toward Sunset Boulevard.

Chapter 29

The night was crystal clear, and an infinity of multi-colored lights sparkled through the picture window. Nolan paced tensely. His usual gray complexion was slightly flushed, and a tic had developed just above his left cheekbone. "God knows there's a hell of a lot of crap that goes with this job," he complained, "but I can abide politics, bureaucracy, public indifference, insufficient budgets, and incompetent personnel." He stopped pacing. "You learn to put up with that shit. I've done my time on the streets. I've seen all the horror. I've been knee-deep in piss, blood, and excrement. That's the job. We chose to protect and serve the citizens, but goddammit, I cannot tolerate fucking *mysteries!*

"I asked you to lay off this case and lean back on our laurels. We intercepted three hundred million dollars' worth of street snow, the greatest drug bust in L.A. history. But you fellows persisted." He paused and clutched the pit of his stomach. "Now we have a full-blown mystery."

He delivered the word *mystery* as if it were the most malignant word in the English language. Jack and Silvio exchanged glances but said nothing. Nolan slid the late edition of the *Herald-Examiner* across his desk toward the two detectives.

"Banner story," Nolan said. " 'Who's killing the porno stars?' It goes on from there, connecting these homicides with the Colombians and the mob. It was all over the six o'clock news." Nolan slumped on his chair. "I have the city commissioner, the mayor, and Chief Gates on my ass!

"The Malibu police turned Candy Lane's death over to us because of that high-grade coke found in her beach house. And having done that, they conveniently went

174

back to policing driftwood. The Hollywood Division turns the Traynor and Stella Pierson killings over to us because of the coke valentine. I explained to His Honor the mayor that we are not a homicide unit. You know what he said? 'Tactical is a crack intelligence unit that handles all manner of criminal activity, and I'm counting on you, John, to solve these valentine murders.'"

Nolan opened his top drawer and removed a blue bottle of Brioschi. He shook some of the white crystalline stomach soothers into a half glass of water, waited for the brew to fizz, and swallowed it in one gulp. He belched, rubbed his stomach, and grimaced. "Well, I'm listening, gentlemen."

Jack rose, walked to the huge picture window, and gazed down at the rainbow of lights blinking their way toward the Pacific.

"You enjoying the view?" Nolan asked sarcastically.

Silvio noticed that the small crescent scar on his partner's cheek seemed to be glowing, and he hoped Jack would contain his anger.

"Here's how it goes," Jack said calmly. "Candy Lane, a haunted, despondent three-gram-a-day addict, teenage star of erotic films, is found shot to death. We determine that she had contact with Cisneros, Whelan, and Davis, which means Maffatore and the mob. She also had connections to the straight film world in the person of Jeff Kellerman. Candy Lane was bisexual. She engaged in a homosexual relationship with Karen Dara and perhaps her director, Sherry Nichols, and Lisa Chang, who introduced her into the Order of Shiva. She was killed with a twenty-five-caliber Beretta up close. All the apparent MO of a suicide." He walked slowly toward Nolan's desk. "But we find a valentine drawn in snow with the initials P. C. and assume it's a suicide note to Pedro Cisneros, with whom Candy may have had an affair. The night of her death Whelan paid Candy five thousand dollars in crisp new one-hundred-dollar bills. That money is missing."

"She may have stopped on the way home and bought five grand worth of coke," Nolan suggested. "Dammit, Jack, don't make mysteries. Traynor and Pierson are homicide victims—but not Candy. The coroner said suicide."

"He also said someone could have pressed that Beretta to her temple, then placed her prints on the weapon."

"Torres also mentioned that the valentine has the traditional earmark of serial killers," Silvio interjected.

"And considering the MO used on Traynor and Stella," Jack continued, "Candy's so-called suicide is certainly open to question."

"Sit down," Nolan grunted. "You're making me nervous."

"You were born nervous."

"Don't get cute with me," Nolan growled.

"Next," Jack said, "I visit Kellerman. He mind-fucked Candy with promises of an acting career. But I don't think he figures in the violent aspects of the case. He gets pussy and snow from Whelan, but I can't prove it. Kellerman is just a random particle, a floating piece of shit that surfaced in a complex case." Jack lit a cigarillo. "Next, I receive an urgent message from the WASP star of erotica, Karen Dara. She comes up to my apartment and tells me someone tried to run her down on the Pacific Coast Highway."

"When?" Nolan asked, displaying a modicum of interest.

"Shortly after Candy's death. Karen puts up a cool, hip façade, but she's scared. She tells me she took part in a séance up at that Shiva place. She communicated with Candy's spirit."

"What?" Nolan said with disbelief.

"It's her religion, John."

"You mean to tell me that she believes that crap?"

"How would I know?"

"Come on, for chrissake." Nolan frowned. "That séance bullshit is the oldest scam in the world. You told me Karen Dara is educated. Bright."

"And complicated," Jack added.

Nolan relit his cigar and blew a cloud of smoke up at the ceiling spots. "Okay . . . okay . . . she communicated with the dead girl's spirit. What did the late Miss Lane have to say?"

Jack sat down alongside Silvio. "I don't know. I stepped on Karen's religion—the way you have, John. And she clammed up. I believe her story about the car incident, but I make it a psycho, a highway freak. Nothing more."

"Have you considered the possibility that she may have hit Candy?" Nolan asked. "I mean, they had an affair, and the Dara woman knows how to use a handgun."

"It's possible. But there's no motive."

"Remember, though," Silvio said, "Karen had no alibi for the time Candy was hit."

"Neither does anyone else in this case," Jack replied.

"But she did accompany Candy to Key Biscayne for that weekend with Cisneros," Silvio said persistently.

"So what?" Nolan asked.

"Anyone who had business with Cisneros may have known too much."

"That's conjecture," Nolan snapped, and glanced at Jack. "Keep going. I want everything up to the moment."

"Traynor and Karen Dara despised each other," Jack continued. "Stella Pierson was a fluff who was about to graduate."

"How do you know that?"

"Traynor told me about his ongoing grudge with Karen. And Stella told us she was going to star in a new film called *Memories of Candy*."

"Lisa Chang and Sherry Nichols confirmed that to me," Silvio added.

"There may have been some inside jealousy between those porno freaks," Nolan suggested. "It looks like an inside thing. All three were killed at close range. No forced entry. No struggle. The killer had to be a longtime acquaintance they knew and trusted, someone who took the time to draw that valentine."

"Silvio has a different theory that may explain everything," Jack said.

"I don't know if it explains everything, but Pepe told me Ordóñez turned down the offer Davis presented in Santa Rosa."

"What offer?"

"Maffatore's compromise to launder an additional four hundred million. These killings may be Ordóñez's way of shutting down the Mafia's porn business."

"Well, it's the best theory we've got," Nolan said. He

came around the desk and sat on the arm of a leather sofa. "If these killings are the opening guns in a war between Maffatore and Ordóñez, it would be a dream come true. The FBI, the DEA, the Coast Guard, the Customs, for chrissake, even the president would have a cause to celebrate. But at the moment it's all conjecture and I've got a press conference at Parker Center in a half hour. What do I say?"

"The investigation is continuing," Jack suggested. "We're pursuing several leads. The coroner will have fixed the time of Traynor's and Stella Pierson's deaths by noon tomorrow. The killings may have international narcotic-smuggling tangents. Give them enough glitter to fill two columns."

"Mention that prick Kellerman," Silvio added. "It gives them a Hollywood connection."

"What about the valentines?" Nolan asked.

"Have Brody give that exclusively to Hunnicutt," Jack said.

Nolan nodded and rose. "What about protection for Nichols and Chang?"

"They're not stars," Jack said. "Besides, you'd have to protect the whole technical crew that worked on Candy's last picture. The one we ought to watch is Karen Dara."

"Whatever you think." Nolan sighed. "But I'm gonna light a candle. I'm gonna make a novena that these porno murders are the first shots in a Mafia-Colombian war. Besides the obvious benefits of having those bastards at each other's throats, we'll be out of the mystery business." Nolan paused. "Okay . . . keep after it and watch yourselves."

Jack sat behind his desk and poured a shot of Bushmills into a paper cup. He looked at the worn, cracked furniture and shook his head. Nolan had not made good on his promise to replace the shoddy furniture.

He swallowed the strong whiskey and felt it warm his stomach. He rose and threw his window open. A sultry night breeze wafted into the lime-colored office.

He stared off at the endless streaming lights at the freeway interchange. They seemed to glow in soft focus.

His eyes were definitely going. He would have to get distance lenses. The desk phone rang sharply. He picked up the receiver. "Raines speaking."

"You wanted to see me?" Karen Dara asked.

"That's right."

"When?"

"Now. Is there a safe restaurant in that Venice swamp?"

"As a matter of fact, yes. It's new. Expensive. And good. But you may know people there."

"So what?"

"You want the town to know you're dining with Karen Dara?"

"Can't you stop hating yourself for one goddamn minute?"

"How soon will you get here?"

"I'm on the way." He paused. "And make a reservation."

"I already have."

The line went dead. He hung up, lifted his jacket off the sofa, and opened the door. The ringing phones and clacking typewriters had subsided in the operations room. He was about to leave when the phone rang.

He leaned across his desk and lifted the receiver. "Lieutenant Raines?"

"Speaking."

"This is Lisa Chang. I tried to get Detective Martinez, but he—"

Jack interrupted. "What is it, Miss Chang?"

"Well, it's about the killings. John Traynor and Stella. I thought you ought to know something." Her voice broke slightly, and Jack knew she was trying to maintain her composure.

"Take your time, Miss Chang," he said warmly.

"It's about Karen Dara. We—that is, me and Karen, and Guru Meli-Ramdas conducted a séance."

"Karen told me."

"Oh." Her response was one of surprise. She cleared her throat and asked, "Did Karen tell you what Candy's spirit instructed her to do?"

"No."

"Well, I probably shouldn't say this. After all, it's my religion, too. But I can't help it. Not after what's happened."

"I assure you whatever you tell me will be kept in confidence," he said, lying.

"Well, Candy's voice pleaded with Karen to seek vengeance."

"Vengeance on whom?"

"Everyone."

"Did Karen respond to that?"

"Not that I remember. It's probably nothing. It was a spiritual connection, but I thought you should know."

"You're insinuating that Karen Dara murdered Traynor and Stella."

"No, no," she replied nervously. "I simply—I—well, I'm frightened. I needed to unburden myself."

"Okay, you told me."

"I'm scared to death, Lieutenant."

"I understand your fear. But it's our belief that you're not in danger. You're not a threat to anyone."

"Neither was Stella."

"Stella was an accident."

"Then you don't think I'm in jeopardy?"

"No. But if you feel threatened, we can place you in protective custody."

"I don't want to be shut away in some cell."

"I can't say that I blame you. My advice is to remain calm and stay in close touch with my office; if I'm out, you can ask for Silvio Martinez or Sergeant Phil Brody."

"Thank you, Lieutenant. I hope you don't mind my calling you."

"Not at all. Good-bye, Miss Chang."

Chapter 30

They discussed the twin killings during the drive from Karen's house to the restaurant. Jack tried to conceal the more horrific aspects of the homicides, but she pressed him for details with a curious intensity, an almost voyeuristic need to be shocked. He finally told her everything. She slipped into a melancholy silence and stared out the window at the passing rows of decaying one-story dwellings. She seemed to snap out of her morose mood as they turned onto Market Street and saw the gaily lit exterior of the restaurant, simply called 72 Market Street.

Two red-jacketed Iranian parking attendants took charge of the GTO. It was past the dinner hour, and a group of well-dressed people stood clustered at the entrance, waiting for their cars. The men ogled Karen as she and Jack crossed the narrow street.

She wore a black silk dress that made a case for simplicity. A string of pearls was draped around her neck, and three slim, Italian gold bangles circled her wrists. Her hair was parted in the center; its thick ash blond waves framed her face, and the scent of expensive perfume clung to her as if she moved in her own sweet atmosphere.

The restaurant was a large, cube-shaped room. Two oversize abstract paintings hung on the cream-colored walls. A spray of Peruvian lilies decorated the piano which was spotlighted at the rear of the room. The decor was a cool mixture of Art Deco and simple contemporary furniture.

They were seated at a rear table close to the piano. The pianist played a medley of Cole Porter tunes with a frozen smile on her face as if she were somewhat dubious about her presence in the room.

A pretty waitress with brutally cold eyes took their

181

order of white wine and fresh oysters to be followed by grilled chicken. Jack lit a cigarillo and had started to say something when the maître d' came over, carrying a bottle of Dom Pérignon. He was followed by a Mexican busboy holding a silver ice bucket.

"Compliments of Mr. Bennett," the maître d' said.

Jack glanced around the room and spotted the gleaming bald head. The TV star waved, and Jack waved back.

"I didn't realize you hobnobbed with the rich and famous," Karen said.

"I did him a small favor some years ago."

The maître d' popped the cork and poured a small amount of the champagne into Jack's glass. He sipped it and nodded. "It's fine." The man proceeded to fill their glasses and placed the bottle in the ice bucket.

"You'd better tell our waitress to cancel the white wine."

"Yes, sir."

They raised their glasses. "Cheers."

"Cheers."

Karen sipped the champagne and said, "What sort of favor did you do for Mr. Bennett?"

"It was a classic case of entrapment. Young boys. A pimp applying pressure. They had pictures. That kind of thing."

"Did you pervert the judicial system?"

"In a sense. The boys were underage. But I despise blackmail. It's one of those crimes I can't handle."

"Did he cool his activities? I mean with the boys."

"I hope so. But I doubt it."

The pianist played "Don't Cry for Me, Argentina."

"Sad song," she said.

"Yeah . . ."

"You look like hell, Jack."

"Haven't been sleeping."

"Neither have I."

"Why did you go up to Shiva?"

"You mean today?"

He nodded.

"When I heard about John and Stella, I just took off.

The compound is circled with barbed wire, and the guru employs heavy security. It seemed a safe place to be."

The waitress served the oysters and asked, "Where did this champagne come from?"

"It was a gift," Jack explained.

"I already ordered the wine," she replied icily.

"Well, these things happen." Jack smiled. "It's the way of the world."

"Enjoy your dinner."

The oysters were fresh, cold, and delicious, tasting faintly metallic with a hint of the sea. They savored the oysters, washing them down with champagne.

Jack noticed a bearded man eyeing Karen and wondered if it was her fine, patrician features that attracted the man's attention, or had he recognized her from a film?

"I didn't mean to come down on the Shiva thing," Jack said. "No one has any right to criticize another person's religion."

"Forget it."

"No. I want to explain. Those Eastern orders are for the most part scams, and I reacted that way. But maybe I'm just down on religion in general. The last time I went to confession the police chaplain said my only salvation was to become a Protestant."

She laughed, and her green eyes glittered.

"I think my uncle talked me out of practicing formal religion when I was just a kid."

"You mean the uncle that went off to fight in Spain?"

"Yeah, the one that got killed at the Ebro."

The pianist played "What's New?"

"Well, people had defined causes in those days," she said. "Black and white." She swallowed the last oyster. "These days everything's gray. Religion. Politics. Good. Evil. All difficult to define and impossible to understand." She removed a cigarette from her blue pack of Gauloises. A Mexican busboy lit it for her. She inhaled and spoke through the smoke. "It's all stainless steel."

The champagne had gone to his head, and he felt light and high. "We've *become* stainless steel," he said, "but we weren't born that way. I came out of the police academy prepared to save the world. My first radio call was a four-fifteen, a domestic quarrel. Man beating his wife. It was an apartment on Romaine Street. I never forgot what I saw in that apartment."

"Why do you do it?" she asked softly.

He shrugged. "People are dying out there for no reason. You try to hold on to the belief that you can save someone. There's nothing noble about it. Its something you've chosen to do. You don't even understand where the desire comes from. After a while you stop questioning your motives. You pay the dentist. You support a family and try to remain sane."

"You seem to have handled it."

"To a degree, but there are things you can never handle."

The waitress served the grilled chicken and refilled their glasses.

The pianist swung into a lively rendition of "Avalon."

They ate in silence for a while. The TV star waved to Jack as he left with a dowdy, overly made-up woman.

Karen said, "I guess you believe me now about that incident on the highway."

"I believed you the other night."

She touched the napkin to her lips. "Why don't you connect the highway thing with these killings?"

"If we assume Candy was murdered. The MO, modus operandi, was an automatic weapon fired at close range, the same MO used with Traynor and Stella, including the valentine and the added touch of explosive bullets. Very professional. The use of a car as a murder weapon doesn't connect."

The waitress collected their plates. "Will there be anything else?"

"I would like a Courvoisier." Karen smiled.

"Make it two," Jack said.

Karen lit a fresh cigarette and said, "You realize that I'm the last bankable, bookable star of erotica."

"I'm thinking of placing a twenty-four-hour watch on you."

"No, thanks. I don't want people dogging my life. I'll go up to Shiva and live there until these killings are solved—until this is over."

"You can't hide, Karen. If professionals are involved, they'll track you to Zanzibar. If it's a nut, a vigilante, we'll have to nail him before he gets you, but those monsters are difficult to track down. You ought to consider police protection."

The waitress served the brandy snifters along with a facedown check.

"I'll take my chances," Karen said, and sipped the brandy. "I'm not exactly defenseless. I've got that thirty-eight right here in my handbag, and I'm not afraid to use it."

"That gun won't protect you. Remember, if Candy was murdered, whoever killed her and the others was someone they knew and trusted."

"But none of the people I work with had a motive."

"Lisa Chang thinks you have a motive—a very strong motive. She said Candy's voice ordered you to avenge her death."

"The fine Oriental mind," Karen said disdainfully. "That was a spiritual contact. Nothing more. It was a metaphysical symbol of a departed soul's unrest. I don't take the spiritual channeling of dead voices literally."

He tossed off the brandy and said, "Don't get upset, but I've got to ask you this. Where were you between two P.M. and six P.M. yesterday?"

"Home. I phoned your office around four."

"You could have made that call from a public booth."

"Right. I called your office to establish a half-assed alibi," she said sarcastically, "then went up to Traynor's and blew them away in cold blood. Okay? Case is solved."

He placed his American Express card on the check, and the waitress picked it up. "Look, Karen, I don't enjoy this, but I'm part of it. And so are you. You're a possible victim and a possible suspect. So is Lisa Chang. So is Sherry Nichols. So is anyone in the film crew who worked on Candy's last picture. Or maybe Silvio's right. Maybe these killings are the opening shots fired in a war between the Mafia and the Colombians. On the other hand, that valentine makes a case for the presence of a weirdo. I don't know. But I have to ask these questions."

The waitress returned with the charge slip and credit card. He added a generous tip and tore his blue copy off.

Karen put her hand on his. "I was at home. I tried you at the office; then I phoned your apartment. I despised Traynor but not enough to kill him. And I certainly had nothing against Stella."

Jack drove slowly through the bleak, dimly lit, deserted streets. The scent of her perfume permeated the car, and her gold bracelets clicked as she fluffed her hair. "What will you do now?" he asked. "I mean, about work?"

"I'm going to try to stay healthy."

"What about money?"

"It's not a problem. The checks keep coming in. My share of cassette revenue. Millions of my fellow Americans light up their dormant sexuality watching me perform."

"Sounds like something I ought to try."

"You've seen my latest and best work, and I was obviously not a smash. You practically threw me out of your apartment." She paused. "Turn left at the corner; there's an emergency access road for official vehicles. You can park on the walkway in front of the house."

He turned onto the broad paved walkway and slowed down as they approached her house. The tall streetlamps glowed soft orange in the ocean mist, and the sea shimmered in the moonlight. The deserted broad beach was dotted with large refuse cans that ran in a jagged line toward the Venice pier. The surf was up, but the roar of breakers seemed to enhance the serenity of the beachside street.

He parked in front of her house and cut the ignition. "I'll wait until you're inside."

She stared at him intently as if trying to perceive the inner man that he kept under tight wraps.

"I don't suppose you'd want to come in?" she asked.

"That would be dangerous. I think I'm in love with the girl in that Spanish poster. I'll walk you to the door."

He came around to her side and opened the door. She got out, turned to him, and smiled. "Could I possibly interest you in a walk on the beach? There's something about the sea and that empty beach at night that's good for the soul."

"I'd like to, but I've got to get back."

"To what? Sinatra and a view of the Hollywood Hills?" She smiled like a child with a special secret. "Well, I'm going whether you come along or not." She kicked her shoes up onto the steps. "Come on," she said. "Take your shoes and socks off. If I get killed out there alone on that beach, you'll never forgive yourself."

They crossed the street in their bare feet. He helped her over the low wall onto the cool, damp sand. They walked beneath a cluster of palms and came out onto the wide moonlit beach.

They strolled along the edge of the foaming surf. She tried to engage him in conversation, but he replied perfunctorily, obviously preoccupied.

"What's bothering you?" she finally asked.

"I was thinking how out of line I was the other night. I wish I could play that one over."

"I told you to forget it. Besides, you were right. I am an emotional cripple. I've always lacked what the French call *amour-propre*."

"You're taking advantage of an illiterate cop. What the hell is *amour-propre*?"

"*Amour-propre*"—she smiled—"has nothing to do with love. It means self-esteem, of which I have very little. Even as a child. Especially as a child. No one's fault. My father and mother were fine middle-class folks. We lived in one of those fly-over towns in Ohio."

" 'Fly-over'?"

"Those invisible villages that seven forty-sevens fly over on their way back and forth from Los Angeles to New York. I was a skinny, cross-eyed, picked-on kid. I was constantly being made fun of, the butt of all butts. Bowing and scraping, trying to ingratiate myself with my peers. After some eye surgery and psychiatry I managed to summon the courage to go to college. I told you the truth about that professor."

"Dr. Mengele?"

"As he was affectionately known." She nodded. "I was

a virgin at the time. My knowledge of sex had up to then been confined to masturbating boys in the back seats of old Chevrolets. That was as far as I would go. To gain favor; to get a date; to see a movie; to . . . well, you get the picture."

She was silent for a moment. Her forehead was furrowed by lines of concentration. The breeze smelled of salt and fish, and a family of sandpipers trotted along the surf, seeking sand crabs.

"That professor really destroyed me," she continued. "He used me, which in itself isn't terrible. I mean, it does take two. But he used me badly. Degradingly. I was like one of those lost, foolish heroines in a modern romance novel. I cried, threatened suicide, and worse. I knew he was screwing my best friend, but I took it. All of it. It was two years of relentless agony. But I managed to turn it around. In the end I made that bastard plead. On his hands and knees. I was like Dietrich in *The Blue Angel*. I made him grovel. I finally recognized my own sexuality. You see, in those two years, my body had developed. My eyes had gone very green, and my hair had turned from mousy brown to ash blond. Something wonderful had happened."

"That would have happened with or without the professor."

"Maybe, but there's a great sense of achievement when you can raise your self-esteem from nowhere to somewhere. Still," she said sadly, "that senior year was the last time I felt good about myself. After college I went to New York and shared an apartment with a fashion model in the East Village. It was the time of flower children, LSD, coffins coming home from Vietnam. Nixon. Lenny Bruce. The Beatles. I tried all the drugs. And I joined all the causes. I was a revolutionary in the midst of a revolution led by self-serving phonies. I modeled for a while and hung around with some fast folks, but the old self-loathing set in. I went from one bed to the next. I couldn't seem to connect emotionally with myself or anyone else. I was about as low as you can get, and the terrifying thing was I couldn't get a fix on what it was that was destroying me."

"Did you try to get help?"

"I spent a small fortune on psychiatrists. Nothing. I finally left New York and went to San Francisco. Larry Getchell asked me how I felt about performing in an erotic film." She paused. "I always had a curious fascination about pornography. It's the ultimate form of exhibitionism and one hell of a power trip. In the beginning it was surreal. I could dissociate myself from the screen image, but after a while it's hell. You reduce yourself to raw meat. I tell myself that one way or another everyone sells themselves, but the truth is sooner or later you despise yourself and everyone around you. That's why so many of us lean on drugs."

"Why don't you stop?"

"I intend to, but it's not that simple."

They moved quickly back as a huge wave broke high up on the beach.

"Tell me about Candy," Jack gently said.

Karen shrugged. "She counted on me, and I failed her."

He stared out at the moonlit sea. "You know, there are those people who want to lose. For whatever reason they require failure. And there's not a damn thing you can do about it." He paused. "An old burned-out cop once told me, 'Don't let the street get you, kid. Those bastards out there have their own demons, and you'll kill yourself trying to cure them.'"

"You're saying we just let it all happen."

"I'm saying we do the best we can."

She stopped, picked up a piece of driftwood, ran her fingers over its smoothness, and suddenly tossed it out to sea. She looked at him and smiled. "Maybe I should have backpacked to France. Taken a room in a pension in Cannes. Written poetry. And lived on Camembert and croissants. I actually did the south of France in '78. High style. With a married man, a famous literary agent. He never read my stuff but said I had the soul of a poet."

"Maybe he was right."

"He was full of empty compliments. He enjoyed having sex with me, which is okay. But why didn't he say that? 'Karen, your poetry is awful, but you're a great fuck. You're worth the first-class plane ticket and some clothes and jewelry.' Why don't men say that?"

"I guess it's considered bad form."

"I probably should have never left fly-over Ohio. Raised kids and collected antiques. My damaged, misguided ego did me in."

She knelt, picked up a seashell, and dipped it in the foam to wash the sand from its perfect fan shape. She rose and turned the shell over in her hand, scrutinizing it as if it were an extraordinary artifact. "All my life"—she sighed— "I've been searching for that magic person, that someone you can tell it all to, and he doesn't say anything, but you know . . . you just know it's going to be all right." She tossed the seashell into the surf and turned to him. "Seeing me on the screen really turned you off. Didn't it?"

"It wasn't the film. Christ, you must think I'm a monk. If anything, the pictures stirred my failing libido. I didn't trust you."

"And now?"

"I'm not sure."

She stared off at the surging black sea.

"Jack," she whispered.

"Yes?"

"In six hours the sun will come up and we never happened." She moved very close to him and stared into his eyes. "You don't have to do a damn thing. Just spend what's left of this night with me."

The moonlight etched the line of her high cheekbones and lit her eyes with a catlike luminosity and turned the color of her hair very pale. And he thought of all the lights, and lips, and eyes, and shoulders, and hands, and haunting songs, and clinging perfume, and all the nights, and all the places, and all the women with whom he had shared magical moments. And he knew a man must never permit those memories to fade. If you once let them go, the lights went out, and your soul dried up and died.

His arms went around her, and she curled into him. He felt her breasts pressing against his chest. The wind sprayed cold, salty drops against their cheeks. They kissed lightly at first, then quickly, over and over. Their mouths locked together, their lips hot and feverish. They gasped for breath, surrendering to the passionate current raging between them.

They clung together in the moonlight on the deserted beach, accidental players caught in the fallout of a savage vendetta they neither understood nor controlled.

Chapter 31

At 3:00 A.M. eastern daylight time the Mafia soldiers struck. The first hit occurred in East Harlem, and like a live match in a dry forest, the flames of violence flashed across the country.

Manuel ("Big Manny") Pachecko, the kingpin East Side coke dealer, was machine-gunned by two men while eating a plateful of hot rice in La Cubana restaurant on 114th Street and Madison Avenue.

Ira Spear, a respected CPA and part-time dealer, was cut in half by a burst of automatic-weapons fire while boarding a train at Penn Station.

Lorenzo Cordera, a Colombian national and major laundryman, was found slumped over a seat in a Times Square porno theater, an ice pick handle protruding from his right eye.

Ramon Contreras and his brother-in-law Julio Cardenas were found alongside the Long Island Expressway, their faces blown away by .45 slugs. Both men had been free on bail awaiting trial in federal court for drug smuggling.

Guillermo Ruiz was found shot to death in his car, on the Merritt Parkway turnoff to Greenwich, Connecticut. State troopers discovered $3 million in $100 bills in the Jaguar's trunk.

Three Colombian nationals were shot to death outside their cocaine refinery, which was blown up in Baltimore Hollow, Long Island.

Luis Herrera and his chemist, Arthur Mendoza, were firebombed while working in a clandestine refinery in Fly Creek, New York.

In Miami two men on a speeding motorcycle fired an RPG rocket into a black Rolls-Royce. The fireball incinerated a kingpin *coquero*, Gabriel Cinfuentes, along with his bodyguard and Cuban mistress.

Acting on a tip, U.S. customs agents seized a Colombian Avianca 747 commercial jet at Miami International Airport. The agents uncovered 1,000 kilos of pure cocaine hidden in boxes of cut flowers.

In Cicero, Illinois, the charred bodies of four Colombian nationals were found in the smoldering ruins of a cocaine refinery located in the basement of a fashionable clothing store.

In Chicago, Roberto Cadiz, Fernando Pinzon, and Luis Arquelo were cut down in a hail of gunfire as the Colombian dealers came out of a Rush Street nightclub.

In Los Angeles Ramon Cabrillo and Julito Carnera were found floating facedown in a fountain on Olvera Street.

A West Side dealer named Chucho Gomez was stabbed to death while sitting on the fantail of his eighty-three-foot motor sailer at the marina. His genitals were stuffed into his mouth. Police discovered five kilos of cut snow and $300,000 in the main cabin's wall safe.

Roland Cannell, director of a Colombian-owned bank in Orange County, was shot to death in a suite at a Newport Beach motel. Cannell never did keep his appointment with a high-priced call girl who had fortunately been delayed by her previous client's inability to maintain an erection. She did, however, arrive at the seaside motel in time to identify the jellylike remains of Mr. Cannell.

Leonardo Sánchez y Sánchez, a Colombian national and member of the World Bank, was thrown from a window of his fourteenth-floor suite at the Sheraton West Hotel. His body hurtled down toward Wilshire Boulevard, trailing a stream of $100 bills. Senor Sánchez's head exploded against the roof of a Yellow Cab. The initial shock of passing pedestrians was instantly replaced by a joyous rush to catch the floating $100 bills. An editorial in the *Los Angeles Times* commented on the extraordinary sight of a police detail unable to reach the remnants of an unfortunate suicide because of the avarice of money-hungry Los Angelenos.

At midnight on August 8 the Colombians struck back

with a ferocity that spared no one: not the intended target, or the target's family, or innocent bystanders. Their victims constituted a who's who of the American underworld: the East Coast president of the transport workers union and six of his organizers; the executive director of a huge Atlantic City casino; the comptroller of a Las Vegas hotel, his wife, bodyguard, and four tourists who had had the bad luck to exit the hotel's side entrance with the comptroller.

Bookmakers and numbers runners were blown up, machine-gunned, firebombed.

Heroin dealers in Harlem, San Francisco, Philadelphia, and New Orleans were hit.

Porno theater operators were taken out. Film laboratories processing X-rated movies were firebombed.

The long arm of Ordóñez's killer squads managed to reach one national council member, Tony ("the Shark") Armatti. His wife and son, daughter-in-law, grandchild, and two bodyguards were also machine-gunned to death while dining in a South Brooklyn restaurant. Two patrons seated nearby were critically wounded.

The war raged on for ten days and nights, and from a media point of view, the conflict had erupted at a fortunate time. There had been no terrorist hijackings, no further reports of presidential cancer or celebrities stricken with AIDS; no assassinations of any importance; no perceptible economic calamities. The baseball strike had lasted only twenty-four hours. There was a dreadful lack of volatile news. The media had been forced to publicize the tragedy of South Africa's racial unrest—an issue that seemed irrelevant to most Americans.

In the face of relative geopolitical tranquillity the media pounced on the gangland violence. Network television presented graphic coverage of the carnage. The internecine warfare made front-page headlines. *Time* and *Newsweek* ran feature stories describing the warfare as a dispute between the Mafia and Colombians over territorial rights to the $100 billion cocaine industry.

On August 21 Angelo Maffatore, Sidney Davis, Vincent Mangano, and four national council members met secretly at a mòtel in Hot Springs, Arkansas.

At the outset of the conflict Sidney prudently sent his wife and two sons abroad for a summer holiday. He had appealed to Don Angelo to permit him to accompany his family, but the old man had refused, explaining that for the moment Sidney's services were indispensable.

The Mafia overlords commiserated over the death of council member Tony Armatti and agonized over the general havoc committed upon the organization. They appealed to Don Angelo to effect a truce with Ordóñez, a truce with honor.

At the same time Rafael Ordóñez was advised by Cisneros that their associates in Ecuador, Bolivia, Peru, and Brazil were demanding a meeting to discuss the financial debacle that had fallen upon the industry. The cultivators of the coca leaf were feeling the pinch as the American market dried up following the killing of dealers and loss of refineries.

Chapter 32

Nolan popped the cork on a bottle of California champagne and filled their glasses. The chief of Tactical was in an expansive mood. His ears still rang with the praise and congratulations of his colleagues. The war between the Mafia and Colombians had delighted all agencies of national and local drug enforcement.

The press had accepted Nolan's theory that Candy Lane, John Traynor, and Stella Pierson had been the initial victims of the war. Tactical's NIFTY squad had been credited with exposing the link between the Mafia's pornographic industry and Colombian money-laundering activities.

"To the war," Nolan toasted, "may it never end."

"Amen!" Silvio exclaimed.

Jack did not join in the toast.

"What's wrong with you?" Nolan asked.

"I hate to be a spoiler, but the war seems to have diminished."

"It's just the pause that refreshes." Nolan smiled. "They're licking their wounds, regrouping. This thing is far from over. My novena has been answered. This outbreak is a divine blessing."

"The Holy Spirit did not participate in this war," Jack replied. "This war was triggered by a third party."

"What does it matter?" Nolan asked. "Major coke dealers are dead. Refineries are in ruins. The price of street coke has shot up to three bills a gram. The Mafia has been kicked in the belly. The Colombians took out key mob men in almost every Mafia-controlled racket. The day this war started should be declared a national holiday."

"I agree," Jack said. "But the fact is we still have

three unsolved homicides on our hands—and maybe more to come."

"Are we back to that?" Nolan sighed.

"It looks that way, doesn't it?" Jack answered sarcastically.

"Well, from where I sit this case is over," Nolan replied emphatically.

"Come on, John, you're not talking to the press now. Colombian hit men don't draw valentines after they blow people away." Jack paused. "We're up against a deranged vigilante, and it's not going to end with Traynor, Pierson, and Candy!"

"And I'm telling you," Nolan responded angrily, "that I couldn't care less about those porno degenerates! They're the toilet bowl of society. As a matter of fact, if you're right, if there is a crazy out there, some vigilante that kicked this war off, he or she has my eternal gratitude."

"You're wrong, John," Silvio calmly interjected. "No one hates those Colombian *coqueros* more than I do. But Jack has a point. We can't turn our backs on a vigilante. Today he takes out porno actors. Tomorrow he goes after proabortionists or people with Spanish names. You ignore something like this, and you're not a cop anymore. You're letting politics get in the way of justice."

"Okay . . . okay . . ." Nolan nodded. "Let's examine the facts. The coroner fixed the time of the Traynor-Pierson killings at between three and four P.M. the afternoon of the fourth. Did you check out Lisa Chang, Sherry Nichols, and Karen Dara?"

"I questioned Nichols and Chang," Silvio replied. "They were together having a late lunch at Dolce Vita. Jack questioned Karen Dara."

"She had no alibi," Jack said. "She phoned my office around four that afternoon. But she could have made the call from the murder site. She claims she was home but has no corroboration."

"Well"—Nolan leaned back and sipped his champagne—"you want to book her on suspicion of murder one?"

"The DA would throw me out of his office."

"That's exactly my point," Nolan said. "We've performed our duty. We questioned the logical suspects, and we've come up empty. The third party theory is conjecture. The porno people were hit by Colombian killers. That's it."

"What about Whelan?" Jack asked.

Nolan's eyes widened in disbelief. "Are you suggesting that Leo Whelan murdered his own stars—that the man would put himself out of business?"

"I think Whelan and Sid Davis can tell us something about the true origins of this war."

"You have all that from Silvio's informant." Nolan sighed. "We know why it started. Can't you, for chrissake, enjoy a first-class victory over these bastards? Can't you take yes for an answer?"

Jack sat on the arm of a leather chair. "So three people who harmed no one, mugged no one, hurt no one are shot to death, and we're drinking champagne."

"Those people are irrelevant!"

"Tell that to Candy's father! Tell that to Stella Pierson's family! And tell that to Karen Dara!"

"You know what I think?" Nolan's face flushed. "I think you have a personal interest in this Dara woman. I can't say that I blame you, but don't make a chump out of yourself."

"As a matter of fact, I am worried about her. She's the last surviving star."

"For all we know she might be your vigilante," Nolan replied. "You told me that she communicated with Candy's spirit, and that spirit or voice, or whatever the fuck it is, demanded that Karen seek vengeance."

"That's true," Jack conceded. "Karen Dara is both a suspect and a possible victim. That's why she's got to be kept under surveillance."

"We've maintained a twenty-four-hour watch on her for two weeks at no small cost to the taxpayers. Would you like me to call out the National Guard?"

Jack's seething anger suddenly exploded. "Fuck you, John! If you want my resignation, it's yours!"

"Hold it! Hold it!" Silvio exclaimed. "You fellows have been together for a lot of years. Don't get into something you'll both regret. We've all been under pressure. Now, take it easy—both of you."

Nolan rubbed his hand wearily across his eyes, sighed, and stared at Jack. "I'll make believe you didn't say that. Now, tell me exactly what you want me to do because I don't know anymore. We've left nothing to chance in this case."

"I want your approval for me to rattle a few bones. I want to question that guru. I want to talk to Sid Davis and Leo Whelan."

"We've been together for fifteen years," Nolan said. "We cut some sharp corners, and I've always backed you one hundred percent. When your former wife was hit, I sent you halfway around the world to nail her killer. I stretched the legal limits of this office to help you. I did that because I consider you family. And speaking of family, you have a daughter to consider. There's a murderous war raging around these porno killings. Sid Davis, Leo Whelan, and that guru may be targets, and I won't permit you to get in the cross hairs chasing down some mythical vigilante. On the other hand, and this is a promise, if anyone else connected to Candy Lane's last film is hit, the gloves are off. You can sleep on that. But for the moment you keep your nose out of it. That's an order."

Chapter 33

A wind-whipped black-green sea crested to a height of 100 feet and roared between the illuminated office buildings lining the western edge of Sunset Boulevard. The dust, filth, and debris of the boulevard had risen to the surface of the dark water.

Karen Dara, naked and numbed by terror, was swept along by the raging current. Candy Lane's nude, bloated body was pinned against her. The dead girl's voice wailed above the screaming wind, "Avenge me, Karen. Avenge meeeee."

The swift tide hurtled them along. Huge plastic breasts, vaginas, and penises swept past them. A raft with a camera crew directed by Jeff Kellerman photographed the two women. John Traynor's and Stella Pierson's ghastly heads emerged from the sea and peered menacingly at Karen before disappearing under the surface. Candy Lane's body slipped away. Karen was alone.

The sound of the wind rose to an earsplitting howl.

And then she saw it.

A cobra appeared from beneath the black water. Its head fanned out, and it rose to a towering height before transforming itself into a mountainous tidal wave. The suction at the base of the wave pulled Karen toward the cresting wall of water. A roaring sound clogged her eardrums. The colossal wave began its downward plunge.

Karen screamed and bolted upright in bed.

Jack grabbed her shoulders as she continued to scream. His arms went around her, embracing her, pulling her to him. Her screams finally subsided. "My God . . . my God . . ." she gasped.

He held her until she stopped trembling.

Her breathing slowed, and she said, "I'm sorry, I'm sorry."

"Just a nightmare." He smiled. "This bedroom is no stranger to nightmares."

Cold beads of perspiration ran down her cheeks and snaked over her breasts, wetting her stomach. She extracted a cigarette from a pack of Gauloises. Her hands trembled as she lit the stubby cigarette and inhaled the strong Algerian tobacco.

"You want to talk about it?" he asked.

She nodded and proceeded to describe the nightmare. She concluded and leaned back against the headboard.

"How about a nickel-and-dime Freudian explanation?" he asked.

"Go ahead."

"Have you participated in any recent séances?"

"Yes, a few nights ago. I tried with the help of Meli-Ramdas and one of his disciples to reach Candy."

"And did you?"

"Yes. It was the same as before. Her voice pleaded for vengeance."

"You may get pissed off at me," he said, "but I've got to prove to you that this supernatural contact is nothing more than a drug-induced scam."

"I know about the tricks. It doesn't diminish the fact that I can reach Candy's spirit. I feel her presence, and that's all that matters." She swallowed some brandy and crushed the cigarette out. "She trusted me, and I let her die."

"That's self-pitying nonsense. I told you that night on the beach. Candy destroyed herself. You're not responsible."

"I was the only one she trusted."

"I've got a badge that says people can depend on me, but I fail them more often than not."

"It's not the same."

"It is the same. You remember my mentioning the first official call I answered?"

She nodded. "A domestic quarrel. You said you never forgot what you saw in that apartment."

"Right. A woman was bent over her husband, sobbing. She held a butcher knife in one hand and a Kotex pad in the other, pressing it against her husband's severed throat. She had cut him from ear to ear."

Karen shook her head and whispered, "Jesus . . ."

"That was my introduction to the street. There are people out there screaming for help, and you show up like some goddamn knight dressed in blue, and people grab you and cry, 'Thank God, you're here,' but there's nothing you can do. Ninety percent of the time it's too late. You spend more time with victims than criminals. You do the best you can and try to shake it off and lead a normal life. The only thing that keeps you going is the fact that you're not responsible. You're at best a minor-chord player in a violent, endless opera that you can't control or begin to understand."

"Why do you do it?"

"Ego. Sheer, unadulterated ego. I suppose in a curious way every cop is an exhibitionist. The uniform. The badge. The gun. You're made to feel special, that somehow you can make a difference. But you pay one hell of a price for that ego ride, and the nightmares are part of it."

They were silent for a moment, staring at the dead eye of the TV set.

"Whelan phoned me this afternoon," she said. "They're thinking about starting a new film."

"When?"

"I guess whenever Leo gets an okay from Davis or Maffatore to begin production."

"That means they expect this war to be over."

"Leo told me that they're setting up a meeting with Ordóñez."

"I figured as much."

He finished his brandy and leaned against the pillows. "Are you going to perform again?"

"I don't know."

"Do you want to?"

She stared at him, and her eyes caught a spill of exterior light. "It's what I do." She paused. "Isn't it?"

Chapter 34

After careful deliberation both sides agreed to meet at the Camino Real Hotel in Cancún, Mexico. The Caribbean resort was safe, neutral, and convenient. Maffatore had leased a private jet for the four-hour flight from Los Angeles to Cancún. Ordóñez had cruised the 1,000 nautical miles from Barranquilla to Cancún aboard his Norwegian-built yacht.

The men were seated at a large table in the poolside restaurant shaded by a white awning. A balmy breeze carried the disparate aromas of grilled shrimp and suntan oil. Musicians wearing gaudy costumes topped by huge sombreros played "Cuando Caliente del Sol."

Maffatore had never before met Ordóñez and was impressed by the Colombian's aristocratic demeanor and impeccable manners. The old mafioso was equally surprised by the change in Pedro Cisneros's appearance. He thought Cisneros had aged dramatically since he had last seen him in the summer of 1981.

The men had eaten a hearty lunch but drunk sparingly of the cold Hidalgo wine. The two chieftains had not addressed the subject of their meeting during lunch, preferring to discuss the weather, the bomb, and the general decline of Western civilization.

The chess game did not begin until dessert and espresso had been served. Ordóñez removed a folded tissue paper from his pocket, placed it on the table, and unwrapped a brilliant emerald. "A token of my respect, Don Angelo." He smiled. "Colombian, flawless, and very rare."

"Ah . . ." Don Angelo sighed. "You embarrass me. I've come empty-handed."

"Take it, please. You have a daughter-in-law, do you not?"

"Yes. She's the widow of my eldest son."

"Present that stone to her. Every woman dreams of possessing a perfect emerald."

"You're very kind," Maffatore replied, and tucked the gift into his pocket.

Ordóñez lit a cigarette and said, "There is an Indian legend concerning a deadly Amazonian beetle called the machaca. It is said that the bite of the machaca is fatal unless the victim makes love immediately afterward."

Maffatore shrugged his narrow shoulders and said, "An interesting legend, but the question is, why did the beetle strike? Why does it choose a particular victim?"

"Ah, Don Angelo, there you have the riddle."

"Yes, the riddle is clear. The answer is not."

"To me, the answer is very clear," Ordóñez replied. "We both have been bitten by the machaca."

Maffatore studied Ordóñez.

Davis eyed both men.

Cisneros looked off at a striking raven-haired girl poised on the diving board above the pool.

The Mexican musicians played "Amapola."

Maffatore leaned forward and brushed a fly from the remnants of his caramel custard. His black eyes then flicked up at Ordóñez. "We did not start this war."

"On the contrary, Don Angelo. Your soldiers struck without warning, without provocation."

"Provocation?" Maffatore rasped. "Your ultimatum had only just expired when your people murdered two more of our pornographic actors. You left me no choice."

"This is the riddle, Don Angelo, because we killed no one. Ohlendorf was standing by in Lausanne, waiting for your response to my proposal. Did you think I would not permit you twenty-four additional hours? I know you cannot act without consulting the national council. I was saddened and shocked when your soldiers hit our dealers in Harlem. At that point I, too, had no choice. If we had communicated directly, this war would not have occurred. You must believe me. We never murdered anyone in Los Angeles."

"Candy Lane was killed even before Sidney met with you in Santa Rosa," Maffatore said.

"Not on my orders."

"Didn't you tell us that films cannot be made without actors?"

"It's true. I did make that observation. It was a mistake, for which I apologize, but it remains to this moment an unfortunate remark. Nothing more."

"Are you telling me we've been fucked over by some third party?" Maffatore asked.

"Exactly. We were provoked into this war by an assassin. A madman. Or possibly agents of the DEA. This war"—Ordóñez sighed painfully—"has caused me grave problems with my growers in Bolivia, Ecuador, Peru, and Brazil. These men represent six million acres of coca leaf. They depend on me to keep our industry healthy and thriving. What could I say to them? Only the truth: that I did not start this conflict and that I would meet with you to resolve our problems. But I have suffered a loss of respect and confidence."

"We, too, have suffered," Maffatore replied. "None of our enterprises escaped your killer squads. Your people even hit one of our council members. Anthony Armatti, a friend of forty years, murdered with his entire family."

Davis felt beads of perspiration snaking down his rib cage. He hoped Maffatore would not press the Colombian drug king too far.

Cisneros chain-smoked and stared off at the bikini-clad women lounging at the poolside.

Maffatore lit a small cigar and asked, "Why is it your people kill innocent women and children?"

Ordóñez smiled. "If Aurelio, my chief of field operations, was here, he would say, 'We are Colombians.' And he would be right. We cannot apologize for the more violent aspects of our nature."

"You see," Maffatore said, glancing at Sidney. "I told you. Blood is everything." The old man then turned to Ordóñez. "It's difficult for me to trust you. I believe a man's blood determines his destiny, and with all due respect, by your own admission, you're cursed with this mestizo blood. You're more dangerous than we Sicilians. And I never trust a Sicilian."

"Perhaps that explains your longevity, Don Angelo. But I don't agree with you about blood. To me, geography determines destiny. If Colombia did not border the Pacific, Caribbean, and Amazon, if we were not six hundred miles from American coastal cities, we would not be in the drug business. If Colombia were situated in Alaska, we would be in the oil business."

"No"—Maffatore smiled—"you would be killing baby seals."

Ordóñez laughed.

Sidney squirmed.

And Cisneros signaled the waiter. *"Dáme una cognac, por favor."*

"En seguida," the waiter replied.

Ordóñez tried to mask his surprise at Cisneros's summoning of the waiter in the midst of a meeting. He knew his cousin was close to a breaking point. During the four-day cruise from Barranquilla Pedro had been reclusive, sitting alone on the afterdeck of the yacht, staring blankly at the sea. He had not even approached the Brazilian girls Ordóñez had invited aboard.

It fell to Maffatore to caution Cisneros. "Careful with these waiters, Pedro. Some of these hotel people work for the Mexican Secret Service."

"Fuck them. Fuck all these greasers. Look, we came a thousand miles to meet with you. Let's stop dancing. We were all tricked, manipulated into this war. Now, let's make peace and find out who did this damage to us."

"Calma, mi primo, calma," Ordóñez said quietly to Cisneros. "Don Angelo is not wrong. You cannot have waiters around us while we talk."

"Forgive me," Cisneros said. "It's very hot. And that goddamn music. And the fucking flies. I needed a drink."

The waiter served Cisneros's cognac and asked, *"¿Algo más?"*

"No, gracias." Ordóñez dismissed him.

The waiter left.

A statuesque redhead wearing a skimpy bikini sauntered past the table and smiled at Ordóñez.

Davis cleared his throat and said, "I agree with Pedro. We've been had. The thing to do now is declare a truce and take steps to protect ourselves."

"Bravo, Sidney!" Ordóñez exclaimed.

Maffatore stared off at the celery-colored sea and the creamy clouds towering above the horizon line. The old man knew the moment of truth was at hand. He mistrusted the handsome Colombian *coquero*. But he had no choice. A deal had to be struck.

"All right," Maffatore said quietly. "Let's say that by either chance or design we were tricked into this war. I'm not so sure. But"—he shrugged—"there is a kind of truth that is so brutally simple it defies belief." He turned to Sidney. "Make our proposal."

Sidney and the don had rehearsed this moment for three days while waiting for Ordóñez's yacht to arrive. Both of them knew their initial proposal would be rejected, and both knew their counterproposal would be accepted.

Sidney spoke slowly, deliberately. "We are prepared to launder an additional billion at the same ten percent rate. In return, we want to establish certain dealerships."

"Where?" Ordóñez asked.

"In Miami, L.A., and New York."

Ordóñez's fingertips drummed the tabletop. "What do you think, Cousin?"

"You can't have Italians and Colombians dealing side by side in American cities."

"I agree," Ordóñez said, and addressed Maffatore. "If you establish dealerships, sooner or later we'll be fighting the Miami war all over again. Besides, I can't be in a position of cultivating the leaf, refining it, smuggling it, and permitting another party to come between me and the consumer. It's bad business."

"Well"—Maffatore shrugged—"it's a standoff."

Sidney waited for a respectable moment and, as rehearsed, said, "Suppose we leave things as they were before the war. But as a gesture of goodwill we agree to launder an additional five hundred million."

There was a momentary pause, and Ordóñez glanced at Cisneros. "Well, Cousin?"

"If it ends the war, I would agree."

Ordóñez drummed his fingers and nodded. "All right, and to show you there is nothing but goodwill running through this hot blood of mine, I will raise your commission from ten to twelve percent. I have only one request. After one year we renew negotiations with the figure of one billion in mind."

"Done!" Maffatore said. "But we must take steps to insure against more killings, against being pushed into another war. Our porno business is exploding in America. The cassette sales are booming. I want to start producing new films."

"You have my blessings, Don Angelo. But the murders of the actors are an American problem. We can't help you there."

"I understand." The old man slowly got to his feet. "It's been a pleasure to meet you after all these years. You are a true mafioso, Don Rafael, a man who shows the way."

Ordóñez rose, as did the others.

"I'm a man like you," Ordóñez said, "a man chosen by destiny to lead my people to a position of power, to a place of honor and dignity that has been stolen from them."

"I have no such ambitions. I never cared for power, and I piss on destiny," Maffatore said. "I have my gardens, my pool, my dog, and a few memories. I'm alone, yes, but sometimes a man ends up this way—alone with simple pleasures."

"There is only one difference between us." Ordóñez smiled. "You have America by the balls; we have America by the nose."

The dying sun bled crimson veins into the indigo sky, and the color of the sea had changed from pale green to mauve.

El Encanto's bow knifed through the gentle swells tossing up a silver spray. The sleek yacht made eighteen knots as it headed on a southwesterly course.

Pedro Cisneros lounged in a deck chair at the fantail. His feet rested on the gunwale. His dark glasses were shoved up on his head. He sipped a rum drink from a hollowed pineapple and stared blankly at the circular bubbling pools cut into the sea by the ship's twin screws.

Ordóñez stood under the awning of the afterdeck salon, having a drink with Aurelio Estrella, the man who directed his killer squads.

"*Por la victoria,*" Aurelio toasted.

"*Salud,*" Ordóñez replied.

They sipped their drinks, and Aurelio said, "We've won a great victory."

"For now . . ." Ordóñez cautioned.

"We have nothing to fear from this old Sicilian."

"Never underestimate a man like Maffatore. To remain alive at the top of a treacherous organization for half a century requires both brains and courage."

Aurelio sipped his drink and, using his glass, indicated the fantail. "Look at how Pedro sits and broods. He speaks to no one. His eyes have madness in them." Aurelio paused. "He is dangerous, Don Rafael."

A warning bell rang in Ordóñez's consciousness, but his manner remained calm and interested. "If there's a problem, you must tell me, without fear and without hesitation."

"Pedro planned the war very well," Aurelio said. "He provided perfect documents for our soldiers. The weapons were in the safe houses. The targets were carefully selected. But on the third night of the war, in the suite at Key Biscayne, Pedro insulted me in front of my men. I said nothing out of respect for you. I understood that Pedro had lost his courage." Aurelio paused and added, "That's why he used *cocaina.*"

"You saw my cousin take the white powder?" Ordóñez asked with genuine surprise.

Aurelio nodded. "We have to deal with him, and quickly."

"When did you see Pedro use the *cocaina*?"

"In Key Biscayne, in front of the men."

"You were right to tell me this, Aurelio."

Ordóñez placed his drink on the bar, propped his right foot up on the arm of a chair, and slipped a gold inlaid .25 automatic out of a holster strapped to his leg.

He slid the chamber back, charging the weapon, and switched the safety off.

"I tell you these things with a sad heart," Aurelio said. "But our cause is greater than any one man."

"Yes. The cause is everything," Ordóñez agreed, and fired three bullets into Aurelio's face. The chief executioner's insulted eyes were wide in disbelief as he slumped to the deck.

Cisneros and three seamen came running into the salon and stopped cold when they saw Aurelio's pulpy remains staining the deck.

"Throw him over the side and clean this mess up," Ordóñez said, and walked to the fantail. Cisneros followed him warily.

Ordóñez stared off at the fiery ball of sun as it slipped below the horizon line. They heard the splash of Aurelio's body as it hit the water.

Ordóñez removed his sunglasses and turned to Cisneros. "Aurelio spoke against you, Cousin. And if a man speaks against my own blood, one day he will speak against me." He paused and sighed. "But that assassin said something that troubled me. He accused you of using *cocaina*."

Cisneros licked his lips nervously. "In Miami. Once. I was exhausted. The planning, the war, the false documents, the weapon procurement—everything fell on me."

"*Cocaina* is a white man's devil," Ordóñez said quietly. "We are Indians. We never use that white powder. If we do, we break our sacred covenant with our god, Manco Capac, and this I cannot tolerate even from my own blood."

"Forgive me, Rafael. I swear to you, it will never happen again. I tried to tell you in Santa Rosa, I'm not myself. I'm very tired. I used the *cocaina* only for energy."

Ordóñez stared steely-eyed at his cousin for a long moment, then finally nodded. "All right. This business is finished. When we return, you will accompany Kurt to Switzerland. You will rest in Lausanne. The Swiss have made an art of resting." Ordóñez smiled. "Come now, I told the chef to cook empanadas and arepas. We'll drink good Santa Tomás wine. And afterward, I want you to take one of those Cariocas. Brazilian women are flowers—open flowers. You have only to touch them." Ordóñez put his arm around Cisneros, and the cousins walked down a gleaming mahogany ladder to the dining room.

A few feet below the ship's wake two hammerhead sharks tore at the bloody remains of Aurelio Estrella.

Chapter 35

"You look great, Dad."

"I should. I haven't done any work for two weeks."

"Have you been to the races?"

"As a matter of fact, I had a rare winning day down at old Del Mar."

"Handicapping like a demon, huh?"

"The master at work."

Jack's arm circled his daughter's shoulders as they strolled through the dappled sunlight filtering through the woods. She seemed to have grown two inches during the past seven weeks. Her long, straight blond hair had turned a very pale color, and her profile was heartbreakingly similar to that of her mother's.

She had introduced him to a rugged square-jawed young man with whom she had shared a summer "friend-ship." Jack was polite but reserved; he still had trouble accommodating the fact that Jenny was inexorably moving off in her own orbit, with her own friends and her own philosophies.

"It's just up there, Dad."

They climbed the steep path toward a ridge lined by deformed, blackened trees.

"The wind changed at the last moment," she said. "If the fire had crossed that line, it would have spread to the camp."

They reached the crest of the ridge and stared at the forlorn landscape of charcoal-colored tree trunks and scorched earth.

"Reminds me of the jungle after napalm," Jack said.

"We've started to reseed the whole area."

"Quite a job bringing the forest back to life."

A slight breeze whispered through the tortured woods stirring paper cups and litter left by the fire fighters.

"Come on," she said. "I want to introduce you to Carmen."

"Who's Carmen?"

"My horse."

She led him along a curving path through a stand of tall pines that permeated the forest with a fresh, exhilarating aroma. The scent reminded him of distant innocence, of sweet things long forgotten. Birds chirped, cicadas buzzed, and squirrels scampered up and down trees.

Jenny suddenly stopped and grabbed his hand. "Look," she said in a hushed voice, and pointed to a clearing up ahead.

A deer stood poised in a shaft of sunlight. Its ears pricked, its luminous black eyes staring at them.

"God . . . he's beautiful," Jenny whispered.

The animal pawed the ground, then bolted off into the thicket.

"You wonder how anyone can shoot something as lovely as a deer," she said, and resumed walking.

As he followed her, the last line of Candy's poem suddenly came back to him: ". . . lost in the lights, /seeking a dream that/would never come true." Candy and Jenny were children of the same generation, and but for the grace of God, or fate, or strength of character, or sheer luck, Jenny might have been swallowed up in the same horror that had destroyed Candy. Their generation was stalked by hype, and drugs, and a venal fast-lane morality supported by sophisticated electronic technology that instantly replayed soul-numbing violence interrupted only by mindless commercials.

They were forced to steady themselves as they descended the steep grade. He watched her move, her chin tilted up, her shoulders straight, her tall, curvy figure maturing into womanhood.

As they approached the stable area, the wind carried the pungent odor of horses, hay, and manure.

"Have you been seeing anyone?" she asked suddenly.

"No one special."

"How's Phil Brody?"

"Same as ever." He smiled. "Phil's the wise old man of the department. I don't work with him as closely as I used to. I have a new partner, Silvio Martinez. He's a veteran narcotics agent."

"You get along?"

"Very well."

They reached the stables, and Jenny ran to a big chestnut mare that leaned out of her stall as if expecting company. Jenny rubbed the mare's nose and slipped her a cube of sugar.

"Isn't she a beauty?"

"Where did she get the name Carmen?"

"Her sire was a Spanish-bred champion show horse, so the owner called this filly Carmen. She doesn't have her father's talent, but she's a terrific trail horse, gentle and smart. I was walking her in the hills. All the kids were strung out behind me. Carmen suddenly reared up and whinnied. I knew she was trying to warn me about something, so I stopped, and about ten feet ahead a big timber rattler came out of the brush and wriggled across the trail."

"Maybe we ought to get rid of our prowl cars and bring back the horses."

"Not a bad idea," she said.

Arm and arm they crossed the campgrounds and strolled toward the guest parking lot. Along the way she introduced him to campers and their visiting parents.

"Well, in a few weeks you'll be back in school," he said.

"I'm looking forward to it. I had a great summer, but I'm anxious to get back. I miss you. I miss you a lot."

"It's mutual, kiddo."

Her arm circled his waist. "Have you heard from Gabriella?" she asked.

"I received a letter about ten days ago," he replied as they entered the parking lot. "I've been thinking about going to Rome during the Christmas holidays. I'd like you to meet her."

"Gosh—Rome! That would be fantastic."

"We'll see."

They reached the GTO, and he asked, "Where's a good lunch place around here?"

"There isn't any."

"Well, suppose we drive down to Santa Barbara and have lunch at the Biltmore Hotel?"

"It's a long drive, Dad."

"I don't mind."

He followed the inland country road due west toward the Coast Highway.

Jenny noticed the tip of a silk scarf protruding from between the console and the armrest. She tugged it free and read the label aloud. "Hermès . . . pretty expensive." She pressed the scarf to her face. "And nice perfume. Who does it belong to?"

"A famous movie star."

"Anyone I know?"

"I hope not. How did you spot that thing?"

"For a cop, you're not too bright. Ladies' scarves go with convertibles, and if the lady in question is someone we can't discuss, you're careless."

"Fold it and put it in the glove compartment." He smiled. "I pity the poor guy who marries you."

"Why?"

"You've hung around detectives too long. He'll have to be a master criminal to cheat on you."

"My husband won't have the strength or inclination to cheat."

The Sunday-night crowd in Prego's restaurant was noisy and lighthearted. Chefs wearing tall white hats stirred the pasta sauce and turned the salmon steaks on a huge grill. The heavy aromas of garlic, perfume, and grilled fish wafted across the room.

Sherry and Lisa had arrived early to ensure getting a window table. Their outward appearance contrasted sharply. Sherry wore a man-tailored gray suit, a white shirt, and a dark red tie, but her face was without makeup, and she wore no jewelry.

Lisa Chang's long, silky black hair spilled over the shoulders of her white dress. Turquoise rings circled three fingers of both hands, and large turquoise earrings dangled from her earlobes. Her luminous almond-shaped eyes were dramatized with blue eyeliner.

They ate fried calamari with their fingers and drank a house Chianti.

"Leo phoned me this morning," Sherry said.

"What about?"

"We're starting preproduction on *Memories of Candy*."

"When?"

"A couple of weeks. I'm going up to San Fran after Labor Day with Jimmy Crane to pick some locations."

"Jimmy's a marvelous cameraman."

Sherry nodded. "I want every frame to be lit like an impressionist painting—soft, filtered, a trace of blue in everything."

Lisa touched a napkin to her lips and asked, "With Stella gone, who's going to play Candy?"

"We'll have to find someone."

"I wish . . ." Lisa sighed. "I wish sometimes I hadn't been cursed with this Oriental face."

"Your face is lovely," Sherry said, and squeezed Lisa's hand. "I'm having the script rewritten. I want it to be sensual, not pornographic. Your role will be expanded. I promise you."

"What about Karen?"

"I'm stuck with that bitch. She is, after all, the only box-office name left."

"I hope I'm wrong," Lisa said, "but I have this nagging feeling that she had a hand in killing John and Stella."

"She's capable of murder," Sherry said. "There's a kind of calculated hatred coiled up inside her. You see it on the screen. No matter what she's doing up there, her eyes radiate a cold, vicious light."

Jeff Kellerman entered with an attractive young girl and was seated immediately. He glanced at Sherry and waved to her. Sherry smiled at Kellerman and muttered, "That prick. He shoots nothing but talking heads. How the hell he achieved this chic critical aura beats me."

"Well, he's a charmer," Lisa said. "He had Candy in the palm of his hand."

"Candy was impressionable. He promised her a straight film," Sherry said, and swallowed some wine. "God, I'd give anything for a chance to direct a straight film."

The waiter served Sherry's salmon steak and Lisa's grilled chicken. "Is everything all right?" he asked.

"Fine." Sherry smiled.

They ate in a desultory fashion as if neither woman wanted the dinner to end.

"Karen is balling that cop," Sherry blurted.

"What cop?"

"Raines."

"I spoke to him," Lisa said. "I told him about the séance. No wonder he was so protective of Karen." Lisa chewed on a wing. "How do you know she's getting it on with him?"

"She mentioned it to Leo. Karen's playing her own game, and if she had anything to do with the killings, what better insurance than having the investigating cop in your pocket?"

"I can't believe any man would find her sexy."

"It's that imperious WASP face, those glittering lime eyes. She's got something special. I've got to give her that," Sherry admitted. "What puzzles me is that she actually believes in that Shiva order."

"I believe in it, too," Lisa said.

"You're different, honey. After all, it is an Eastern religion."

"Spoken like a true racist."

"Has anyone helped you more than I have?"

Lisa stared into Sherry's eyes and squeezed her hand. "No one."

Lisa removed her hand as the waiter refilled their glasses. "Will there be anything else?" he asked.

"I'd like a double espresso," Sherry said.

"I'll stay with the wine." Lisa smiled.

Sherry shook her head in dismay. "I've always been intimidated by Karen. I hate working with her, but there's no choice."

"There's always a choice," Lisa said.

*   *   *

Silvio and Pepe were seated in the darkness of the
half-empty balcony. In its heyday the old movie palace had
been the sight of splendorous and opulent premieres; its
history went all the way back to vaudeville. The theater
now survived by showing X-rated films and selling X-rated
cassettes in the lobby. On weekends "live" sex acts were
featured on the same stage upon which Jolson, Buster
Keaton, and W. C. Fields once performed.

"What happened in Cancún?" Silvio asked in a whisper.

"Don't look at me," Pepe whispered nervously. "Watch
the screen."

"It's been two weeks, Pepe. It's been quiet for two
weeks."

"I can't help you."

"Just tell me if they made a deal."

"Look at that broad down there in the third row,"
Pepe whispered excitedly. "She's whacking that guy off."

"Don't fuck around with me, Pepe," Silvio said
ominously.

"Look, I got nothing to tell you."

"You better talk to me, Pepe."

"Aurelio Estrella was hit." Pepe sighed.

"Who the fuck is he?"

"*Was*. He *was* Ordóñez's chief executioner. He was
also my connection. He gave me the *Ave María* tape."

"Why?"

"He wanted to be the number two man. *Ave María*
was Cisneros's idea. Aurelio was looking to nail Cisneros."

"Why was he hit?"

"I don't know. But when Ordóñez and Cisneros came
back to Barranquilla, Aurelio wasn't with them." Pepe
shifted his long legs. "I gotta split."

Silvio grabbed the dealer's arm. "Just tell me, is the
war over?"

Pepe felt the pressure of Silvio's fingers squeezing his
forearm. Silvio was in a dangerous mood. Pepe knew he
had to give him something. The trick was to respond but
without being specific. "Shit, you're a fucking cop," he
whined. "You see any killings in the past two weeks? You
see any porno people gettin' hit? You see any coke dealers

gettin' clipped? Now let go of me. Christ, it's Sunday night. Don't you have a woman? Or a house, or a kid, a dog, a cat—anything?" Pepe paused. "Listen, you keep pushing like this and they'll have to put speed bumps in your coffin."

"Did they make a deal?" Silvio pressed.

"They made a deal." Pepe sighed.

Chapter 36

The dark green Pacific was flecked with silver, and surfers rode the curling swells. It was late afternoon, and the coast traffic was light.

Silvio drove the GTO, and Jack scanned the passing signs.

"I hope you know what you're doing," Silvio cautioned him. "Nolan's orders were to stay out of it."

"I just want to interview the guru. Hell, I may join the order."

"Bullshit. You want to destroy his credibility in front of Karen Dara. You're antagonizing Nolan for nothing. If she believes in that crap, you're not going to change her mind."

"It's not just Karen. The guru futzed Candy's voice. I want to find out why he had that voice ask for vengeance. It's important that we know."

"Why?"

"His followers believe that they're communicating with the dead. And if that dead spirit asks for vengeance, and a disciple kills someone, the guru is an accessory to murder. A religious scam is one thing. Incitement to murder is another."

They stopped at an intersection and watched a tall, shapely blond girl carry a surfboard across the highway.

"You think Karen hit Traynor and Pierson?" Silvio asked.

"I don't know, but she admitted the guru supplies opium and grass to help induce contact with the afterworld, and opium fucks up the psyche pretty good."

"Absolutely," Silvio said. "Opium is a murderous drug.

I've seen addicts shift from stupor to violent hallucinations in one pipe."

The crosswalk cleared. Silvio pressed the accelerator and shifted smoothly through the gears. They drove north for two more miles before Jack exclaimed. "There it is! Slow down, and hang a right at that sign."

Silvio down shifted and swung the convertible onto the access road. Steering carefully, he followed the winding drive for 200 feet before pulling up alongside a Mustang parked on the shoulder of the road.

A cloud of dust settled over Jack as he got out of the Pontiac and walked to the Mustang.

He stuck his head in the window and greeted the two NIFTY detectives. They were the same pair who had staked out the factory on Los Angeles Street. The older, hefty detective, Stillwell, sat behind the wheel. His short-sleeved shirt was drenched in perspiration, and the ground below the window was studded with cigarette butts. The younger man, Reisman, seemed unperturbed by the heat. It had been Reisman who decoyed at the factory, stumbling drunkenly across the street and pissing on the loading dock wall in full view of the Colombian *coqueros*.

"How you guys holding up?" Jack inquired.

"Hot as a rat's ass in here," Stillwell grumbled.

"Any traffic?" Jack asked.

"Karen Dara arrived at ten thirty-five. The only other vehicle was a black Buick with a uniformed man driving—guru's security guard, I guess. He left about twelve-thirty and came back a little after two."

A distant tumbler clicked in Jack's memory bank. "A *black* Buick?" he asked.

"Black as opposed to white." Stillwell nodded. "You want the plate number?"

"No. You get any pictures?"

"Snapped off a roll of rich and famous—wives and girlfriends of stars and one prominent actress. The guru has a wealthy clientele."

"When do you get relieved?" Jack asked.

"Fitz and Santoro come on at five. Cantini and Simmons have the dog watch." Stillwell sighed. "I hope this Dara dame is worth it."

"She's worth it." Reisman smiled. "I've seen her films."

Jack walked back to the Pontiac and opened the door on the driver's side. "Out, amigo," he said.

Silvio stared at him quizzically.

"Wait for me with the boys. I won't be ten minutes."

"What for?"

"Come on, Silvio. This is my thing."

"That's bullshit."

"Out!" Jack insisted. "If the guru's attorney files a complaint, I don't want you involved."

"I'm going up there with you," Silvio replied firmly. "You can see him alone. But he's got muscle up there. Now, get in."

Silvio drove up the steep, curving road in low gear, trailing a cloud of red dust.

They reached a low ridge close to the summit and stopped at a pair of huge wrought-iron gates. A stocky uniformed guard appeared.

"Private road, fellas," he said. "You're trespassing."

Silvio flashed his badge. "Detectives Martinez and Raines—Brother Meli-Ramdas is expecting us."

The man stared at them, snapping his chewing gum. "I'll check it."

He walked slowly to a panel control box adjacent to the gate, opened the box, and picked up a phone receiver. He spoke briefly, hung up, pressed three buttons on the panel, and the massive gates swung open.

The late sun illuminated the single ruby eye atop the pyramid-shaped temple of Shiva. Wooden bungalows and large canvas tents were situated on either side of the temple.

Silvio backed into a parking stall so that the front of the GTO faced a large bungalow marked "Meditation Center."

"I'll be waiting here," he said as Jack got out. "You have no warrant, so take it easy."

Jack noticed several guards carrying walkie-talkies and armed with .45 automatics lounging outside the temple.

A plain-faced white-robed girl came out of the bungalow door and greeted him. "This way, please."

* * *

The room was bare except for a small table piled with publicity pamphlets. The blades of a ceiling fan were laced with cobwebs. A worn Persian carpet covered the dusty wooden floor. The grimy windows were closed. A burning incense candle introduced a sweet aroma into the stale air.

Wearing a turban and draped in a purple velvet robe, Guru Meli-Ramdas sat on his haunches in the center of the carpet. He was a slightly built man with bright eyes, coffee-colored skin, and a long gray beard.

"Fetch Brother Raines a stool," Meli-Ramdas said to the girl.

She left abruptly, bowing and clasping her palms together.

"Tea?" the guru asked.

"No, thanks."

"What may I offer you?"

"Just some answers."

"Of course. My life has been devoted to answering questions. Cosmic questions."

"My questions aren't that weighty."

"All that remains unanswered is weighty." The guru smiled.

"Spare me your philosophy, brother. I'm hip to the movement from the time Maharishi Saraswati left his Indian cave and set up his ashram in L.A. He made a hell of a score, but the greatest guru gig of all time was Jim Jones and his famous Kool-Aid."

The white-robed girl reentered and placed a low stool on the rug. She bowed to the guru and left.

"You conducted a séance some weeks ago," Jack said, "with Lisa Chang and Karen Dara. You reached the departed spirit of Candy Lane."

"Departed *soul*," the guru corrected him.

"Right. As I understand it, Miss Lane's soul demanded vengeance for her death."

"That is true."

"And that demand was directed to Karen Dara."

"That is also true."

Jack shifted his weight on the stool. He had begun to perspire in the fetid heat of the room, and he fought to contain his rising anger toward the patronizing attitude of the beady-eyed scam artist.

"Have you conducted any séances for Miss Dara since that time?"

"Yes, indeed. We attempt to reach the soul of Miss Lane at least three times a week. We are not always successful, but we try."

Jack rose and walked to the table and picked up a pamphlet bearing the guru's photograph. "May I have one of these?"

"Of course."

"You mind if I smoke?"

"I wish you would refrain."

"Tell me, brother," Jack said warmly, "is the opium-grass combination smoked, injected, or swallowed?"

"Are you referring to ceremonial opiates required to reach the other world?"

"I'm referring to the illegal drugs you supply to your disciples."

"I follow the prescribed dictates of the goddess Shiva. Some religions use smoke, wafers, holy water, and wine. The Order of Shiva uses pure herbal opium seed and untreated marijuana. To my knowledge, neither one is illegal when utilized in a theological ceremony."

"I'm afraid you're wrong, brother. The purpose is irrelevant; they're both illegal drugs."

The guru's watery brown eyes blinked, and his bony shoulders shrugged. "Perhaps I have been misinformed by my attorney."

"Misinformed, my ass! You're dealing hard drugs. That's a felony worth fifteen to twenty-five years in this state. But I'll make a deal with you. I want you to produce the sound machine you use to re-create the voices of departed souls, and I want you to bring one of those séance chairs in here and show those hidden springs to Miss Dara. I want her to get an inside look at your scam, and in return I promise not to produce a warrant for your arrest."

"Arrest?" the guru asked incredulously.

"For the distribution and use of illegal drugs," Jack replied.

The guru did not respond.

The room fell silent except for the buzzing of flies climbing up the grimy windowpanes.

"All right . . ." The guru nodded and took a bell out of his robe and shook it loudly.

The young girl in white appeared. "*Porti Karen*," the guru ordered.

The girl palmed her hands and backed out of the room.

"It will not be necessary to expose the devices used in the séance. I will freely admit to their use," the guru said. "You see, brother, spiritual contact with the departed is only aided by these devices. They help the inner soul reach that exalted transcendental state. By themselves these devices would not be effective. The living spirit and the departed spirit must be cosmically orchestrated. It is my humble task to bring these forces together. I am merely a servant of the goddess Shiva."

"Who recorded Candy Lane's 'voice'?"

"One of my disciples."

"Why did you have the recording demand vengeance?"

"I was directed to by the goddess Shiva."

"I know. But I'm asking you *why*?"

"The goddess desires that her children be free of perversion."

"You mean pornography?"

"In the case of Sister Dara, yes."

"And the goddess desires that Miss Dara wipe out all her colleagues?"

"Ah." The guru smiled. "You interpret *vengeance* as violence. This is wrong. Candy Lane's soul is, in fact, pleading with Sister Karen to achieve purity. You cannot accept the words of departed souls literally."

"Why didn't Candy's voice demand that Lisa Chang seek vengeance?"

"I am only a servant of the goddess. I do not question her wishes."

Jack paced for a moment before asking, "How much do you charge your disciples for religious comfort and drugs?"

"Ah, brother, you said we would not discuss drugs."

"Okay . . . what's your fee?"

"I depend upon the largess of my disciples."

"That black Buick your guards use—did they by chance follow Karen down the highway the night of that first séance?"

"It is possible one of my people tried to protect her since she was in an exalted state of mind."

"By *exalted state of mind*, you mean, high on opium?"

The door opened, and the guru rose.

Karen, wearing a white linen smock, stood just inside the room. She stared icily at Jack. "What are you doing here?"

Jack turned to the guru. "Tell her."

"The officer wishes me to inform you that the voice of Candy Lane was recorded by Sister Carnelia and that the movement of furniture in the séance is abetted by mechanical devices."

"And," Jack said, wiping the perspiration from his face, "the Buick that ran you down on the Coast Highway belonged to one of his gunsels who was probably high and sexed up on opium."

"I have no knowledge of this." The guru smiled. "This is sheer speculation."

"Speculation or not"—Jack glared at Karen—"it's a pretty good bet. You're not stupid. You get the scam. This little bastard's been feeding you opium and guilt through a bullshit religious ceremony. That's why you're having nightmares. Now, get your clothes on, and let's get out of here."

"You've got some goddamn nerve coming up here and throwing your weight around," she replied angrily. "This is a recognized, licensed religious order, and you're intruding. Trespassing. What the hell makes you think I care about the how and why of this order? That part has no relevance to me. I feel Candy's presence in séances. That's all that matters to me."

"Well"—Jack removed his jacket and draped it over his arm—"maybe you require the courage of Shiva to go around knocking off your colleagues."

"Good-bye, Jack," she said quietly. "And call off those bloodhounds. I'm a big girl. I'll take care of myself."

"Whatever you say," Jack replied, and derisively added, "Sister."

Karen waited for him to leave before addressing the guru. "I'm sorry for this," she said apologetically.

"It's nothing. The material world haunts us all. Come, let us kneel and pray. Sister Carnelia is preparing the pipe. We will pray for peace."

They knelt together on the Persian carpet and chanted in the language of Esperanto, "*Se placas porti paco.*"

Chapter 37

The valley lights glowed like a luminous necklace draped around the distant foothills of the San Bernardino Mountains. Ignoring the splendid view, Leo Whelan paced the living-room terrace of his Encino Hills house, speaking angrily into the amplified phone console.

"Goddammit, Eddie, what the hell is so tough about finding some local talent?"

"AIDS! That's what." The answering voice belonged to Ed Berlfien, Whelan's San Francisco production manager.

"Did you say AIDS?" Leo asked incredulously.

"Yeah. People are afraid to perform."

"Tell me, Eddie, since when did this become a zero-risk world? Besides, you know goddamn well no one that didn't pass a physical ever worked in a picture of mine. I operate just like the straights." Leo paused. "Now, what about the casting?"

"Finding a beautiful blonde that can double Candy is tough."

Whelan knew that Eddie had already found a candidate and was figuring a price that would accommodate a kickback.

"How tough?" Leo asked.

"Ten thou a day."

"Jesus . . . who is she? Madonna?"

"Her name is Stephanie Storm. She's a featured dancer at Gino's. She's a knockout. Broadway legs. Playboy tits. And a smile that would make the ayatollah forget Mecca."

"She a druggie?"

"How would I know?"

"Can you send me some pictures?"

"You gotta see her, Leo."

"Okay, I'll be up in a couple of weeks with Sherry Nichols and Jimmy Crane." There was a pause as Leo extracted a cigar from his jumpsuit and bit off the end.

"You still there?" Eddie asked.

"I'm lighting a cigar."

Leo blew the smoke up toward the terrace lights and addressed the speaker. "I need a castle, Eddie."

"What?"

"A castle. It's for a film to follow the Candy Lane story."

"Why a castle?"

"I want to make an expensive, high-gloss picture—a porno that will cross into the straight world. The story is based on the Edgar Allan Poe classic 'Masque of the Red Death.'"

"I don't know that one."

"It's set in the eighteenth century. There's a deadly plague in the land—like AIDS, only worse. The royalty and nobility are holed up in this castle. The moat is up. They can't leave, and they can't let anyone in. As time passes, this costumed nobility becomes savage, crazed. They're trapped in this castle with time running out. They got to get it on now. They're surrounded by death. I want costumes, jewelry, that Madame du Barry hairdo, wigs, Louis the Fifteenth furniture—the works."

"You have the rights to this story?" the muffled voice inquired.

"Don't worry about the rights. Fuck the rights! Get me a castle."

"I'll find something up in the wine country. I like the idea, but the title stinks."

"We have time to worry about the title, for chrissake."

"No one's gonna see a picture called *Masque of the Red Death*. You've got to come up with a title."

Leo sighed. "I have a working title, Eddie. But you don't tell a soul."

"I'm like a stone. What is it?"

"*Deep Moat*."

There was a beat of silence before Eddie exclaimed, "*Deep Moat*! That's sensational! That's a twenty-five-million-dollar title."

"Glad you like it. Now, get the castle, and don't lose that kid—Stephanie Storm."

"It's under control."

"Good-bye, Eddie."

Leo walked over to the small table and took the receiver off the speaker cradle, hung it up, and depressed the button, cutting the connection.

He placed his cigar in an ashtray and checked his watch. It was 9:45. He had to shower and dress. Jeff Kellerman's limousine would be arriving any minute. The director was hosting a party in his Coldwater Canyon house to celebrate the start of a new film. Leo had provided some fluffs to dress up the event, and Kellerman had in turn invited Whelan to the gala event.

Leo was feeling somewhat euphoric after the long siege of violence and business disruptions.

Sidney Davis had filled him in on the meeting at Cancún. A truce was in place. Ordóñez had denied any involvement in the Los Angeles killings. But Leo wasn't sure. The murders and the valentine signatures bore the bizarre stamp common to Colombian hit men. Leo recalled a cheating dealer whose throat had been cut and a tie had been knotted through the hole where the dealer's Adam's apple had been. The murder had been labeled the "Colombian Necktie." But the porno killings no longer concerned Leo. A truce was in effect, and production could be resumed.

He was grateful that Karen Dara had been spared. She was the sole surviving major star, and her presence in the upcoming pictures guaranteed top-drawer theatrical bookings and huge cassette sales.

Some weeks ago Karen had told him about her personal relationship with Jack Raines. She had cautioned him to keep the matter confidential. She did not want to hurt Raines professionally. She was relating the information to let Leo know that even the police were puzzled by the murders, and perhaps he should take steps to protect himself. He thanked her for the information, but the call had unnerved him. It was probably his own paranoia, but her advice had the earmarks of a sugar-coated threat. She had always made him edgy. Karen Dara was an enigma wrapped in an icy smile.

He picked up his cigar and had started for the bedroom when the doorbell chimed.

"Fucking limos are always early," he muttered to himself, and lumbered to the door. He peered through the peephole. Somewhat surprised, he sighed, unbolted the lock, and opened the door.

"Come on in; fix yourself a drink. I'm running late, but I'll—"

There was a deafening crack. Leo crashed against the bookcase, feeling as though a blowtorch had been ignited deep inside his belly.

The flame and smoke came at him again.

He clutched his stomach and screamed as a geyser of blood spurted from between his fingers. He slumped down the wall into a sitting position, staring up at the black hole of the muzzle. It moved slowly closer, finally pressing against the pulpy mass protruding from his belly.

"Why?" Leo moaned. "Why?"

The muzzle belched flame. The sound booms echoed, bouncing off the walls. Leo's body jerked three times, and he fell over onto his side. A trickle of blood oozed out of his mouth, staining the hardwood floor. His eyes were glazed but open. The last image they flashed to his dying brain was that of a light snowfall. . . .

Chapter 38

The coroner's ambulance, the print van, and the photo lab truck had departed the murder site at 2:50 A.M. The press vehicles remained parked in Leo Whelan's circular driveway, along with Jack's GTO, a Van Nuys police unit's prowl car, Gabriel Torres's Toyota, and an incongruous, gleaming black limousine. TV crews had set up a bank of lights in anticipation of an on-camera interview with Raines. Journalists huddled in small groups, smoking and chatting.

Inside her TV mobile van Gloria Hunnicutt reclined on the sofa. She hoped Raines would be more forthcoming tonight than he had been in the past. She despaired of having to go through Brody for her information—not that she objected to turning a small trick on the wizened detective. But it was an annoyance and, in a sense, a diminution of her importance.

Raines and Silvio were in the master bedroom, sifting through the last of the drawers and closets. Silvio slammed the bottom drawer of a huge armoire. Jack came out of the walk-in closet.

They glanced at the huge bed. "I guess this is all of it," Silvio said.

Resting on the bed was a bankbook, a stack of canceled checks, and a thick leather-bound phone directory.

The directory contained names of casting directors, film technicians, actors' agents, film distributors in Cleveland, Chicago, San Francisco, and New York. The only names relating to the case were those of Sidney Davis, Angelo Maffatore, Jeff Kellerman, Sherry Nichols, Karen Dara, Lisa Chang, and Candy Lane.

"Come on, let's talk to Gabby," Jack said.

They entered the living room and glanced at the chauffeur pacing nervously on the terrace.

"We've kept that guy a hell of a long time," Silvio noted.

"He'll survive."

Torres peered at the chalked body outline. The dark bloodstains on the hardwood floor contrasted sharply with the snow-white valentine.

"Curious," he said. "Candy Lane, John Traynor, and Stella Pierson were hit in the skulls by slugs from automatic weapons. Their deaths were instantaneous. But Whelan was shot by a thirty-eight revolver, five times, in the belly. Someone wanted to inflict a lot of pain. It's a slow, brutal death. The liver, pancreas, kidney, and stomach walls rupture, yet the heart continues to receive blood. It takes a long time to slip into a coma."

"Are you saying that Whelan was singled out for torturous death by the killer?" Jack asked.

"Looks that way."

"What about the valentine?" Silvio asked.

"Ah . . ." Torres said with interest. "The chemist tells me it's one hundred percent pure hydrochloride cocaine—uncut and lethal. A couple of snorts, and you go into seizure and coronary thrombosis. It electrocutes the brain."

"Where would anyone get one hundred percent coke?" Jack asked.

"Only at a refinery," Silvio replied, "before it's cut and packaged."

"That would indicate Colombian involvement," Jack suggested.

"Maybe," Gabby said. "But the valentine has been constant from the beginning. To me it's the signature of a serial killer. Then again"—he sighed—"the killer could have used it to throw us off."

"Can you fix the time of death?" Jack asked.

"No problem. The chauffeur found him shortly before ten. He called the paramedics. They arrived at ten-fifteen. Whelan was still clinically alive. The paramedics administered morphine. Whelan died at UCLA emergency an hour later. I would say he was hit minutes before the chauffeur arrived—between nine forty-five and ten."

"How can you be that exact?"

"If he had been without morphine longer than fifteen or twenty minutes, he would have gone into metabolic shock and expired." Torres snapped his medical bag shut. "I'll run the slugs through ballistics. But it looks like a standard Smith and Wesson."

"Karen Dara has a thirty-eight," Silvio remarked.

"See if you can get her to let you test-fire it," Torres suggested. "You guys look like hell. Go home and get some sleep."

The stocky coroner left, carrying his bag, trudging toward the door like an old-time doctor leaving a patient's house after a late-night visit.

"Better give Nolan a call," Jack said.

"It's almost four," Silvio cautioned.

"Wake him up. He's got to know about this before he turns on the morning news."

"Okay." Silvio nodded and walked toward an alcove.

Jack approached the chauffeur, who was now seated in a white leather chair, sipping a cognac.

"Your name is Adalan Hasbani?"

Beads of sweat oozed out of the chauffeur's forehead, and his black eyes darted nervously around the room.

"I asked if your name is Adalan Hasbani," Jack repeated.

"Yes, yes—Hasbani. I told all this to the police."

"I'm in charge of the case, so you have to tell me. What time did you arrive?"

"A little before ten. I'm never late." His speech was laced with a Middle Eastern accent.

"Who sent you?"

"Mr. Kellerman."

"You mean Jeff Kellerman?"

"Yes, the film director." He pronounced *film* as "filim." He wiped his forehead with his sleeve. "I was to collect Mr. Whelan and bring him to Mr. Kellerman's house."

"What was the occasion?"

"A party."

"You work for Kellerman?"

"No. I work for Cinema Transportation."

"Now, take your time. I want to know exactly what happened when you arrived."

The chauffeur swallowed some brandy and chewed his lower lip. "This is very difficult for me. But I'll try to be precise. The door was open. I called Mr. Whelan's name. Several times. There was no answer. I came in. I saw the lamp had fallen. I smelled a sharp smell like smoke."

"You mean gunpowder?"

"Yes. I walked toward the lamp. And then . . ." His lips quivered. "I saw Mr. Whelan. He was on his side. His coverall front was soaked with blood, and yellow matter was sticking out of his belly. Blood was coming out of his mouth. I saw that valentine. I couldn't move. I stood there for a moment."

"Did you touch anything?"

"No, sir."

Silvio came out of the study and nodded at Jack.

"What did you do?" Jack asked the sweating chauffeur.

"I ran outside to the limousine. I used the car phone. I called nine-eleven. I gave them the address. I stayed in the car until the police and paramedics came."

"When you came up the hill, did you notice any cars coming down?"

"There was one."

"What kind?"

"We passed quickly. It was dark."

"Your business involves cars; light or dark, you can still tell the difference between a Toyota and a Mercedes."

The chauffeur shifted uneasily in his chair. "It was a big sedan."

"Goddammit!" Jack exclaimed. "Sedan doesn't mean a fucking thing to me. Was it foreign or American?"

Silvio knew Jack was right on the edge. He hoped the chauffeur would say something to calm his partner.

"American," the chauffeur replied tensely. "Yes, it was American—perhaps a Lincoln."

"Could it have been a Cadillac?"

"Perhaps."

"Did you see the driver?"

"It was a woman."

"White? Black? Old? Young?"

"I—I . . . couldn't tell," the chauffeur stammered. "Only that the driver was a woman—a white woman; not very old."

"Get up, Mr. Hasbani."

The man struggled to his feet. "Can I go now?"

"You have a phone number and address?"

"I gave it to the police."

"Where were you born?"

The chauffeur's eyes flicked from Jack to Silvio. "I was—I was born in Teheran."

"When did you enter the United States?"

"Two years ago."

"You have a green card?"

"Please. I have a—a visa. A tourist visa."

"How come you're driving a commercial vehicle?"

Silvio grabbed Jack's arm, took him aside, and in a hushed voice said, "If you asked everyone in the city for a green card, it would be a ghost town."

"I'm tired of these people taking jobs away from native-born Americans. We've got a hundred thousand black kids out of work in this city."

"Fuck it, Jack. We're up to our eyeballs in multiple homicides. Let the customs people worry about illegal aliens. I was once an illegal, too."

Jack stared at Silvio for a beat, then turned to the chauffeur. "Go home, Mr. Hasbani. I warn you not to speak with any of those press people out there. Get in your limousine and go back to the garage. You understand?"

"Yes, sir." He paused. "I thank you, Officer. I plan to apply for citizenship. My family was murdered in Teheran. My father was a banker. We were educated, refined people. I don't want to be involved in this."

The chauffeur left. Jack walked to the portable bar, poured three fingers of scotch, and knocked it down.

"What do you make out of that car business?" Silvio asked.

Jack shrugged. "Thousands of people live up in these hills."

"But he passed a big American sedan only minutes after the killing. Karen owns a Caddy."

"It's a reach. What interests me is that lethal coke. Come on, let's get out of here."

Silvio walked directly to the GTO while Jack delivered a brief statement to the press. The journalists complained, but the late hour had taken its toll, and they gave up quickly. Jack started toward the GTO as Gloria Hunnicutt came out of the TV mobile van.

She smiled and offered him a cigarette.

"No, thanks. You never quit, do you, Gloria?"

"Some people have accused me of employing certain unsavory tactics to get a story. But my real secret is my discipline. I'm relentless."

"That's certainly true. I have to give you that."

"Can you give me anything else?" she asked coquettishly.

"Why not? But it's from an 'unnamed but reliable source.' Agreed?"

"Absolutely."

"The murder of Leo Whelan follows the pattern exhibited in the deaths of Candy Lane, John Traynor, and Stella Pierson."

"Including the valentine?"

Jack nodded. "Complete with the initials P. C."

"Anything else I should know?"

"Yeah. Whelan was on his way to a party at Jeff Kellerman's."

"Why would Kellerman invite Leo Whelan to a chichi Beverly Hills party?"

"You're a bright girl, Gloria. You tell me."

"I would guess Whelan provided some dress extras for the party."

"I would not disagree with that conclusion."

"You don't like Kellerman, do you?"

Jack stared off at the chalky light beginning to seep into the night sky. "Let's skip it, Gloria. I'm dead tired, sweetheart."

"Do you have any suspects?"

"Not a clue."

"You'll let me know?"

"You treat Nolan right, and I'll treat you right."

"This could be the start of a beautiful friendship."

"Spare me the *Casablanca* dialogue." Jack smiled wanly. "There are still certain things I consider to be sacred."

Chapter 39

"Okay, okay," Nolan grumbled. "You were right."

"I haven't said a word," Jack replied wearily.

"The commissioner called first thing this morning," Nolan continued. "He said, 'We bought your theory of Colombian hit men, John. We accepted as fact that these porno actors were the initial victims in a war between the Colombians and the mob.' But now"—Nolan looked at the men—"now the commissioner sticks the knife in. He says a child could perceive that we're faced with a serial killer. There's a vigilante loose out there." Nolan glanced at Silvio. "The commissioner paraphrased what you said to me a couple of weeks ago. He said, 'Find the killer, John. Because today it's porno people, tomorrow it's car sales-men, next week it's politicians.'" Nolan stopped pacing and waved his arms. "Then I get a call from Sidney fucking Davis. 'What's happening, John?' he asked. 'A month ago your man Silvio Martinez roughs up Leo Whelan; now Whelan's dead. Do you protect citizens, or do you harass them?'" Nolan sank into his chair and relit his cigar. "I don't mean to hassle you fellows. I know you've been up all night. I know you're tired. But we've got to nail this thing. Thank Christ, that Hunnicutt dame went easy with us this morning."

"Maybe we ought to get Brody involved," Jack suggested. "He's the best street-corner criminologist on the force. It was Brody who cracked the freeway serial killer in '79."

"I already have him studying the case file," Nolan replied.

"It's too bad." Silvio sighed. "For a while there we were in great shape."

"You bet your ass we were," Nolan concurred. "It was nirvana. We had come off a sensational drug bust. The porno killings had been chalked up to the war. The heat was off, and those city hall bureaucrats were bowing and scraping."

"And," Silvio added, "we had the pleasure of sitting back and watching those two organizations swimming in their own blood."

"Goddamn right," Nolan replied. "We were on vacation, for chrissake."

"Not quite," Jack said, and dropped the guru's publicity handout on Nolan's desk.

"What the hell is this?"

"A mailing piece extolling the virtues of Guru Meli-Ramdas."

"You went up there against my orders?"

"Yes, I did, John. I had to let him know his scam, his bullshit séances, his prerecorded voices of the dead might incite his disciples to murder. I wanted to know why he had Candy's voice order Karen Dara to seek vengeance."

Nolan studied the Shiva publicity sheet and spoke through a cloud of smoke. "You think the guru incited Karen Dara to murder?"

"It's possible." Jack shrugged. "I ran a make on Brother Meli-Ramdas." Jack read from a telex. "Meli-Ramdas, aka Kassim ben Gafga, a Pakistani national. He was busted by the French Deuxième Bureau for dealing drugs in Marseilles. He served two years, left France, and entered the United States in '78. He operated a religious order in Portland, Oregon, and split when a Mrs. Belgrave accused the guru of forcing her daughter into white slavery. He set up the Zuma location in '81." Jack turned to Silvio. "You have those pictures?"

Silvio nodded and placed a manila envelope on Nolan's desk. "These thirty-five-millimeter proof sheets were shot and developed by our stakeout crews."

Nolan removed the proofs and scanned the frames. "Christ, this is a who's who of show biz women." He paused and glanced at Jack. "What did Brother Meli-Ramdas say when you warned him about incitement to murder?"

"He said that I misinterpret the word *vengeance*. He equates vengeance with purity."

"Did you confront Karen Dara with this?"

Jack nodded. "She told me to take a walk. She considers the drugs and trick devices irrelevant. Her spiritual contact with the departed soul is all that counts."

Nolan's fingers drummed nervously on the desk. "That Cadillac coming down the hill minutes after the killing is interesting."

"That Cadillac is a mirage," Jack replied. "The chauffeur was so tense it could have been a Sherman tank that passed him."

"Maybe so, but I make Karen Dara a prime suspect."

"Why would she torture Whelan?" Silvio asked. "The MO used to kill Whelan differs from the other killings. Whelan was gut-shot five times. Someone wanted him to suffer."

"Besides," Jack added, "this is the first time we've seen a hundred percent pure, lethal coke."

The phone buzzed, and Nolan pressed a button on the console. "Yes?"

"Deputy Barnes calling from the mayor's office."

"I'm in a meeting," Nolan snapped, and got to his feet. "Well, what do we do? We've got to do something."

"We're going to visit Angelo Maffatore," Jack said.

"Maffatore . . ." Nolan whispered the name as if it belonged to some ancient deity. "What the hell for?"

"Because Sidney Davis is with him up at the Bel-Air villa."

"How do you know that?"

"I phoned Davis's office. It's a chance to question them both."

"About what?"

"Tell him, Silvio."

"Pepe told me Maffatore and Ordóñez met in Cancún two weeks ago. They discussed the murders of the mob's porno stars. We ought to know what they know."

"Are you telling me that we require the assistance of Angelo Maffatore to solve a string of murders?"

"What's the difference?" Jack asked. "We use their informers all the time."

"What about Karen Dara?" Nolan asked.

"I'm going to see her tonight. We've got to test-fire her thirty-eight."

"You think she'd use her own gun to kill Whelan?"

"No. But we can't assume anything."

"Do we still have an around-the-clock watch on her?"

Jack nodded. "She was up at the order all night."

"Then how could she have hit Whelan?"

"There may be back roads out of that place. We can't ring the whole mountain."

Chapter 40

The high ceilings and windowless walls of Angelo Maffatore's study seemed to have been transported across the ages from the Spanish Inquisition to twentieth-century Bel-Air. Baroque Spanish antiques rested on black hardwood floors, and grotesque canvases of a bleeding Christ, before and after crucifixion, hung on the walls.

Sidney Davis and Don Angelo sat opposite each other at a long distressed-oak table. The old man had summoned Davis to the villa shortly after hearing of Leo Whelan's murder. Maffatore sipped some sherry and stared accusingly at the dapper attorney.

"I don't understand," Maffatore said. "Why is it you continue to ignore Ordóñez's Indian mentality?"

"I'm aware of your theories about bloodlines and racial traits, and maybe there's something to it," Sidney replied. "But Ordóñez is not a simple Indian. You've met him. You've heard him. He perceives himself as a messiah, a saint."

"I never met a saint I trusted."

Sidney spoke in a pained, solicitous manner. "I respect your feelings about Ordóñez. But why would he travel a thousand miles to effect a truce and then, only two weeks later, have Whelan hit? Ordóñez's dealerships have been destroyed. His American refineries are in ruins. His growers are by his own admission upset with him. Why would he persist in a war that jeopardizes an American market worth a hundred billion dollars?"

"You've just stated all the reasons why that Colombian madman had Leo killed."

Sidney loosened his tie and shook his head. "Forgive

me, Don Angelo, maybe I'm slipping into mental infirmity, but your logic escapes me."

"Think for a minute," Maffatore replied. "Ordóñez's business is in the crapper. We hurt him pretty good. When a man is sitting in the middle of ruins, what the fuck has he got to lose? His spic mentality demands vengeance. He wants us on our knees. Now he kills Leo. He keeps hitting our key people. Who are we gonna hit? We're out of targets. But he's got our whole national organization to go after."

"I'm sorry, but I disagree. Whelan was hit by the same lunatic who murdered Candy and the others. The line is very clear. The method is similar: the coke valentine; the fact that every victim knew the assassin. They opened their doors to their killer. It's not Ordóñez's people."

"You're thinking like an American," Maffatore replied. "I give you the benefit of a lifetime's experience with spic mentality, and you don't listen."

"I'm not trying to be adversarial," Sidney calmly replied. "You're my client. I've given you my opinion. It would be easy for me to agree with you, but it would be dishonest."

Maffatore glanced at a painting of Christ bent over, bleeding, wearing the crown of thorns, bearing the great wooden cross up the Via Dolorosa. The old man got to his feet slowly, walked to a portable bar, and poured another sherry. "Mangano phoned early this morning," he said. "The council believes Ordóñez tricked me into accepting his truce. Mangano is positive the Colombians hit Whelan. The council thinks I'm slipping."

Sidney rose, came around the far end of the table, and draped his arm around Maffatore's bony shoulders.

"I have nothing but respect for you, and I sympathize with your position. But ask yourself, why didn't they hit Whelan when the war was on? He was a key man. Why wait until after a truce exists?"

There was a soft knock at the door. "Come in," Maffatore said.

The butler entered and said, "Detectives Raines and Martinez are here."

Maffatore glanced at Davis.

"It's all right," Sidney said. "This is one of those rare occasions when it suits our purpose to cooperate with the law."

Maffatore nodded to the butler. "Show them in."

Jack and Silvio entered the brooding baronial study. Both of them were sweat-soaked from the desert heat that had blanketed the city.

"Take off your jackets," Maffatore said affably, and turned to the butler. "Bring the boys some iced tea."

Maffatore sat down opposite the detectives. Sidney remained standing.

"You know my attorney, Sidney Davis?" Maffatore asked.

"We've met before," Jack said. "This is my partner, Silvio Martinez."

"Well, what can I do for you fellows?" the don inquired.

"We wanted to talk to you about the murders of your porno stars and last night's killing of Leo Whelan."

Sidney crossed to the table and said, "Let's get the facts straight, Lieutenant. My client is a silent partner in Leo Whelan's Galaxy Films Distribution Company. He is not engaged in the manufacture of X-rated films."

"Spare me your sanctimonious horseshit," Jack replied. "We've got a sheet on Don Angelo's porno activities all the way back to *Deep Throat*."

The butler entered and served the iced tea in frosted tall glasses, each garnished with a sprig of mint.

Waving the butler out, Maffatore said, "Mr. Davis is absolutely correct. I have limited investments in erotic films. Nothing illegal about that."

"I don't give a shit about the porno stuff," Jack replied. "I'm trying to track a vigilante, a serial killer. We came here to ask your help."

Maffatore shrugged. "You know what I know. Galaxy Distribution made a lot of money with those actors. We were hurt by their deaths."

"Did you meet with Rafael Ordóñez in Cancún two weeks ago?" Silvio asked.

Sidney interrupted before Don Angelo could respond. "My client spent a brief vacation at the Camino Real Hotel in Cancún, Mexico."

"Your client, my ass!" Jack exclaimed. "You crossed the line a long time ago, Counselor. You've been consorting with known criminals. I've got enough on you to initiate disbarment proceedings. But I'm not interested in reforming the legal profession. I'm trapped in a lousy piece of irony. I'm pursuing a complex case, and if I crack it, your client will be back in the porno business. In effect, Counselor, I'm working for Don Angelo, and I don't enjoy it for one fucking minute!"

"Fine," Sidney said. "Now I suggest we facilitate this interview by agreeing to simple ground rules. This conversation is off the record. My client is a concerned citizen who has opened his home to you in order to aid you and the department in an ongoing investigation into multiple homicides. Furthermore, his lawyer was not present during the discussion." Sidney glanced at the don. "I'll be out on the terrace."

Maffatore nodded, and Sidney left.

"He's a good boy," the don said. "Too nervous at times, but a good boy."

"Tell us about Cancún," Silvio said quietly.

"We spoke, Ordóñez and I. We spoke about many things."

"Was Cisneros with him?" Silvio pressed.

"Eh." Maffatore smiled. "You know a lot, Mr. Martinez."

"I know you made a truce with Cisneros in '81 at that same hotel."

"Is that so?"

"Yeah. The Colombians stopped you from dealing. They made you laundrymen."

"How did you come by all this information?"

"I was blessed with the services of a very dedicated agent, a brave young woman who was murdered by Ordóñez's assassins."

"Well, the past is the past." Maffatore sighed. "As to the recent Cancún meeting, I met with Ordóñez, and we settled our problems."

"Did you discuss the porno killings?" Jack asked.

"Yes. We both agreed it was the work of a third

party, someone who tricked our organizations into open warfare."

"You believe that?" Silvio asked.

"More or less."

"You have any idea who this third party might be?"

"I personally believe it's a vigilante. A maniac."

"So," Silvio said, "you rule out the Colombians?"

"When it comes to Colombians, I never rule out anything."

"You sound like Dr. Goebbels." Jack smiled. "I wouldn't think a man like you, a man of the streets, would be a racist."

"I'm not a racist, Lieutenant; I'm a realist. When I asked Ordóñez why his soldiers hit innocent people, he said, 'We are Colombians.' "

"Tell me, Don Angelo." Jack used the respectful title for the first time. "How badly has Leo's death hurt you?"

"Businessmen are replaceable. It's the loss of stars that hurts. The young girl, Candy Lane, was a phenomenon. She captured the public imagination overnight. Difficult to replace. But fortunately we still have Karen Dara."

"You're fairly certain Ordóñez had no hand in these killings?" Jack pressed.

"Let's say this, Lieutenant. When you have the misfortune of doing business with Colombians, you can never be certain of anything."

"Thanks for your time."

"A pleasure."

Maffatore's eyes narrowed against the bright sunlight as he entered the terrace and joined Sidney at a canopied garden table.

"They're in the dark," Don Angelo said. "But they agree with you. They believe the killings were committed by a third party."

"They have no leads?"

"None. I want you to phone Ordóñez. Tell him we hold him blameless in Whelan's death. I don't want him preparing for another war. If we have to fight again, I want to hit him fast. I want him to be relaxed."

"I'll get in touch with Ohlendorf," Sidney said.

"It's better for you to speak directly with Ordóñez."

"I disagree. If anyone talks to him, it should be you."

"No . . . if I speak with him, it makes the Whelan killing too important. Ordóñez will think I'm suspicious of him."

"Let me start with Ohlendorf," Sidney suggested.

Maffatore stared off at the clouds of steam rising from the pool below the terrace. "All right." He sighed. "Speak with the German, and after you reassure him, tell him Ordóñez has an informer here in L.A."

"How do you know that?"

"Martinez knew all about our meeting in Cancún: the time, place, everything. He's a veteran of the Miami wars. He's running an inside Colombian informer, probably a dealer."

There was a sudden sound of barking, and the Irish setter bounded up the lawn, sprinting toward Maffatore. The dog leaped up and placed his paws on the old man's chest.

"Easy, Red, easy," Maffatore cooed. The dog removed his paws, and the old man bent down and hugged the setter. "You see, Sidney, the dog loves me. This is a pure thing. This is an emotion you can trust."

Jack and Silvio left the house under the watchful eyes of two bodyguards and walked slowly to their car.

"You were too polite to that old bastard," Silvio said.

"Maybe so, but I understand men like Maffatore. He was an immigrant raised at the Mafia's tit. He never knew any other system. It's men like Davis that I despise. He's educated, bright, successful. A man with choices, a man who knows the rules."

Chapter 41

Karen threw the glass terrace doors open, and the fresh sea breeze smelled faintly of salt. "A drink?" she asked.

"A chilled vodka would be nice."

"You look awful."

"Leo Whelan." He sighed.

"People should have the grace to be murdered at a reasonable hour," she said as she prepared their drinks.

He nodded and stared at the propaganda poster of the girl standing defiantly on the Madrid barricade.

"You really have a thing for that girl, haven't you?"

"Maybe it was the influence of my uncle—I don't know—but I've always wished that I had been there."

"No you don't. It was a venal war, glamorized by Hemingway. The Spanish Republic was betrayed by Chamberlain, Roosevelt, and Stalin." She handed him a vodka and lifted her gin and tonic. "Cheers."

"Cheers."

She lit a Gauloise and said, "I'm sorry I lost my temper with you, but you were out of line."

"Yes and no; there's a law against incitement to murder."

"I'm not a fool, Jack. There's a degree of madness in every religion. You take the best and ignore the rest."

· "Can I have one of those?" he asked, indicating the pack of Gauloises.

"Help yourself."

He lit the stubby cigarette and said, "Let me give you a little history on Brother Meli-Ramdas."

She walked to the sofa, sat down, crossed her long legs, and swung her foot up and down impatiently.

"Meli-Ramdas is a convicted felon," Jack said. "He was busted for drug dealing in Marseilles. His real name is Kassim ben Gafga. He's an illegal alien. He ran his Shiva scam in Oregon until some young lady's irate mother had him run out of town."

"Every innovative religious leader from Jesus to Joseph Smith has been run out of town."

"I've heard of the first guy, but who was Joseph Smith?"

"He invented the Mormon religion and got lynched for his troubles. I know it's difficult for you to comprehend, but I happen to find a strong sense of tranquillity in the teachings of Shiva."

"Can we talk about last night?"

"What time last night?"

"Between nine-thirty and ten."

"You know where I was. Your bloodhounds must have reported to you. I was at the order. You can check with Brother Meli-Ramdas."

"Sure I can," he replied sarcastically. "Anyone else see you up there?"

"Oh, fuck off, Jack." She rose, crossed to the bar, and freshened her drink.

"If you don't cooperate with me"—he sighed—"some homicide bull from central will serve you with a warrant, handcuff you, and take you down to Sybil Brand Detention Hall, where you'll be printed, stripped, and tossed into a holding cell."

"I did not murder Leo Whelan or anyone else, and I resent your threatening me."

"On the contrary, I'm trying to help you, and I would appreciate your letting me test-fire your thirty-eight Smith and Wesson."

"Why?"

"That was the make of the weapon used to kill Whelan."

"You actually believe I used my own gun to murder Leo?"

"No."

"But you have to check it out?"

"Right."

She put the drink down, turned abruptly, and stalked

out of the room. He sipped his drink and studied the Spanish poster. It was evocative and compelling. He could smell the acrid bite of cordite and hear the scream of shells.

"Catch." She stood in the alcove and tossed the gun at him. It fell at his feet. He bent down, picked it up, and stuck the muzzle in his belt.

"Be careful," she said icily. "It's loaded."

The phone rang sharply. She walked to the bar, lifted the phone receiver, and turned her back to him. "Yes, I read the script," she said. "It's fine. But I'm not doing the picture." There was a pause as she listened to the voice on the other end.

"You do that at your own risk!" Karen exclaimed angrily, and slammed the receiver down. "That was Sherry Nichols. They're starting preproduction on *Memories of Candy*."

"I take it you're passing up that epic."

Karen nodded. "I still have a few thin moral lines I won't cross. Sherry threatened to insert that scene from Candy's last film."

"What scene?"

"The sequence of Candy and me in the circular bed. I believe you're familiar with the scene."

She crossed to the open terrace doors and stared off at the beach and shimmering sea. After a moment she turned and stared deeply into his eyes. "Do you really think I'm capable of mass murder?"

"No, but then I wouldn't think you'd be working in X-rated films either."

"Answer my question."

"I'm in a business that's famous for surprises, and technically you're a prime suspect."

"Why?"

"We've got all night to discuss that one."

"Really? You mean it's okay for you to make love to a potential mass murderer?"

"What the hell do you want me to say?"

"Nothing, Jack. Absolutely nothing. If you need it that badly, I'll give it to you. We'll call it a public service." She moved close to him. "You know what I think? I think you're hooked on me, and it's tearing you up. And you probably wish we had never slept together."

She took his face in her hands and brushed her lips against his, lightly and rapidly, then deeply, crushing her mouth against his. She pulled away and whispered, "Now get the hell out of here."

She closed the door, bolted it, and set the chain latch. She walked back into the living room, feeling mixed emotions. She had wanted him to stay, but for some inexplicable reason it was important that she maintain her dignity with him.

She closed and locked the terrace doors and doused the lights. She looked off at the twinkling lights of the Venice pier and the moonlit sea, and she remembered the night she had walked with him on the deserted beach. But sentimentality was a luxury she could not afford.

She entered the bedroom and took a joint out of her handbag. She wished she had some opium, but the grass would have to do. She lit the joint and held the smoke in her lungs. She repeated the process five times and felt the dope's heady rush. She slid a cassette into the stereo. Neil Diamond sang "You Don't Send Me Flowers." The song had been a favorite of Candy's. She listened to the first few bars, then opened the top drawer of her bureau and took out a heart-shaped gold pendant. She turned the pendant faceup in her palm, and tears welled up in her eyes as she read the engraved message: "For P. C. with all my love—Candy."

Chapter 42

Pale morning mists rose from the jungle floor and turned gold in the sunlight. The cousins stood in the clearing, watching a section of the newly designed warehouse being hammered atop the forty-foot frame. The dimensions of the warehouse were equal in size to two football fields. A colonnade of floor-to-ceiling wooden bins ran the length of the warehouse. Indian craftsmen cut sheets of thick glass matching the width of the bins. Latches were screwed into the glass panels, which were then attached to all four sides of the bins, effectively transforming them into airtight chambers.

"Once this is finished, our American currency will be safe from the rats," Ordóñez said.

"But what good is our money sitting here in the jungle?" a tanned and fit-looking Cisneros asked.

"Well"—Ordóñez smiled, the sun glinting off the lenses of his sunglasses—"it's a temporary haven."

They began to walk toward a white Corniche Rolls parked at the crest of the dirt road. "Kurt succeeded in washing eighty million last month," Ordóñez said. "The American bankers have been surprisingly cooperative."

"Why not?" Pedro shrugged. "They make twelve percent while the cash sits with them, and if they're caught, the fine is minimal."

Ordóñez waved to a group of Indian workers unloading bales of coca leaf.

"What about this Whelan business?" Cisneros asked.

Ordóñez stopped and turned to his cousin. "You look like a new man since you returned from Lausanne. Why worry about this?"

"Maffatore wants to speak with you."

"To what purpose? Davis's message was clear. Don Angelo acknowledges we had no hand in Whelan's murder." Ordóñez resumed walking. "What is there to speak about?"

"It would be a gesture of goodwill for you to speak with him."

Ordóñez shook his head. "You don't understand the Sicilian mentality. Don Angelo will regard my call not as a sign of courtesy but as a sign of complicity."

"Why would he suspect us?" Cisneros asked. "After all, it's in our interest to see that his pornographic business remains healthy. We have six hundred million dollars waiting to be washed."

"In the Sicilian mind, logic takes second position to vengeance," Ordóñez replied.

"If that's true, he may be looking for an excuse to go to war."

"Let him do what he wants. To hell with it. We've lost our important dealers. Our key American refineries are in ruins. Who is he going to shoot? We have to rebuild. And we will. But there's no urgency. Western Europe is opening up to us. In the meantime, the Americans are paying three hundred a gram."

"But we may lose the average American. The middle-class customer cannot afford the inflated price."

"When a man is hooked, he'll find the money. We're fine. We're going to take a holiday. We'll go to Leticia and take the *Jacaranda* down the Amazon to Manaus. We'll cast our lines for those six-hundred-pound catfish. We'll drink Dom Pérignon. We'll make love with Carioca girls. Then we'll fly from Manaus to Rio. I've booked the presidential suite at the Copacabana Palace. Kurt will meet us there. He's bringing a group of European dealers with him. I have everything in hand, Cousin."

They halted as a giant lizard slithered across the road.

"There is one thing," Cisneros said as they resumed walking. "Davis said we have an informer in Los Angeles."

"Since we eliminated Ramon and Julito, the informer has to be Pepe Montoya," Ordóñez replied. "Once we reorganize, we'll present him with a Colombian necktie. In the meantime, send Davis a gift for his information."

"These killings in Los Angeles stay in my mind," Cisneros persisted.

"I urge you to forget it. This is an American thing. The Americans are famous for their homicidal maniacs and their cheap hamburgers. The Soviets are famous for their parades and their gulags. So much for the two great powers. That's why we have such a magnificent opportunity. Nothing can stop us."

Chapter 43

A silent crowd of women and small children had gathered on the sidewalk in front of a single-story dwelling. The treelined residential street was located on the wrong side of the Santa Fe tracks that bisected Beverly Hills.

The women held handkerchiefs to their mouths and nostrils in a vain attempt to filter the sickening odor radiating from inside the house. The crowd murmured as the old man got out of his car. The aged landlord blinked in the bright sunlight. He sniffed the foul air, and as he shuffled toward the front door, a distant horror stirred in his mind.

Herman Mittleman had purchased the house in 1968 with "reparation funds" he had received from the West German government. Mittleman was a survivor of the infamous Bergen-Belsen concentration camp; his left forearm still bore the tattooed inmate's serial numbers. He had rented the house to Sherry Nichols three and a half years ago and considered the young woman an ideal tenant. Her checks were never late, and her complaints were minimal.

Mittleman had spent a long weekend in San Diego and upon his return found numerous messages on his answering machine from Miss Nichols's neighbors. The content of the messages were similar: A foul odor coming from the Nichols residence was permeating the street.

He opened the front door and stepped inside the foyer. The hall lights blazed, and a rush of ripe, putrid air took his breath away. The old man instantly recognized the stench of decaying flesh. He pressed a handkerchief to his nose and walked slowly down the hallway to the bedroom.

Chapter 44

Sidney Davis was seated at his desk with the phone receiver cradled to his ear, listening to Angelo Maffatore ranting on the other end of the line.

"I warned you," Maffatore rasped. "Never trust a spic, especially one who thinks he's a saint. We shook hands with that bastard Ordóñez two weeks ago. Then Whelan's clipped. Now they hit Sherry Nichols. How do we get back in business? We got one goddamned star left—Karen Dara. We have no producer, no director."

"Don Angelo," Sidney said calmly, "all the media reports claim her death was caused by an overdose of drugs."

"What the fuck does it matter how they killed her? She's dead!"

Sidney's long experience with emotionally overwrought clients helped him control his rising anger. "Are you suggesting that the police lied to the press?" he asked.

"You have a short memory, Sidney! The police called Candy Lane a suicide!"

Maffatore raved on about blood, Indians, and spics. Sidney waited for the tirade to conclude before calmly replying, "I'm not questioning your instinctive mistrust of Ordóñez, but he has absolutely no interest in keeping us out of production. On the contrary, how can we launder his narcodollars if we're not in action?"

"I'm telling you, Ordóñez hit Whelan and Nichols!"

"Well, I disagree. In my view, he never hit any of our people, and he's not preparing to start a war." Sidney paused, removed his feet from the desk, and leaned forward. "Ordóñez is vacationing. As we speak, he's sailing down the Amazon with Cisneros."

There was a momentary pause while Maffatore pondered Sidney's remarks. "How do you know that?" he asked.

"Ohlendorf told me. And by the way, he expressed Ordóñez's appreciation for our tip concerning the L.A. informer." Sidney felt his persuasive skills were slowly turning Maffatore around. "My advice," he continued, "is to remain calm. And let the police handle things."

"Easy for you to say," the don replied, somewhat subdued. "Mangano called. Vince thinks we've been had."

Sidney felt the moment of decision was at hand. He had adopted an obsequious attitude for too long. Raines had labeled his position accurately. He *had* become an unofficial but active member of an underworld organization. *Well, so be it*, he thought; the time had come to assert himself.

"Did you hear me?" Maffatore whined. "Vincenzo thinks that spic made a patsy out of me."

"One of these days Vincenzo might find himself wearing a Colombian necktie," Sidney bluntly replied.

"What did you say?"

"I thought I was quite clear."

"Who the hell do you think you're talking to? Where do you come off saying that?"

"I'll tell you where I come off. My involvement with you exceeds that of a client-attorney relationship. The fact is I am your *consigliere*—all right. It's my choice. And I assume full responsibility for my professional decisions. But you, too, have a choice. You either start accepting my advice or get someone else. I say this from my heart. I have nothing but respect for you, and I know you're worn-out, exhausted. But you are in charge, Angelo." For the first time Sidney dropped the respectful "Don." "I advise you to assert yourself with Mangano and the council; if not, we, and I say *we*, will find ourselves in an endless, no-win conflict with Ordóñez."

There was a long pause before the don replied, "All right, Sidney. We'll let the police handle this for now. But if one more of our people gets hit, all bets are off."

Sidney hung up, feeling a strong sense of relief and pride. He had finally stepped up to a career decision he had made a long time ago. There were grave risks, but there were limitless possibilities. The tentacles of the Honored Society, of the Unione Siciliana, stretched all the way to the Oval Office. And all his life he had harbored political ambitions. He would have to exert extreme caution, but it was a damn sight more challenging than holding an actor's hand at three in the morning. He glanced at the banner headline in the *Herald-Examiner:* PORNO DIRECTOR DEAD OF OVERDOSE. The accompanying article mentioned the fact that the police had not ruled out the possibility of foul play and that Sherry Nichols might have become the fifth victim of a porno serial killer.

He quickly turned the pages to the financial section. Kurt Ohlendorf had, as a gesture of goodwill, urged him to buy Canadian gold maple leaf coins. The former director of the Reichsbank had served some cruel masters in his time, but the cadaverous German was a fiscal wizard. Sidney jotted a note on his reminder pad to phone his broker in the morning. He rose, walked to the window, and glanced down at the traffic moving along Sunset Boulevard. Yes, he mused, in an uncertain world gold was an indestructible commodity.

Chapter 45

The smoke of cigars and cigarettes drifted up into the ceiling spotlights in Nolan's office. The tension in the room was palpable. Nolan, Jack Raines, Silvio Martinez, Phil Brody, and Dr. Eugene Harris, director of forensic psychology, were concentrating intently on Gabriel Torres's autopsy report on Sherry Nichols. The rumpled coroner folded his facts sheet, placed his cigar in an ashtray, and continued wearily.

"The decedent ingested a large quantity of lethal hydrochloride cocaine, went into instant heart seizure, and died of coronary occlusion. Decedent's tissue specimens contained vaginal emissions of libidous sputum—female blood cells—indicating cunnilingus was performed on decedent the evening of her death."

"What about the valentine?" Nolan inquired.

"Chemical tests prove the quality matches that which she ingested and is similar in every respect to the coke found at the Whelan death site."

"Have you fixed a time of death?" Jack asked.

"The decomposition makes it difficult, but my best judgment is that decedent expired in the late evening this past Thursday, certainly no less than four days before her body was discovered."

Nolan knocked some ash off his cigar and glanced at Dr. Harris, who was standing at the huge window, peering thoughtfully at the sprawl of city lights.

"Doctor . . ." Nolan prodded.

Harris turned and faced the room. He was a handsome, balding man whose kind brown eyes reflected eternal optimism.

"First, let me preface my remarks by saying that

260

forensic psychology is a relatively new and imperfect science. What has emerged in the last decade of research into the pathology of serial indicates certain similar behavioral patterns. In principle, most serial killers are sane. They create mythological 'voices,' 'music,' 'satanic signs' to mask their total lack of conscience. They are driven to kill by sexual frustration, a desire for notoriety, or vengeance, and in some instances a combination of all three. They strike in what appears to be random fashion; however, their victims almost always bear similar symbolic features.

"Theodore Bundy killed college-age girls with black hair parted down the middle, the image of a teenage girl who had rejected his advances in high school. The Hillside stranglers chose young girls with well-developed breasts. The mutilation and torture were centered on the mammary glands, indicating strong oedipal pathological hatred for women. Back in history, Jack the Ripper murdered aging prostitutes. It's a pretty safe guess the Ripper's mother was the focus of his pathology."

The men stirred restlessly as the doctor walked slowly to the center of the room. "However, these porno homicides do not correspond to the usual profiles associated with serial killers." Harris continued. "The serial killer almost always employs the same weapon, be it a gun, a knife, his hands, a hammer, an ax, or poison. He or she mutilates or marks the victims.

"In this instance you have five victims killed by a variety of handguns, with the exception of Sherry Nichols, who was murdered by lethal cocaine." The doctor paused and said, "In my opinion, none of these homicides was sexually motivated."

"Why not?" Brody asked.

"The absence of mutilation and the varying ages, sexes, and physical divergence of the victims would seem to rule out a sexually motivated killer."

"But are the killings connected?" Nolan asked.

"Absolutely. They're connected by profession and carefully planned. The victims and their killer were known to each other. In my view, your killer is an individual capable of masking enormous inner rage. I would have to conclude that he or she is motivated solely by vengeance."

"Vengeance for what and against whom?" Silvio asked.

Harris smiled. "That, my friend, is an unanswerable question."

Nolan got to his feet and said, "Thank you for your help, Doctor."

"I repeat, forensic psychology is an imperfect science. I've given you my professional diagnosis, but I caution you not to jump to any quick conclusions."

Dr. Harris started out, and Torres rose. "I'm going with you, Doctor."

Nolan sat down, and stared up at the lights for a moment, then swiveled around and faced the three detectives.

"Okay. Point one. The killer and victims knew each other and shared a professional bond. The killer has access to high-grade coke and knows how to use handguns. The killer exhibited lesbian sexual techniques in the killing of Sherry Nichols. Harris diagnoses the motive to be vengeance. The single suspect who satisfies all those categories is Karen Dara."

"We test-fired her thirty-eight," Jack said. "The ballistics didn't match the slugs used to kill Whelan."

"So what?" Nolan replied. "She could have acquired a Saturday night special and taken a back road out of the Shiva compound, come over Coldwater into Beverly Hills. Visited Sherry, balled her, given her the coke as a gift, and left her in a state of coronary seizure. I want Karen Dara picked up."

"I've already ordered the surveillance unit to place her in protective custody," Jack said.

"When?" Nolan asked, surprised.

"I radioed Stillwell before we started this meeting."

"You're certain she was up at the Shiva place?"

"According to Stillwell, she's been there for the past week." Jack paused. "You realize that you're going against Harris's advice."

"What do you mean?" Nolan asked.

"He warned you about jumping to quick conclusions."

Nolan glared at Jack and shook his head in dismay. "You've developed a close relationship with this woman, and that personal involvement has blurred your objectivity."

"That's bullshit, John. I've always considered her a possible suspect, but no one has ever come up with a logical motive."

Nolan drummed his fingers on the desktop for a moment, then asked Brody. "You worked on the vagrant killer and the freeway killer—what do you think?"

Brody shrugged. "I'd have to meet the lady. But off the top, it looks too pat, too convenient. Serial killers don't operate in straight lines. We've never gotten a print at any murder site that matched a file print of a felon. The vagrant killer and the freeway killer had prior convictions for minor sexual offenses. This woman is absolutely clean. She's educated, financially secure. And from what I've heard and read, she is relatively stable."

"Anyone engaged in porno acting is abnormal."

"That's personal prejudice, John," Brody responded. "It's not factual and has no basis in law."

"Hold it!" Silvio exclaimed, and turned to Jack. "Did you ever run a make on her?"

"I checked motor vehicles, voter's registration, IRS, Social Security," Jack replied. "There is nothing in state or federal records indicating past criminal activities."

"But did you check her real name?" Silvio asked. "Her birth name? These porno people use stage names."

"Her state records go back to 1974," Jack said. "She was twenty-two in 1974. Even if she used another name prior to '74, what the hell would we discover?"

"She might have had a juvenile conviction," Nolan stated. "She might have done time. She might have exhibited childhood violence. Who knows?"

"He's got a point," Brody said.

"How do you check?" Jack asked. "If her birth name was Mary Jones and she attended Ohio University or some high school in Columbus, how do you connect Mary Jones to Karen Dara?"

"Easy," Nolan said, and pressed a button on his intercom.

"Yes, sir?" Nolan's secretary responded.

"Get me Ira Kosstrin at State Department Intelligence. You'll find his office and home number on the Rolodex. Tell him it's an emergency."

"Yes, sir."

Nolan released the button and said, "They have passport records on an ITC computer. They can track the issuance of passports back to the original. Citizens are required to furnish legal certification of birth records the first time they apply."

Jack paced.

Silvio smoked and rubbed his wrists nervously.

Brody peered out the picture window.

Nolan's chair creaked as he rocked back and forth.

The passage of time seemed interminable and excruciating.

The secretary's voice suddenly came over the speaker. "Ira Kosstrin is on the line."

Nolan picked up the receiver. "Hello, Ira. Listen, sorry to disturb you, but we're in a bind. I've got to check the passport history of a woman named Karen Dara." Nolan paused and spelled it. "D-A-R-A. Right. . . . We've got to trace her passport issuances back to the original." He paused. "As far as we know—native-born, state of Ohio. Have your man phone me at this number. It's my direct line." Nolan knocked some cigar ash into the ceramic tray. "I'm in your debt, Ira. I know it's after ten back there, but this is an emergency. . . . Right. . . . Bye, Ira." Nolan hung up and said, "A matter of minutes."

"I've got a bad feeling about this," Jack said.

"Why?" Brody asked.

Jack shrugged. "Just intuition. It's like a pinched nerve. I can't explain it."

"What the hell is it?" Nolan asked.

"I have this uneasy feeling that we're sitting on the wrong end of a sputtering fuse."

"Shit!" Nolan exclaimed. "You're the one that pushed. I tried to tell you to lay off. I might have urged the commissioner to assign a special homicide unit."

"I know," Jack said. "You're right. I did press. I kept equating Candy with my own daughter, and once I'd met her father, I was hooked. The case became personal."

Nolan's phone rang. He grabbed the receiver, picked up a pen, and held it poised over a notepad.

"This is John Nolan. Yes. Go ahead, Mr. Bellwood."
Nolan paused. "I understand. We're starting from the
most recent issuance."

Nolan repeated the data aloud as he made the nota-
tions. "October 14, 1981. Passport issued in L.A. Name,
Karen Dara. July 23, 1976. Passport issued in San Francisco. Karen Dara. April 2, 1971. Passport issued in Day-
ton, Ohio, to Karen Dara, who had legally changed her
name from original birth certificate produced by subject."
Nolan glanced at the men and paused dramatically before
saying, "In the name of Paula Cahill. Spelled C-A-H-
I-L-L. Thank you, Mr. Bellwood. I appreciate your help."
Nolan hung up, leaned forward, and triumphantly said,
"Paula Cahill. There's your P. C."

The sudden silence in the office was instantly jarred
by a loud buzz from Nolan's phone console. "What is it,
Mary?" Nolan inquired.

"Sergeant Stillwell calling in for Lieutenant Raines."

Jack came around Nolan's desk and lifted the receiver. "Yeah, Frank?" He listened and sighed. "Christ,
okay. Place Guru Meli-Ramdas in protective custody, and
come on in."

Jack hung up and said, "Stillwell, Reisman, and two
highway patrolmen searched the temple, the tents, the
bungalows but failed to locate Karen Dara. The guru
claims she was in a prayer meeting."

"She obviously took a back road out of there," Nolan
said.

Jack glanced at Silvio. "Get over to Lisa Chang's and
maintain surveillance. I'll meet you there later. Phil, you
come with me."

"Where are we going?"

"Venice. She's either on her way home or on the way
to Chang's."

"*If* she's our killer," Brody cautioned.

Nolan slammed his fist on the desk and roared, "There
are no ifs! Bring her in!"

"We don't have a warrant," Jack replied. "All I can do
is confront her with the evidence and have Phil record the
interrogation."

"Suppose she clams up?" Brody asked.

"Keep her under surveillance," Nolan replied. "I'll get in touch with Judge Imperato; by noon tomorrow I'll have a bench warrant served on her for five counts of murder one."

Chapter 46

It was a moonless dark night, but the sea was aglow with the lights of private boats that bobbed in a wide semicircle around the brilliantly illuminated Venice pier. A crowd of spectators lined the walkway, watching a high school marching band play its way onto the pier.

As the two detectives walked toward Karen's front door, Jack asked, "What the hell's going on?"

"A pre-Labor Day festival," Brody said. "Marching bands. Fireworks."

"What are they celebrating?"

"Who the fuck knows? It's Venice."

Jack rang the bell and said, "Let me do the talking."

Karen opened the door, and in the portico light she appeared haunted, hollow-cheeked, and pale. She neither greeted them nor acknowledged their presence in any way. She simply turned and led them into the living room.

The drapes were partially drawn across the sliding terrace doors, permitting a view of the beach and sea.

"This is my partner, Sergeant Phil Brody," Jack said.

She nodded at Brody and said, "I want you both to understand I agreed to this inquisition because I'm fed up with suspicion and surveillance. I'm also"—she glared at Jack—"and this may come as a surprise to you, fearful for my life. Now, ask your questions."

"Do you mind if Sergeant Brody takes notes?"

She crossed to the wet bar and said, "I wouldn't care if Mr. Brody wrote a novel."

"Sometime tomorrow a sheriff's officer will serve you with an arrest warrant," Jack stated. "The warrant will charge you with five counts of murder in the first degree."

"I'll wear something appropriate." She sipped the gin and sighed. "I assume there's some legal basis for this warrant."

"We determined that your birth name is Paula Cahill."

"So what?" she said, unperturbed.

"The initials P. C. appeared on all those valentines."

"Anything else?"

"You're familiar with the use of handguns. You probably had access to lethal-quality coke, the stuff used to kill Sherry Nichols. And you knew all the victims."

She shook her head, looked into her glass, and whispered, "Jesus."

"In the time frame of Candy's death you claimed to be at home, but you have no proof," Jack said. "You claimed to be at home when Traynor and Pierson were hit, but again without corroboration. At the time of Whelan's murder you were presumably up at the Shiva order, but there are back roads out of that place, so our surveillance unit could have missed you."

"What was my motive for killing Candy?"

"Jealousy or maybe a mercy killing. The goddess Shiva might have instructed you to put Candy out of her misery."

"Terrific. I do Candy a service by killing her, then become an avenging angel for having killed her." She paused. "What do you think, Mr. Brody?"

"I'm listening."

She crossed the room, drew the window drapes apart, and looked off at the activity on the pier. There was a muffled fireworks explosion followed by a brilliant shower of crimson lights. She turned from the view, crossed the room, sank into a deep leather chair, and sighed. "Shall I start at the top?"

"Any way you like."

"Thank you." She sipped the drink and said, "The night we finished shooting Candy's last film, I came home and phoned her. I was worried about her. I knew she had bought a gun."

"How did you know that?"

"She told me."

"When?"

"At a party, the previous week at Kellerman's. She

did a lot of coke and threatened suicide. The gun and her depression were on my mind the night we finished shooting. I phoned her twice and got her recording. I decided to drive out to Malibu."

"What time?"

"One, one-fifteen. Her car was parked in the breezeway, and all the lights were on. I rang the bell repeatedly. No one answered. I went down the access staircase and came around the beach side of the house. Candy was standing on the terrace. She was naked, holding a small automatic in both hands. She relaxed when she recognized me, but she was wired, snow-blind. I tried to talk her into letting me have the gun, but she refused. I did manage to take the five thousand dollars out of her purse. I knew she'd use it to score coke. I pleaded with her to let me stay the night. It was a long, sad, disjointed conversation. She said she loved me but asked me to leave. That was the last time I saw Candy. By the way, when her father returns from Europe, he'll find a money order for five thousand dollars waiting for him."

"Are you saying that Candy drew the valentine, then committed suicide?" Jack asked.

"Yes. The valentine with P. C. was her final farewell to me."

"Why didn't you tell me this when I first questioned you?"

"I didn't think anyone would believe me."

"Why not?"

"Come on, Jack, don't patronize me. Motives are easily invented by hungry prosecutors. You want to hear a few? Candy and I were sexual degenerates. I was insanely jealous of her. We were drug addicts. I shot her in a moment of rage. Shall I continue?" She brushed a spill of hair from her cheek. "I just felt too vulnerable to admit I was with her at the end."

Jack nodded. "Okay . . . let's say Candy was a suicide. You then participate in drug-induced séances. You hear her voice demanding vengeance. You systematically take out Traynor, Stella, Whelan, and Nichols."

"That's sheer conjecture, and you know it."

"What I think doesn't count. There are people in high

places who are convinced that you became an avenging angel. Serial killers are known to listen to voices. Besides, you had a strong motive for killing Whelan and Nichols."

"Oh?"

"They were going to cut your love scene with Candy into a new picture, a story that you felt exploited her. I was here when Sherry called. You said, 'You do that at your own risk!'"

"And you regard that as a death threat?"

"It's a threat."

"What I meant was that I would take legal action to prevent them from using that clip. My contract prevents Whelan from doing just that. And I have a damn good attorney." She tossed her drink down and said, "I think you had better leave now. You're an empty man. A shameless son of a bitch. You insulted me, you made love to me, you attacked my religious beliefs, and now, under the guise of being a concerned friend, you come here and accuse me of mass murder." Her voice thickened, and tears welled up in her eyes. "The sad thing is that I trusted you. I really did. But I don't blame you. I blame myself. I was wishfully thinking something that never existed." She shook her head in disbelief. "I must have regressed to some childhood fantasy. How could I have ever expected you to consider me anything more than a stand-in for a lonely night?" She sighed audibly. "Now, please take Mr. Brody and his notepad and go back to those men in high places."

Her eyes radiated a hopeless defiance, the kind of defiance endemic to lost causes. It was the same tragic defiance displayed by the girl in the Spanish poster.

Jack and Phil walked toward the GTO and saw a glittering shower of scarlet stars blossom against the black sky, briefly illuminating the fleet of private boats circling the pier. The high school band's martial music carried on the Pacific breeze.

Brody got behind the wheel, and Jack sat alongside. They turned right at the corner and entered a narrow street lined by scarred tenements. Brody drove for fifty feet, then abruptly pulled over to the curb, slid his window down, and cut the ignition.

"Something wrong?" Jack asked.

"I think she's telling the truth."

"You don't know her. She's an actress, and I don't mean just porn. Don't be conned by her cool, sad elegance. She made a first-class horse's ass out of me. She knocked those people off. She may not have been legally sane, but she's a killer."

"You're wrong. You're not reading the facts. Forget what she looks like. Forget you made it with her. Forget what she is and what she does. Forget Nolan's pressure to close this case. I may have an edge because I've got some distance, and I look at the facts, and they don't add up. First place, if she killed Candy, why would she draw her own initials in that valentine? Karen's smart—very smart. She'd figure that sooner or later we'd have made her birth name. Besides, she had no motive to hit Candy. She loved her. She tried to help her. She explained the missing five thousand. She admitted that she contacted the dead girl's spirit. My guess is she felt in some way responsible for Candy's suicide."

A muscular youth on a motorcycle with a pretty blonde clinging to his back roared down the street.

"You're not far off," Jack said. "We took a walk on the beach one night. She told me exactly that. She said Candy trusted her, and she let her down." Jack lit a cigarillo, inhaled deeply, and sighed. "She still could have hit the others. There sure as hell was no love lost between Karen and the rest of that bunch."

"That's an assumption based on nothing. There's no way that Karen would have clipped them, drawn a valentine, and left her own initials. Doesn't make sense. The killer used the valentine and the initials in a copycat fashion to throw us off."

"But Karen could have figured that one out," Jack persisted.

"So could anyone else connected with Whelan's production staff. Outside of the valentine, these homicides have none of the usual symptoms associated with serials. I see a professional here. Traynor and Stella Pierson were hit by explosive bullets, not easy to come by. Whelan was the only victim who was gut-shot, tortured. In the case of

Sherry Nichols, you're getting thrown by the fact that she had a lez number before snorting that lethal coke. I make the sexual activity a coincidence. Maybe Lisa Chang did a number with Sherry earlier that evening. The killer waited for Chang to leave, then entered and gave Sherry the coke as a gift."

Jack puffed nervously on the cigarillo. "But Karen still fits. She could have balled Sherry and given her the dope."

"When was the last time you nailed a street dealer peddling one hundred percent pure coke? You can get that quality only at the source."

"You're back to a Colombian involvement," Jack said. "And maybe you're not wrong. Ordóñez's hit men may have kicked it off and, despite the Cancún truce, kept it going."

"It's a possibility; no one can outguess those fucking Colombians. But that's a stab. I don't want to throw you. All I'm saying is these homicides don't add up to a serial or even a vigilante. They were too designed." Brody spit a piece of tobacco leaf out the window. "I don't know who hit those people or why, but I'd bet my pension that Karen Dara is not your killer. And if Nolan serves that warrant, we're all gonna look like a bunch of assholes. That's my opinion, but it's your case."

The interior of the car was silent. The sounds of fireworks and music drifted on the wind. Jack felt a cold, queasy sensation balling up in the pit of his stomach.

"Let's go back, Phil."

They circled the block, parked directly in front of Karen's house, and got out of the car.

Karen stood at the terrace doors, staring at them.

The glass suddenly fragmented into a spider web, and Karen's face exploded.

"Get in there, Phil!" Jack screamed. He turned toward the beach and saw a dark figure sprinting away from the low wall toward the surf.

Jack pulled his .38 and dashed across the street. He jumped the low wall and saw the figure toss what appeared to be a rifle into the sea.

Jack fired on the run. The .38 bucked in his hand. The shot went wild. The running figure raced along the surf, heading toward the Venice pier. Jack's shoes kicked up the sand as he cut diagonally across the beach toward the pier.

Star shells, fired from a barge at sea, screamed skyward, exploding in glorious colors. The crowd surrounding the pier oohed and aahed as the brilliant colors burst from the rockets against the black sky.

Jack closed the distance to the pier, his legs pumping effortlessly, fueled by a rush of adrenaline.

The running figure disappeared into the dark underbelly of the pier. Jack kept coming on. He could see the tide surging in under the pier, crashing against the supporting cement pilings.

A cabin cruiser hovered perilously close to the pier. A group of revelers on board concentrated their attention seaward in anticipation of the next fireworks display.

Jack heard the distant wail of sirens. He knew Brody had summoned the police and paramedics, but it was too late to save Karen.

The running figure splashed into the tide below the pier and disappeared behind the cement pilings. Jack ran in a zigzag pattern. Ten yards of hard-packed sand still separated him from the pier's underside. He saw a yellow flash from deep inside the dark pilings, and a spout of sand erupted to his right.

He plunged into the dark water under the pier and slipped his left arm around a piling just as the tide rushed at him.

He clung to the piling and shielded his body, waiting for his eyes to grow accustomed to the semidarkness.

The powerful lights illuminating the pier reflected off the sea, casting a vacuous, streaky light beneath the pier.

Jack shivered in the cold waist-high water, his teeth chattering uncontrollably. He held the .38 above the incoming tide and peered intently at the cement pilings. From above, he heard intermittent explosions of fireworks muffled by martial music and the throb of the cabin cruiser's engines.

He knew the killer lurked behind a piling no more

than ten feet ahead. Beyond that point the level of incoming tide would be above the assassin's head. He measured the distance to a center piling and waited for the surging tide to recede. He took a deep breath and, holding the .38 above his head, bellied into the water. Kicking furiously, he swam fifteen feet and wrapped his left arm around the piling. The tide was chin-high. He peered into the murky darkness, his gun hand trained at a piling to his right and slightly ahead. His pulse raced, and a sharp pain throbbed above his left eye. He felt stoned from the rush of adrenaline. He grinned madly as he listened to the constant chatter of his teeth. He felt as though he were trapped in a Daliesque nightmare: the patriotic music; the applause of the revelers watching the fireworks; the ominous throb of the cabin cruiser's idling engines; the surging black water; the noxious odor of gasoline . . . and the shadowy circular pilings, behind which lurked a mass murderer. He gulped the air. He was hyperventilating. A cresting wave loomed up at the head end of the pier, rolled in, and smashed its way down the cement pillars. Jack clung to the piling as the wave roared past. The suction of the receding tide pulled at him, but he managed to maintain his position.

A sudden crack and yellow flash flared from the darkness. A piece of cement exploded inches above his head, and he felt the instant sting of chips splitting the skin on his forehead. A puff of gunsmoke rose from behind a piling up ahead to his right. He steadied himself and squeezed off a shot at the smoke-shrouded piling. The crack of the round rang in his ears, and the sharp bite of gunpowder filled his nostrils. From the beachside the sound of wailing sirens was profound.

He shouted into the watery darkness, "You hear those sirens! The cops will be swimming right with us! Come on out!"

A powerful surge of incoming tide broke against the pilings, throwing up bursts of sea spray.

He saw the dark figure slip from behind a piling and drift into a spill of light radiating from the cabin cruiser idling close to the pier. The figure grabbed at a piling, securing himself but unable to escape the overhead light. The figure's face was now clearly discernible.

Jack froze in shocked disbelief. His heart pounded wildly as if it would burst from his chest. His gun hand trembled. The incoming tide licked at his parched throat. He swallowed a mouthful of seawater. His eyes riveted on the face in the light.

Braced against the piling, gun hand extended, chest-high in the water, was Silvio Martinez.

Silvio shouted above the cruiser's engines, "I had to do it. I had to keep those bastards killing each other!"

Jack stared at Silvio in muted horror, as if a demon had risen up out of the sea.

"I had to keep the war going," Silvio shouted. "They're poisoning the country, the country that took me in! I did it for America! I did it alone. I had them killing each other—the mob and the Colombians. I've got to keep them killing each other!"

It all fell into place with brutal clarity.

Silvio's eyes shone with madness. "You hear me, Jack," he shouted again. "All alone—fucking alone!"

Jack gasped, pumping air into his lungs, desperately trying to activate his vocal cords. "Sil-Silvio." He struggled. Then, slowly finding his voice, he shouted, "It's over now! You can't kill everyone! No man can do it alone. Toss that gun away, and come in with me!"

The yellow flash and crack issued simultaneously from Silvio's revolver. Jack felt the hot sting of the slug as it creased his cheek. Silvio fired again and moved out of the light, grabbing a piling close to the idling cabin cruiser. Jack tracked him but could not bring himself to fire.

Above them the portly skipper of the cabin cruiser drained his fourth martini. A drunken couple danced on the fantail. A pretty dark-haired girl popped a champagne cork and drank the foam from the bottle. The band on the pier played "Hello, Dolly!"

"You people hear somethin' sounded like gunshots?" the skipper asked.

The pretty girl licked the foam from her mouth and shook her head. "Unh-unh, but you get this boat any closer to that pier, and we're gonna think we're on the fucking *Titanic*."

The heavyset, balding skipper poured another martini from a thermos and wiped his hand on his Hawaiian shirt. "I'll take her out," he said, and staggered off toward the flying bridge.

Beneath the pier Silvio steadied himself against the tide and fired twice. Spouts of water erupted inches from Jack's face. No longer restrained by thought or emotion, he fired at Silvio's silhouetted figure. The crack reverberated under the pier, echoing from piling to piling.

Silvio's head bobbed between the piling and the aft hull of the cruiser. "You got two left!" he shouted. "I got half a clip!"

The inebriated skipper of the cabin cruiser placed his martini on the shelf above the instrument panel and, ignoring all maritime safety procedures, thrust both power levers forward. The tachometer needle climbed instantly to 1,500 RPMs. The sleek craft shuddered and lurched forward. The revelers on the fantail were thrown to the deck as the twin screws bit into the sea.

No one on board heard Silvio's screams as he was sucked into the whirling blades of the screws. Watching helplessly, Jack heard a final scream as Silvio disappeared below the surface. The cruiser's engines emitted a charcoal cloud of exhaust as the craft moved off.

Jack let go of the piling and swam toward the residue of bubbling circles.

A star shell exploded, and the sea lit up in a brilliant green flash.

Jack saw Silvio's torso surface in the trough of the forming waves. He changed direction and swam toward the body, closing the distance rapidly.

Silvio's eyes were open. His body had been severed just above his waist. A fountain of blood pumping out of the truncated torso stained Jack's face and hands. He trod water and grabbed Silvio's arm. Stroking with one hand and kicking furiously, he gained the crest of a forming wave and felt himself being raised up and thrust toward the beach. He rode the wave in until his knees scraped the bottom. Still clutching Silvio's arm, he struggled to his feet and staggered onto the beach.

He stood there for a moment like a wounded sea creature: beached; blood-smeared; gasping for breath. He glanced seaward and saw a colorful burst of Roman candles. The people on either side of the pier applauded the pyrotechnical display. The high school band played "Hooray for Hollywood."

He turned and saw the flashing red, white, and blue lights of prowl cars that had converged in front of Karen's house.

He glanced down at Silvio's bloody remains. The corpse reminded him of luckless GIs who had stepped on antipersonnel mines. Holding Silvio's arms, he dragged the truncated body up onto the rise of the beach, all the way to the high ground under the palms, close to the low wall. He stood there for a moment, listening to his own breathing. He was unable to move or think, but he wished someone would cover Silvio. The passage of time became amorphous, and he couldn't tell how long he stood there before he heard the footfalls.

Brody vaulted the low wall and puffed his way up to him. "She's gone, Jack," he said, then paused and examined Jack's face. "Christ, you're sweating blood drops."

"Cement chips. I'm okay."

Brody then saw the grotesque remains of Silvio lying in the sand at Jack's feet.

Brody crossed himself. "Oh, Jesus." His face turned chalky, and he moaned, "Oh, Jesus Christ!"

"He was cut in half by a cabin cruiser," Jack said hoarsely. "I should have made him after Whelan. He gutshot him because Whelan had called him a spic. That was also the first time lethal coke showed up. Silvio took that snow out of the *Ave María* bust, the same snow he gave to Sherry Nichols. He had access to all the victims, but I should have made him after Whelan."

"That's a tough call," Brody said. "How can you make your partner a killer?"

"He started the killings after Candy's suicide," Jack said in a monotone. "He used the valentine to make it look like a serial or a vigilante."

"But why hit the porno players?"

"To keep Ordóñez and Maffatore at war. He kept yelling, '*I did it for America. I did it alone.*'"

Brody glanced at Silvio's grotesque remains and said, "Christ almighty, what a way to die!"

"Silvio was killed a long time ago"—Jack sighed—"on a hot Miami night." He paused and said, "Give me a cigarette."

Jack inhaled and felt the speed surge of nicotine. "Call it in, Phil. Police officer killed in the line of duty."

Brody's eyes widened, and he murmured, "Line of duty . . . How can I do that?" He asked, "How do we explain Karen? How do we explain Silvio?"

"We radioed Silvio to meet us at Karen's place. He was killed while aiding me in the pursuit of unknown assailants, in all probability Colombian hit men taking out the last porno star."

"Christ, I don't know, Jack."

"Nolan will buy it. The press will buy it. Maffatore may even buy it. A continuing war between those bastards will be a legacy for Silvio. What the hell's the difference?"

Brody stared at Jack for a long moment then and sighed. "Okay."

"Thanks, Phil."

"What for? That's the way it happened."

"Yeah . . . Get a blanket. Cover him up."

Jack walked down to the surf and strolled along the beach toward the spot where he and Karen had first embraced. He remembered the light in her pale green eyes and the fine line of her cheekbones, and the soft brush of her lips, and the sweet scent of her perfume.

He remembered the slight tremor in her voice when she had said, "All my life I've been searching for that magic person, that someone you can tell it all to, and he doesn't say anything, but you know . . . you just know it's going to be all right."

A glittering shower of red, white, and blue stars exploded against the night sky, defying gravity for a few seconds before bursting into dazzling blue pieces of luminous light cascading down, growing dimmer, and vanishing.

He started slowly back toward the pier and stopped abruptly as he noticed a shiny metallic object protruding from the sand. He knelt, picked it up, and brushed the sand from its face. He stared at the distinctive DEA badge with its golden eagle emblazoned at the top and Silvio's service number engraved at its center. In that moment he thought of Silvio as a fallen soldier in a war that had been lost to public indifference. Jack fought back the tears as he tucked the badge into his pocket.

On the pier the band struck up a stirring rendition of "Stars and Stripes Forever."

SPECTACULAR ENTERTAINMENT ALL SUMMER LONG!
SUMMER SPECTACULAR FREQUENT READERS SWEEPSTAKES
WIN *A 1988 Cadillac Cimarron* Automobile or
12 other Fabulous Prizes

IT'S EASY TO ENTER. HERE'S HOW IT WORKS:

1. Enter *one* individual book sweepstakes, by completing and submitting the Official Entry form found in the back of that Summer Spectacular book, and you qualify for that book's prize drawing.

2. Enter *two* individual book sweepstakes, by completing and submitting two Official Entry Forms found in the back of those two Summer Spectacular books, and you qualify for the prize drawings for those two individual books.

3. Enter *three or more* individual book sweepstakes, by completing and submitting—in one envelope—three or more Official Entry forms found in the back of three or more individual Summer Spectacular books, and you qualify not only for those three or more individual books but also for THE BONUS PRIZE of a brand new Cadillac Cimarron Automobile!

Be sure to fill in the Bantam bookseller where you learned about this Sweepstakes . . . because if you win one of the twelve Sweepstakes prizes . . . your bookseller wins too!

SEE OFFICIAL RULES BELOW FOR DETAILS including alternate means of entry.

No Purchase Necessary.

Here are the Summer Spectacular Sweepstakes Books and Prizes!

BOOK TITLE	PRIZE
On Sale May 20, 1987	
ACT OF WILL	A luxurious weekend for two (3 days/2 nights) at first class hotel, MAP meals—(transportation not included) Approximate value: $750.00
MEN WHO HATE WOMEN & THE WOMEN WHO LOVE THEM	Gourmet food of the month for 6 months N.Y. Gourmet Co. Approximate value: $750.00
VENDETTA	Schrade Collector's Knife set Approximate value: $750.00
On Sale June 17, 1987	
LAST OF THE BREED	Sharp Video Camera and VCR Approximate value: $1,600.00